I0781075

PERCEVAL THE ALTRUISTIC

Also by
Robert G. Lee

What's the Big Idea?

Perceval the Altruistic

AND HIS AMAZING DISCOVERY OF THE LONG-LOST SECRET TO HAPPINESS

ROBERT G. LEE

WordCrafts

Perceval the Altruistic is a work of fiction. All references to persons, places or events are fictitious or used fictitiously.

Perceval the Altruistic
Copyright © 2024
Robert G. Lee

ISBN: 978-1-962218-80-1

Cover concept and design by Jonathan Grisham for Grisham Designs.

All rights reserved. No part of this book may be reproduced, stored in a retrieval system, or transmitted in any form or by any means—electronic, mechanical, photocopy, recording or otherwise—without the prior written permission of the publisher. The only exception is brief quotations for review purposes.

Published by WordCrafts Press
Cody, Wyoming 82414
www.wordcrafts.net

To Begin

Once upon a time there was a living, breathing, oxymoron known by all as Perceval the Altruistic, who lived in the bustling village of Kingston, which was nestled in the middle of humanity's last, best hope: the tiny country known as Goodania.

Before life dealt this human dichotomy a severe blow via the crap stick, he somehow defied the odds and was universally acknowledged as being not just excessively rich but also a decent human being as well.

Prior to his great role reversal, Perceval was married to Gwendolyn the Exquisitely Beautiful. Sadly, his wonderful wife was undeniably gorgeous on the outside but a little less than radiant on the inside.

When not stewarding his great fortune or spending time with his brood of children, Percy spent more than a few waking hours with his loyal best friends, Richard the Conveniently Brave, Stephen the Sarcastic, and Todd.

Only our hero knows exactly when, but sometime after the upcoming harrowing tale and, no doubt, mainly because of it, Perceval unwittingly uncovered the long-lost, much sought after secret to happiness. One would think people would have been ecstatic over Percy's life-changing discovery. Or at the very least, act mildly interested. But the hard, cold truth is the secret to true happiness involved, frankly, a lot of work, so most of the good folks of Kingston weren't particularly interested.

But all of that's not even close to the main thrust of the story that follows.

His discovery is thrown out there as an ironic icing on top of the huge pile of smoldering refuse onto which Perceval one day found himself unceremoniously flung.

The happiness fiasco notwithstanding, this story also has some rather juicy elements of unrequited love, longing, injustice, betrayal, role reversals, and the agonizing search for a reasonable explanation for it all.

In other words, what most of us have come to expect from simply living life.

Not Perceval, however. What happened to him blind-sided the man and shook him down to his very core. He never expected any of what follows. Truthfully, how could any of us?

Chapter One
The Town Gathers

Our story begins on Naming Day Eve, when Perceval the Altruistic was awarded the King's greatest prize, the much-coveted life achievement recognition platter.

With Naming Day being the biggest day of the year, it had become a local tradition to stretch out the festivities by finding the one person who had most lived up to their namesake and bestow upon them the life achievement award the night before the naming festivities.

This happened despite the fact that the honorees were usually not entirely done either living or achieving.

It is also worth mentioning that the annual award was perpetually doled out to those who lived up to what would be considered *positive* namesakes. Never once was the King's platter given to Darcy the Dim, Peter the Procrastinator, or Bartholomew the Belligerent.

It was everyone's opinion that Percy should have won the honor every year for at least the past decade, but the other annual tradition in town was having Percy turn down the award by claiming he already had plenty of perfectly good platters.

Perceval's other pat answer was that since his name actually meant *persecution*, and by all accounts he had yet to see a single day of hardship, he could hardly be considered a worthy candidate, as opposed to the scores of other people who actually lived up to their names. At which point he would give the committee a short list of much more viable candidates and promise to pay for the entire celebration out of his own pocket.

Ironically, the one year when he finally acquiesced and was

dragged kicking and screaming to his own celebration, was the very year his name became synonymous with persecution.

What apparently was lost on the award committee, was that all of Perceval's contrived reticence surrounding his acceptance of the award was based on his inconsequential first name. His actual namesake described him perfectly. Up until the award ceremony at least, Percy was known far and wide as selfless, benevolent, and goodhearted.

If you've never been to a life achievement banquet, you are heartily encouraged to kiss up to whomever you need in order to snag an invitation. Then make arrangements to travel to Goodania in the height of spring and marvel at the wonderful excess on display.

When the authorities finally conned Perceval into accepting his honor, he did so under the pretense that the affair would encourage and inspire his fellow men and women to go and do likewise with their own lives.

In truth, the main reason to attend the opulent soiree was to gorge oneself with a virtually unlimited supply of food and drink.

All culinary needs were provided, whether the guest chose to indulge in one of the seemingly unlimited varieties of meats and their byproducts, or if they were of the more modern thinking group who only partook of the plant-based offerings (most of which were specifically designed to imitate the taste of meat and their byproducts); no one left the festivity hungry.

Accompanying the endless piles of sustenance, casks of fermented wine and barrels of ale were uncorked and liberally poured before the celebration tent was officially open and, as a matter of course, continued until a short time before dawn.

As a result, the next day's naming celebration was pushed back from its original morning time slot to an hour much later in the day when the majority of villagers could finally open their eyes and walk in a forward direction without noticeably stumbling.

With Perceval's backing, this particular affair was like no other. Row after row of wooden tables and benches were lined up under the protection of the largest and most opulent tent anyone had ever seen. Torch chandeliers hung from the rafters to light the way for both the attendees and dozens of servers who silently flitted back and forth picking up empty plates and goblets and occasionally righting the overly inebriated guests.

It was common knowledge that the place to be as the party commenced was at the entrance to the celebration tent. Crowding around the impressive hand-carved wooden stage at the far end happened after the meal, but at the start, watching the long line of guests enter was well worth the potential neck spasms caused by craning one's neck to see around the sea of fellow guests and to ogle the incoming parade of pseudo royalty.

For many, the highlight of the life achievement gala was watching the who's who of the village as they preened through the entrance dressed up in their very finest regalia. Some took months and spared no expense to design and sew new outfits for their entire family just for this one night.

Thomas the Tailor was rarely seen at the celebration because he was either home, totally exhausted from sewing for several weeks straight, or was at his shop letting out the sleeves or the bust of some awkward teenager who had experienced a last-minute growth spurt.

This year, as was every year in recent memory, the most anticipated surprise of the evening would be the eye-popping gown worn by Perceval's wife, Gwendolyn the Exquisitely Beautiful.

One can hardly imagine the pressure she must have felt year after year to outdo herself, but her ability to astound and titillate with her hip-slimming, bodice-tightening, bosom-enhancing creations was the stuff of legend.

At this celebration, in honor of her husband's award, she managed to astound one and all with her most glorious creation yet. The fabric of her billowing gown was the most brilliant royal blue, with accents of yellow and white peeking out from her corset, petticoats, and shoes.

The train of her gown extended a good ten feet behind her. It was so unwieldy that she had hired two handmaidens whose sole job was to adjust and fluff her garment throughout the night. The overly fussy underlings would slap and shoo away anyone who dared to inadvertently traverse a line that intersected with Gwendolyn's flowing dress.

To top off the walking work of art, a triple strand of translucent pearls draped down the beauty's long neck. Her honey blonde tresses were intricately curled and arranged in such a way upon her head that many a woman standing in her vicinity could only pray the ground would open up and swallow them whole in order to save them from the debilitating horror of comparison.

And since the good woman amazingly still retained her girlish figure after bearing Perceval five healthy children (none of whom had yet to arrive at the party), Gwen was the object of unbridled lust from the men and unmitigated scorn from the women of Kingston.

In the coming months, Gwendolyn would often close her eyes and ruminate on the stolen glances of wanton desire and irrepressible envy she'd catch when people thought she wasn't paying them any mind (but, truth be told, she was always looking).

Perceval, however, could not have cared less about how he looked. He slipped his lanky frame into the exact same rumpled ruffled shirt and long black topcoat he wore to every single event in recent memory.

Gwendolyn begged him to get a new outfit. She even arranged for the tailor to design a coat that would match her gown, but Perceval wouldn't hear of it. He stubbornly insisted it would make him appear to be proud.

When close friends and acquaintances gently ribbed him about the well-worn, classic nature of his attire, Percy would shrug off their teasing and veiled insults by merely saying he had better use of his resources than to replace what was already working perfectly well.

Then he'd give a sideways nod to his ostentatious wife and say, "Besides, I believe Gwendolyn more than makes up for the two of us!"

Which endeared him to the people of Kingston, but not particularly to his spouse.

The man of the hour was considered handsome by the standards of the day in that he still had all of his limbs, fingers, toes, and the majority of his teeth. Not to mention he had managed to retain most of his dark wavy hair, though it was starting to show signs of grey around the temples.

After he heard of the threshing accident where Andrew the Farmer's beard got caught in the gears of his hay baler (which managed to rip out every hair from his chin by the roots) Perceval kept his beard trimmed close to his face. Unsurprisingly, Andrew the Farmer now did so as well.

On this grand day, all the notables of Kingston came to praise Perceval, press the flesh, and be seen as people who are meant to be seen.

Besides Perceval's best friends, one of his favorite guests was the town sheriff, Augustus the Giant, who, as fate would have it, topped out the measuring rod at barely a tick over five feet.

In the days to come, Augustus' keen sense of fairness and unwavering commitment to justice wouldn't be able to save Perceval from an unruly mob. In fact, those very attributes would actually condemn his friend to a heretofore unthinkable public humiliation.

One of the responsible parties in Perceval's upcoming condemnation was the tight clique who, as was their practice, tirelessly attempted to draw attention to themselves while wearing the veil of abject humility: the town's religious scribes.

On this night the learned men were done up in their most luxurious finery, looking as if they were in a competition to see who could feign the most piously dour expression while managing to balance their ornate bejeweled headpieces for the longest time without toppling over.

The scribe's main competition for attention were the namesake givers. While this group of smartly dressed women offered no competition in comparison to the scribes' preening plumages, they still managed to make everyone nervous because of their unilateral power to revoke or add to anyone's namesake at will. That, and their unmistakable delight in wielding such power over the masses.

Outdoing those two formidable groups, in not just the level of their collective volume, but attitude and numbers as well, were the village's attention starved, recently entitled teens.

One interesting development of late was the rising power of the younger generation.

In the past, many elders would not tolerate anyone who preferred to speak rather than to be told when they were allowed to do anything more than be spoken to.

But the winds of popular opinion had changed, and the youth of the village were gaining and asserting more power than they'd ever experienced before.

There seemed to be an inexplicable groupthink the up-and-coming generation possessed that was simply flabbergasting to their elders.

The ultimate consequence of this development was a quite puzzling and unwelcome shift of power from the solemn, measured wisdom of the village's elders to the teens' seemingly uncontrollable group tantrums.

Sometime after Perceval's life celebration banquet, it was one of those spleen venting, foot stomping, breath holding tantrums, led by a particularly vexed scullery maid's influence, that was the driving force that led to Percy's arrest and his humiliating stint in stocks just off the town square.

Chapter Two
The Awards Ceremony

Well into the evening, after most of the attending guests had consumed their fill, Brother Bob made his way over to Perceval.

As celibate brothers of the cloth go, this particular monk was universally well liked. He had a wicked sense of humor and a twinkle in his eye that accompanied a droll and dry delivery. In addition, the affable man was usually chosen as the go-between whenever the fragile egos the religious scribes unconsciously wore as their protective coverings needed to be massaged or placated.

The balding, portly monk coughed to get Perceval's attention.

The man of the hour turned around to see his friend. "Brother Bob! How wonderful to see you. Your order's ale is of particular note this year."

The brother nodded. "By the King's grace, after so many complaints concerning last year's batch, we switched Brother Theodore to kitchen duties."

Perceval's face puckered at the memory. "It was a bit sour, wasn't it?"

Brother Bob shuddered. "You're entirely too kind. Our dogs refused to drink it." He cocked his head and looked his friend in the eye. "Shall we blather on about the weather or discuss how much weight I've lost?"

Perceval took the hint. "May I assume you're in charge of the unneeded puffery to come?"

"Your perception is uncanny."

"May I also assume you're here to urge me to start the proceedings?"

"Most of the guests are filled to the brim and, I suspect, within the hour that will turn to excess. If we desire thy acceptance speech to be heard over the din of the inevitable drunken revelry, I suggest we begin your public flogging."

"Worried about falling flat, are we?"

"I have so little to live for. I need only be discovered here to fulfill my dream of being one of the King's royal jesters."

Perceval looked around. "While I would pay my weight in gold to see thee dance around in tights, I beg thy indulgence."

The Monk shrugged his shoulders. "Thy children have yet to arrive."

"I know of a thousand and one things which could have held them up. But it's not like any of them to at least try to get word to me. Not a pigeon, a messenger, nothing."

Brother Bob nodded. "My dreams of fame and fortune can wait."

Perceval was relieved. "For not too much longer. Who knows, a bridge may have washed out, and they won't arrive for another day!"

As Brother Bob walked off, the smile on Perceval's face was replaced by a look of concern. He loved his children more than anything on this earth, and even briefly entertaining the idea of losing just one of them filled him with more dread than he could bear.

He pushed the morbid thought out of his brain, forced a smile, and turned to face the never-ending line of well-meaning, compliment-effusing neighbors.

After another half an hour of pressing various flesh, and finding himself forcing an increasingly tired frozen smile, Percy caught Brother Bob's eye. He excused himself from the latest fawner, made his way to the stage at the front of the tent, found the fretting organizers, and reluctantly nodded, signaling his agreement.

Immediately, Thomas the Tenuous grabbed the rope attached to the stage curtain and pulled (albeit, as one would expect, a bit tentatively), revealing the waiting orchestra.

The band, lounging half-alert in a somewhat inebriated state backstage, took their cue and quickly settled into their chairs. Clarence the Conductor raised his baton, and the ten-piece ensemble of flutes, lyres, and drums began to play, more or less in time and in tune.

Hearing the music, a roar went up from the crowd. Seeing his half-drunken peers rush to get their seats, Perceval shook his head, ruing his regrettable decision to agree to this debacle.

Brother Bob patted his old friend on the back. "It shouldn't be as bad as ye fear."

Perceval looked up and nodded. "Nay, I suspect it will be much worse."

Near the back, in the corner of the immense tent, Richard the Conveniently Brave, Stephen the Sarcastic, and Todd began rhythmically clapping and shouting, "Per-cy! Per-cy! Per-cy!"

Soon the entire crowd found their seats and joined in the rallying cry.

Gwendolyn had to fight her way to the front, doing her best to retain her dress, her handlers, and her dignity. Arriving by his side, she shot her husband a look that said, *A little more warning next time, please.*

Perceval's look of distress curtailed her caustic attitude. "Oh, with the King as my witness, there shall never be a next time!"

Gwendolyn patted her husband's arm. "It will all be over before you know it."

Their conversation was cut short by the sound of the crowd bursting into applause. The band had reached a crescendo and ended with a big flourish as Brother Bob made his way to the front of the stage.

The monk signaled for one and all to settle down. Perceval pulled out a bench for his wife and waited for her to sit.

She shook her head and muttered under her breath, "I can't."

"You can't what?"

Gwendolyn spoke through clenched teeth and said, "Sit down in this!"

Keenly aware all eyes were on him; Perceval smiled and spoke without moving his lips. "Why not?"

"My corset be too tight! I can barely breathe let alone sit. Just stand with me. No one need know."

"Is thy beauty worth suffocation?"

Mercifully, Brother Bob put a stop to any possible public snit between the two. "Good evening! I bring thee greetings from my brothers at the Our-King-Is-Bigger-Than-Your-King Monastery. And bed and breakfast."

Perceval laughed along with the crowd. He exhaled, put his arm around his wife, and steeled himself for what he assumed would be a tame but still horribly uncomfortable roast.

The reality was he was about to experience a complete and total shift in the trajectory of his life.

The majority of people are never prepared for the proverbial rug to be pulled out from underneath them. But not a living soul could have been prepared for the way Perceval's entire home and hearth came unceremoniously crashing down upon his shoulders.

And so, the unwanted and unwarranted persecution of Perceval the Altruistic began.

Chapter Three
The Messengers

Brother Bob opened the very large, gold-leafed, leather-bound book that had been placed on the podium before him. "Let us begin with a reading from the King's Sacred Book of Accumulated Wisdom, starting with the letter H for humility.

'And lo, fear and respect for the King be the beginning of wisdom. For the art of being truly humble be not thinking less of oneself, but rather, to be not concerned about oneself at all. For when one doth begin to believe thy silver-tongued friends and colleagues as well as thine own puffery, then thou art on a slippery slope of self-deception that leads to conceit and avarice and boorish behavior until thou art a pain in the rear end to live with. And behind thy back, one and all, far and wide, shalt call thee a big doody head.

For be it not so, there art two kinds of people. Those that art humble and those that art about to be.'

"Thus ends today's reading from the ever-so-slightly abridged King's Sacred Book of Accumulated Wisdom."

As one, everyone in the crowd called out by rote, "As it has been said."

Brother Bob gently shut the religious tome and continued, "And lo, many, many, many-many-many years ago, there doth be a man born of woman who came to be known throughout the land as Perceval the Altruistic.

"How the fates aligned to shape and mold the young Perceval into one who ist truly altruistic, be a mystery for the ages. Merely ask Silvia the Selfish, Corine the Coveter, or Reginald the Rear-End-Of-A-Donkey, and they shalt shrug their collective shoulders in wonder.

"For much doth brother Perceval have to be not humble about! At last count this loyal and faithful servant of the King doth have at least six thousand sheep, four thousand horses, and untold number of swine and cattle, which is reputed to be far less in number after feeding the entire town at his own party.

"But that be not all! He doth also own the majority of farmland in the county, and the bakery and the theater and the new printing press! Perhaps the better question might be, what doth thee not have thy fingers in, good brother Perceval?"

The kindly monk glanced over at Perceval, who, in return, only gave back a guilty shrug.

Brother Bob continued. "When thy doth add in his many fine children, countless servants, faithful friends and his long betrothal to Gwendolyn the Exquisitely Beautiful, it be quite easy to see why everyone in the goodly village of Kingston doth hate thee with a fire rivaled only by the dung heaps of the Outskirts."

At that, a roar went up from the crowd, and Perceval's friends started in again with their chant, "Percy! Percy! Percy!"

Brother Bob waited a few moments for the revelry to die down, then began again. "And lo, whilst thy honored guest's financial holdings art known and envied throughout the kingdom, his many acts of largess and kindness art not."

Hearing the surprising road the monk was about to go down, Perceval's eyes went wide, his head shook from side to side and a guttural "Oh, no…" escaped from his lips.

"Didst thou know that Perceval the Altruistic be responsible for providing daily food and drink for the downtrodden living in the Outskirts?"

At that revelation, Gwendolyn shot her husband a look, murmuring under her breath, "Since when?"

"He ist also the major benefactor for the tiny hut project, giving basic shelter for those who be down on their luck. And thy food pantry. And thy shoes for tots initiative. As well as the cows without milkers program."

Seeing the row his words had caused the guest of honor, Brother Bob did his best to put the proverbial cat back in the bag. "And many various and other insignificant charities that need not be revealed here. For as it says in the King's Sacred Book of Accumulated Wisdom, 'thou shalt keep thy works of charity a secret and let not even thy wife know what thy left-hand art be doing.'"

If Gwendolyn's eyes were daggers, Percy would have been drawn and quartered on the spot. Her angry whisper cut through the din of the party and could be heard by all in the tent. "For the love of the King! You said you cut back!"

Perceval could only shrug. "I did! From what I wanted to do!"

Sensing all eyes were upon them, Gwendolyn pasted on a well-honed forced smile as she muttered, "Thou art ever so dead."

Perceval acknowledged the awkward nature of the moment by gesturing to Brother Bob and saying, "Please, continue with thy kind thrashing."

The nervous titter from the audience was cut short when a messenger strode into the tent, shifting the crowd's focus away from the monk.

The paid courier pushed his overly large, feathered cap to the side, unrolled an immense piece of parchment and proceeded to dramatically shout out his decree with the authority of one who did this for a living.

He began, as did all couriers, with, "Hear ye, hear ye, a message of utmost importance for Perceval the Altruistic from thy goodly physician, Derek the Healer. While thy hemorrhoids are, by far, the largest in the land, they art not life-threatening and be of no major concern. Try eating more fiber and sitting on pillows."

The announcement momentarily confused Percy until he saw his best friends in the back doubled over with laughter. Knowing this was just the beginning, Perceval could only blush a little and laugh along with the crowd.

As if on cue, another courier entered the celebration to make his announcement. This one was even more flamboyant than the first. "Hear ye, hear ye, a message of utmost importance for Perceval the Altruistic from thy goodly put upon physician.

"And lo, while thy bowel stoppage be both uncomfortable and doth cause excessive malodorous gas, it be nothing to be concerned about, other than possibly being responsible for thy giant hemorrhoids and thy extreme unpopularity in confined spaces."

While the townsfolk hooted and hollered, a third messenger entered the tent. This particular costume was exaggerated to the point of buffoonery. Percy could only imagine what was in store for him this time.

The courier unrolled his decree and began. "Hear ye, hear ye, a message of utmost importance for Percy the constipated and keeper of many hemorrhoids from thy woefully underpaid physician."

Perceval looked over and caught the eye of Derek the Healer. The doctor defensively threw up his hands and shook his head.

Seeing the doctor's denial, Todd stood up and shouted from the back, "Skirt not thy blame, good doctor! Ye know all too well all the messages forthwith art from thee!"

At that, Percy's third or fourth best friend and lifelong drunken tormentor plopped back down on his bench. His pals clapped him on the back and shoved a pewter mug of ale in front of him, which he promptly downed.

The courier continued without missing a beat. "Whilst thy good doctor hast seen many a wee willy over the course of his career as a healer, he hast never, in all his days, seen a willy quite as wee as thine. And whilst there be nothing medically wrong with having the world's williest wee willy, the good doctor doth wonder how thou didst manage to have quite so many children, seeing as how ye be quite handicapped below the belt, both forward and aft, if'n ye catch me drift."

At this, his friends started a new chant, "Wee willy Percy, wee willy Percy!"

While the whole town joined in the chorus, from the youngest toddler to the most ancient crone, Perceval could only shake his head and chuckle along with the crowd.

Gwendolyn, however, felt humiliated and nothing but contempt for everyone within eyesight and earshot, especially her husband. She stomped her foot in the dirt. "Put a stop to this! Now!"

Percy had to yell to be heard over the commotion. "Sweetheart, I'm afraid this particular horse be out of the barn!" He patted his wife's arm. "It will all be over before ye know it!"

Unfortunately, truer words had never been spoken.

When a fourth messenger stumbled into the tent, a shout of glee erupted from the crowd as they continued their drunken chant. "Wee willy Percy! Wee willy Percy!"

But this messenger was dressed as a common worker and held a decidedly different countenance than the others. His forehead was caked with dirt and sweat, his clothes were blackened with mud.

He saw Perceval, stumbled towards him, and fell at his feet. "Good master, I bring horrible tidings!"

Perceval helped the young man to his feet. "Catch thy breath, my good man and tell me of my latest ailment!"

Percy fully expected this to be an elaborate set up for yet another practical joke from his friends, but when he looked into the messenger's eyes, he saw only terror. He signaled for a servant to bring the exhausted man a drink.

After sloppily draining the contents of his mug, the man wiped his mouth with his sleeve and in between breaths to suck in air, he spit out the following:

"At sunrise, a group of murderous thieves ran aground in dozens of boats on the north shore. They proceeded to kill every one of your faithful servants, burned your crops to the ground, and made off with all of thy livestock they couldst carry, killing whatever they couldn't fit on their boats. I, alone, survived the attack and ran all the way here to tell ye!"

Before Perceval could ask a single follow up question, another harried man burst into the tent. He cried out from the back, "Master Perceval!"

Sensing a sudden bad turn of events, a hush fell over the crowd.

The second servant rushed to the front of the tent, bending over when he arrived, putting his hands on his knees in order to catch his breath. "Master… Perceval… I bring terrible tidings!"

"Catch thy breath, my goodly servant, and speak."

After a few moments, the man was able to croak out, "I come from the mountains to the east, where thy cattle and sheep graze. Early this morning an earthquake, the size of which I have ne'er felt nor seen, shook the ground with the force of a thousand cannons. The earth opened up and swallowed all of your livestock and servants. I, alone, escaped to tell ye of this horrible calamity."

Not more than a moment after the latest servant shared his crushing news, another made his way into the tent.

Were it possible, this one looked even worse than the previous two. His clothes were charred tatters. His hair matted down by sweat and soot. His face blackened to the color of coal.

Perceval's friends got up from their seats, rushed over to the man and caught him as he collapsed. They half dragged him through the parting sea of horrified onlookers to his destination by the stage.

A fear had gripped both Perceval and his wife. Her nails dug into his forearm, but he was oblivious of any pain other than a rising grave concern.

Perceval spit out, "Word from the west?" (As that was where his children had gathered to prepare for his award ceremony.)

When the messenger shook his head, Percy noticeably relaxed. "Tell me, good man, from what calamity have you escaped?"

The servant looked up with eyes filled with remorse. "I bring ye terrible tidings from your vineyards to the south. There was a storm. Fire fell from the sky. All your vineyards… Your faithful servants… The barns and vats… all gone. I, alone, escaped the firestorm and ran all the way to tell ye of this disaster."

When the servant finished speaking, Perceval patted him on the back, gestured to a few of his servants to take care of all the exhausted men and turned his eyes to the tent entrance.

When no one entered, Perceval and Gwendolyn let out a sigh of relief. "All right, they are but material things. We can rebuild—"

His words caught in his throat when a lone figure haltingly walked into the stunned gathering.

There was no urgency in this man's gait. He appeared almost reticent to even enter. And when he did, he appeared afraid to come in more than a foot or two.

Brother Bob jumped off the stage and ran over to the man, hoping he was merely a lost traveler. When he saw tears streaming down the stranger's face, he knew better.

Falling into the monk's arms, Brother Bob held the man as he sobbed. All watched with rapt attention while the servant unburdened himself by whispering into the holy man's ears. When he was done, Brother Bob turned back to face his friend.

The monk's eyes welling up with tears said all that needed to be said.

Perceval softly uttered, "From the west?"

Brother Bob nodded.

Before anything else could be said, fearing the worst, Gwendolyn let out a piercing scream and fell to her knees.

There are moments in a man's life when time has no meaning. These are the moments when either joy or sadness holds you so tightly in their grasp that nothing else in the world can distract you from the experience at hand.

At that exact moment, Perceval couldn't hear the wails of his wife. He wasn't aware of his body, or of the space, or of the crowd watching him. As he made his way over to his friend, all he saw were the monk's sorrow filled eyes.

Perceval pleaded, "Surely not all of them?"

Brother Bob's words were measured.

"A tornado. The house collapsed."

And with those five simple words, Perceval the Altruistic's happy and reasonably carefree life came to an abrupt end.

Chapter Four
The Eviction

Some two weeks after the deaths of his beloved children, Perceval still felt as if he was living outside of his body, somewhere far, far away, walking through an endless fog.

Each corner of his formerly happy manse held a different memory of a different child, and each recollection took his breath away.

People say grief comes in waves, and with each passing day the tide of woe moves a little further out from shore.

This was not the case with Perceval. He was drowning under the weight of his sorrow and wasn't sure if he would ever make it to the surface to see daylight again.

Unfortunately, today he was needed. Gwendolyn shook him back to this side of reality. "Percy! Do something! They're taking everything!"

He came up out of his stupor long enough to see four burly men lift up his family's wooden dining table and heft it through the kitchen doors. Before he could make any sign of protest, he saw a carving on the back leg etched in a decade earlier by their middle child, Chaucer, and was immediately lost again in his ocean of grief.

Fortunately, his best friends had dropped by that day to help, and they tried their best to run interference.

The sad truth was that the bank had taken possession of the house and everything in it to cover the losses of their many co-investments with Perceval. Something Gwendolyn couldn't or wouldn't understand.

Deep down in his mind, Perceval had a vague feeling that

he should probably fight to hold on to at least a few of his possessions, as he might be grateful for them down the road. But at this moment all he wanted to do was burn down the entire house as every board and tile reminded him of his unfathomable loss.

On top of which, every time Gwendolyn's shrill voice cut through the afternoon air with another, "Percy! Do something!" he fought the urge to take her to the nearest cliff and give her the slightest loving shove. Thankfully, even in his current state he knew that was probably an overreaction.

He wanted to shout, "How canst thee care about any of this? That's the couch where Galahad made castles as he fought off countless dragons. I hope they splinter it into a thousand pieces! That's the chair where I rocked both Charity and Angela through their bouts with the croup. I never want to see it again! That's the bed where we made our children! How can you even bear to look upon it? Throw it into the sea where it can sink to a watery grave which is exactly where I want to be!"

But he said none of these things to his wife, knowing he would only be adding to her grief. Instead, he kept them inside and let them fester along with the rest of his simmering rage.

Gwendolyn, however, couldn't keep a lid on her fury. She railed against her husband's apparent indifference. "Why dost thou just stand there and do nothing? Stop them! Go to the King! Have him stop them! If thou art such a loyal servant, surely he can save us!"

That was the proverbial last straw for Perceval. He snapped at his wife and regretted it almost immediately. "Foolish woman! Shall we accept good from the King and not adversity?"

Upon hearing her diminished husband chastise her, especially when he was clearly in the wrong, Gwendolyn could only stare at her husband. "I don't even know who ye are!"

To which Percy shrugged as he watched his wife turn and storm out of the room. "On that, dear wife, we both agree."

Near dusk, the workers had finished clearing out their house of every painting, tapestry, pewter plate, and mixing bowl and had managed to pile everything that wasn't nailed down into four separate carts, each one precariously teetering higher than the others.

The designated leader of the repossessors came over with a check list. "Beggin' yer pardon, sir, but there ain't no cows or horses in the barn. All we see be a few chickens and one angry rooster."

It took all Perceval had to answer the man. "Yea. I let the servants take their pick of the livestock. It seemed only fair after working for us for so many years as I be no longer able to provide for them."

The man sighed as he nodded. "I'm afraid they weren't yers to give."

Perceval felt the blood rush to his face. He wanted to dress the man down and put him in his place but knew any words said in anger here would be ill advised.

Instead, he simply dismissed the man and his coworkers with a wave. "Please communicate to thy employers ye did thy best to complete my bloodletting, but out of compassion for friends who have devoted their lives to me, I experienced a moment of largess."

Not quite grasping his meaning, the man's brow furrowed. Percy clarified. "I gave away the farm. Bring on the rack!"

The man continued, "There also be the matter of the King's book."

Perceval was known to be in possession of one of a handful of complete handwritten copies of the King's Sacred Book of Acquired Wisdom. It was a massive artifact, bound in thick brown leather with brass hinges.

But it was not the rarity of the piece, nor the value, nor the exquisite ornate colorful calligraphy that made the book so precious to Perceval. What made this opus absolutely priceless were the signatures and handprints of his children enclosed within.

Over the years, Perceval used this family treasure to teach his offspring to read. When each child had mastered the King's English, they read aloud an entire chapter of their own choosing to the whole family and, upon completion, signed their name at the end.

In addition, at the back of the book, under the family history section, all of Perceval's children had blackened their hands with soot and left their handprints.

There was no way Perceval was ever going to give up his most prized possession. Especially since this was now his only record of his dearly departed children.

Knowing the likelihood of the bank's request, before their henchmen came over he had wrapped the sacred book in one of his tunics, tied it up with a thick rope and hid it under a pile of straw in the barn.

Now, staring the man in the face, Perceval told a bald-faced lie. "I'm afraid it was destroyed in a small fire sometime last year."

The worker stared back at Perceval for a few moments, nodded, rolled up his parchment check list, stuffed it in his vest pocket, and grunted.

As he turned to leave, he tipped his hat, "Sorry fer your loss, sir. Yer many losses."

Perceval appreciated the small but brief display of humanity. He bowed before the gentleman. "And I appreciate thy graciousness. I can only imagine this can't be easy for thee, a job where thou art paid to kick people when they're down."

The man laughed at Perceval's comment. "Hey, that's rich! You feelin' sorry for me! Me boys'll enjoy that! Stay safe, sir; there'll always be danger about when you've no wealth to protect ye."

Perceval watched the crew as they tied down the last of his worldly goods and prepared to leave. "Wise words! I shall do my very best. Thank ye, my good man."

As the overstuffed carts lumbered away, Gwendolyn ran after the bank's professional thieves, sobbing as she trailed along behind her prized possessions, hoping against hope that her armoire might wiggle free of its binding and land in her arms so the two of them could run away together and start a new life in a land filled with beautiful petticoats and gowns.

She cried out as she ran, "Perceval, do something!"

Stephen the Sarcastic pushed back his thick shock of untamable dirty blond hair, waited until Perceval's wife was out of earshot and said, "Well, that went better than expected."

Despite himself, Percy let out a burst of laughter.

Over in the dirt pit between the house and the barn, Richard the Conveniently Brave wheezed as he heaved a final log onto a pile of wood large enough to burn for most of the night while Todd rhythmically scraped his flint until a spark caught the grassy kindling underneath.

Within moments, flames shot up through the bonfire, its pops and crackles drawing the men to its warmth. They circled the fire and sat on four of the many stumps surrounding the pit.

Worried, Todd indicated Percy's wife on the road behind them. "Think she'll be all right?"

Perceval nodded. His speech was slower than normal, almost forced, as if forming words took more effort than he had to give.

"Her sister lives a furlong away. Either she'll stay there or come marching back, spitting fire. I'd put my money on her sister. If I had any money."

All the men muttered their agreement.

In better times they would have laughed, clinked their mugs and taken a swallow, but there were no libations tonight.

After a long silence, Stephen said, "Well, at least ye have your health!"

This time Perceval didn't laugh. Earlier that morning he noticed several red welts on his legs, and by midday his entire back felt as if it was on fire. He hadn't examined himself yet, as it wasn't anywhere near the top of his latest concerns, but he had a sneaking suspicion his body had recently added injury to his many grievous insults.

Richard was the next one to speak. "I believe ye have the crap stick."

It was a regular part of life in Kingston that one had to walk out in the world to get from one place to another. As one did, inevitably, one had to walk through a daunting amount of mud and manure to get to where one was going.

As a matter of course, every home or business had what was commonly known as a crap stick leaning against the entry door. Once you scraped off the majority of earth and dung from one's shoes, admittance was granted.

This everyday occurrence became a metaphor for life between Perceval and his friends. Every time they met, no matter where they were, they quickly did an assessment of all in attendance to determine who got to hold court first.

If someone's parent had just been gored, or a plague had wiped out their family, or a fellow noticed they'd recently lost a leg, they'd be granted permission to speak before the others.

The size of one's woe determined whether or not anyone else even got a chance to utter their own petty grievances over the course of the evening.

It was always considered a wonderfully calamity-free time when no one claimed the right to the crap stick. This was not that day.

What happened next was not unexpected, but it was uncomfortable, nevertheless.

Believe the generalization or not, it is generally accepted that women are almost without exception better at accepting raw emotion from others.

Men, especially at this particular time and place, did not put a high priority on honest expressions of pain or sorrow. They tended to bury most of their uncomfortable, embarrassing emotions well below the surface and covered them up with joviality, drink, raucous sport, and carousing.

Perceval was well past the pretending stage. When his friend lightly tossed the conversation his way, Percy lowered his head and convulsed as he sobbed.

He had uncharacteristically cried many tears over the course of the past two weeks. Traveling west to see the house where all of his beloved children perished almost destroyed him. Remembering each of their faces and their specific mannerisms brought bitter tears on a regular basis.

But this cry was different.

Enough time had passed that sorrow was unceremoniously shoved aside by the bully known as anger.

Perceval threw his head back and let out a primal scream of rage. To say his friends were taken aback at this raw, unfiltered expression of pure, unadulterated pain would be an understatement.

They expected their old friend to have a few bad days, but nothing like this. The three men shot worried glances at each other. None of them had the slightest idea what to do. At that very moment, to a person, they all wished they were absolutely anywhere else in the kingdom.

Their discomfort increased when Perceval started to grouse and grumble a guttural stream of barely concealed venom.

"May the day I was born be cursed of all days. Nay, may the day I was conceived be cursed! That my father's seed would have been spilled on the ground! For this is the reward I have so earnestly sought? This is how all my toil and trouble are repaid? May the King find it in his heart to strike me dead! For my life is forfeit! I hold not onto any semblance of hope or desire or charity! I am one of the walking dead. Save me from this body of death!"

Stephen the Sarcastic ran through about five different snarky responses in his head but, fortunately, had the good sense to hold them all in.

Richard the Conveniently Brave did not feel this was one of those times when courage coursed through his veins, so he held his tongue.

Only Todd was foolish enough to answer. He stumbled around for an appropriate response and could only come up with a tone deaf, "You don't mean that!"

The denial of his feelings did little to endear Todd to Perceval. It only solidified the persecuted man's true desire to cease to exist, if only to no longer have to deal with people who, at the moment, he considered to be such insensitive fools and idiots.

His retort left little ambiguity. "Oh, but I do, dear friend. I mean it with every fiber of my soul."

Coupled with his emotional pain, the physical discomfort Percy had begun to feel earlier, centered around his legs and back, was now spreading up and over onto his arms, neck, and the back of his head.

Richard was the first to notice it. He pointed to a large red welt peeking out from Perceval's tunic. Without thinking, he pointed at the growing sore and said, "What's that?"

Even in the flickering firelight, all the men could see something was wrong. They craned their necks to get a closer look at the ever-increasing red sores on their friend's face and neck.

Perceval sat up straight, untied his sash and winced as he pulled his tunic up over his head, revealing a body literally covered with red, pulsating blisters. "My body be on fire!"

Once the other men saw the extent of Perceval's infection, they recoiled with revulsion. Richard sucked in air and said, "Oh, Perceval…"

"That bad, eh?"

Stephen stepped closer to the fire for a better look. "No, worse! Whatever it is, you're covered with it!"

Richard looked away as his stomach turned, "It be not leprosy. Came on too quick. Boils, I'd say."

Todd couldn't hold it in any longer. The question that had been burning inside his brain since the award ceremony came tumbling out. "For the King's sake, Percy, what on earth did ye do?"

Once he broached the unutterable topic, the others felt a brief sense of relief, which lasted all of about ten seconds. After that, the vehemence behind Perceval's reply made them all want to cower and hide.

Perceval could scarcely believe what his friend had just uttered. He recognized the ignorance behind the question, but it still managed to knock the air out of his lungs. He was incredulous.

There were daggers in Perceval's eyes and brimstone on his tongue. He threw out each word as if he were dropping two-ton boulders off of a castle wall in the hopes of crushing the enemies down below. "What… did… I… DO!?"

Perceval's flash of anger made Stephen and Richard sit straight up. They had all thought of the question, but only Todd was insensitive enough to actually ask it.

Sadly, they were all in for it now, and nothing could be done other than to steel themselves for the oncoming venting of Perceval's spleen.

Todd, however, was not as perceptive as his two friends. He managed to completely miss Perceval's unmistakable 'back off!' signals.

Like the clueless idiot that he was, he continued. "How can you not see the obvious? All the calamities must have a reason! Things like this don't just happen! And now the boils! Perceval, my friend, what have ye done? The King would never allow such sorrow to land on any of his subjects unless they, somehow, were at least partly to blame!"

The fair-weather friend looked to his friends for support. "Be I wrong? Art thee not thinking the same thing?"

At this, Stephen and Richard did their best to distance themselves from Todd's sweeping accusations.

When people were first introduced to Todd over the years, their first question was predictably why he wasn't given a namesake on Naming Day.

But after spending a few minutes with him, the reason became abundantly clear. Todd was just Todd.

There was nothing remarkable about him, either in the positive or negative column. He just was. He was neither hot nor cold. He certainly lacked a high level of intelligence, but he wasn't a complete dullard, either. His looks were nondescript. His height, average. His smile, unremarkable. The bland-as-toast man spent his unobserved, passionless life treading water in the lukewarm pond of mediocrity.

But this was the day that changed all that. From this day forward, Todd became the first person in Kingston to have his namesake delivered before his moniker. After this particular exchange, Todd was known far and wide as Can't-Believe-He-Said-That-Todd.

Sadly, the name fit. For years people knew that Todd always talked first and if his brain eventually caught up, so much the better. But it was never expected. He was just Todd. Todd the sort of stupid. Todd the on the outskirts of smart. But this was the namesake that finally stuck. It fit him perfectly.

Mainly because Todd tended to double down on awkward questions. Most people catch on when their foot has been fully inserted into their mouths, but not Todd. He was oblivious to social cues.

Can't Believe He Said That Todd was the guy who asked the inappropriate query and immediately followed it up with an even more embarrassing question.

Despite the accuracy of the descriptive handle, eventually the people of Kingston tired of Todd's long pre-namesake and shortened it to the more serviceable Todd the Odd.

After Todd's latest accusation, Perceval shook his head and shrugged his shoulders. "I suppose I'm relieved I can finally admit it. I've been carrying this burden for so long. I knew in my heart of hearts it was only a matter of time before my litany of crimes was discovered and my well-deserved punishment wouldst be carried out."

Stephen the Sarcastic sensed what was about to pour forth. As did Richard. Only Todd took the bait. He leaned forward expecting a confession of the highest order.

Perceval started softly, steadily increasing in volume, as if he wanted all the world to hear. "Why, it was only last month that I took a bag full of kittens and puppies down to the river, filled the bag with rocks and threw them in, gleefully laughing at their drowning yips and mews. The week after that I gouged out the eyes of at least a dozen babies and threw them in after the kittens and puppies. On Tuesdays I like to molest fair young maidens. Wednesdays I save for raping widows and tormenting orphans. But Thursdays are my most favorite day of all. On that special day I rape a widowed orphan maiden, gouge out her eyes, tie her up in a sack and throw her into the river. Oh, now that I say it out loud, I can only pray that the deaths of my children can somehow balance the unconscionable atrocities that I have committed!"

Even Todd, in his perpetual state of dim, couldn't miss the excessive sarcasm Perceval was tossing his way. He groused, "No need to be a complete arse about it."

Stephen tried to ease the tension a bit with, "I can't wait to hear how you fill your weekends."

Clad only in his linen undershorts, Perceval leaned back on his haunches. The fire flickered across the oozing open sores on his chest. His hooded eyes stared at the imbecile across the pit. "Oh, Todd, I've always suspected thou wert dim, but now, without the aid of wine or ale to excuse away your true limitations, I can finally see what a complete and utter moron ye are."

Richard totally agreed with Perceval, but still made a half-hearted attempt to defend their idiot friend. "Now, see here, my good man. Todd may well have overstepped his bounds, but don't let your pain color—"

Perceval cut off his conveniently brave companion. "Overstepped his bounds? Art thou suggesting that anything I could have done would be worthy of the punishment I have received? Art thou also suggesting that the King be so cruel that he would mete out so terrible and callous a punishment on anyone in his kingdom?

"Be he not good? Be he not the very definition of grace? My King may well be behind my calamities, but only to enact a design of his own making that is somehow for my benefit! Never in a thousand years would our King dole out such a heartless sentence! I be innocent, I tell you! And so be our King!

"I have no hidden secret life. I'll grant you, my shortcomings art without end. If you need further proof of that, merely ask my wife for the current list. But as to the reason for my litany of bad tidings, I swear on my mother's grave and all that is holy, I be not the cause."

Off in the distance a flash of lightning and a low rumble of thunder punctuated Perceval's declaration of innocence. A few moments later, rain began to fall. Softly at first, but that soon gave way to a deluge, dampening the fire's roar.

Perceval closed his eyes and hung his head. "Go! Find a warm bed and a woman to hold. Nothing can be done for me."

The three men slowly rose to their feet, torn between wanting to stay with their friend and the desire to do exactly what he had suggested.

Grasping at straws as he rubbed his gaunt frame to ward off the sudden chill, Richard said, "Perhaps in their haste, the crew left a blanket in the house—"

Perceval was more adamant the second time. "Go! Before my tongue reveals what I think of the other two of you! Nothing is to be done for me. Come back when I am of my right mind."

The shivering men scampered off to their horses. Stephen shielded his eyes from the stinging rain. "Yea! That be exactly what we shall do! Soon you'll be right as rain, and we'll take you out for a weekend you'll never forget—to help you forget!"

Perceval nodded and waved them off. "Go!"

The three men did just that, leaving Perceval in the now soggy, smoldering fire pit.

He listened until the sound of galloping hooves was drowned out by the cacophony of the thunderstorm. He struggled to his feet, waited for the feeling to return to his legs and trudged through the mud to his barn.

Going into the corner of one of the barn's empty stalls, he dug out the King's sacred book from under a pile of hay. Fortunately, it was wrapped in a thick tunic. Percy kicked the rest of the loose straw into a pile, untied and then spread the old robe out over his makeshift bed, slowly dropped down onto one knee, and ever-so-cautiously laid down on his side.

Using his family heirloom as a pillow, Percy curled up into a ball, winced in pain once or twice until his mattress of straw was not poking through the material into his sores, and shivered as he waited for sleep to overtake him.

Chapter Five
The Visitors

Perceval the Altruistic was awakened the next morning by the sound of a man impatiently clearing his throat.

Cracking one eye open, Percy could see he had a number of visitors. Six sullen, somber men in dark robes surrounded his woefully uncomfortable bed of hay. The prickly pain throbbing throughout his extremities quickly reminded him he was in no mood for niceties. He winced as he yawned, "Please excuse my appearance. I'm afraid I've just recently run out of caring."

One of the scribes towering over Perceval asked with concern in his voice, "Art thou, by any chance, infectious?"

"Thank ye so much for caring. I don't believe so. But at this point anything be possible. Doth thee desire a hug?"

As one, each of the men took a small step back. Another deep voiced man echoed the anxiety of his colleagues. "If this be not a good time for you, we can always come back."

By nature, Perceval wasn't a rude man, but at this time he discovered he had less than zero tolerance for fools. He neither got up nor moved. He had finally found a semi-comfortable position and wasn't about to ruin that by shifting around on his stable bed. He muttered, "I'd offer you a chair, but it appears they have all run off with our table."

Another scribe tried to assert his authority. "See here, good man, we've come out all this way to comfort you. The least ye can do is sit up and greet us eye to eye."

A laughing cough escaped Perceval's lips. "Comfort me? Somehow, I seriously doubt that. Your group be not known for comfort. Condemnation, yes. Ye have that in spades. Condescension, belittling, arrogance, you've mastered arrogance. But unless I miss my guess, comfort is the last thing ye will be bringing me today."

He knew he was ruffling the feathers of this proud group of peacocks, and in no small way, he found it immensely enjoyable.

In the time it took for his heart to skip a beat, Perceval came to the stark realization that he was done holding his tongue. He had spent a lifetime bowing and deferring to the over-inflated self-opinions of others, and frankly, he was ready to put that particular habit to bed.

Over the years, out of a sense of decency and a respect for the King's social order, he'd smiled through endless prattling and silly declarations from people who couldn't form a coherent thought unless it was written out ahead of time for them.

The scribes were the worst. There are small, insignificant men in the world who have a great need to feel important. Perceval found that strong leaders who truly had power and wealth seldom spent their days showing it off.

The people who bragged about their holdings, or worse, put on a show of their newly found (and usually severely leveraged) assets were the ones who were most to be pitied.

For the few starved-for-approval men who didn't have the wherewithal or the connections to acquire wealth or prestige, those poor fellows inevitably became scribes.

Scribes spent their days pontificating about and extrapolating endless rules and regulations from the King's Sacred Book of Acquired Wisdom, but seemingly spent very little time applying the King's advice to their own lives.

Sadly, rather than spending the bulk of their days lifting up their fellow man, they were all too preoccupied with pointing out where others had fallen short of their vaulted ideals.

Whereas the King had unfailing grace, the scribes were miserly. Theirs was an order of rigidity and fundamentalism.

As such, their organization only seemed to attract other

small-minded men who sought to wield power over the masses through intellectual and social intimidation. All while feigning a holy air of pained concern.

Perceval was sick of it.

He was also at the end of his proverbial rope. After all, what could they do to him that hadn't already been done? When you've been stripped down to the bones as he had, all threats of public humiliation tended to lose a touch of their power.

On top of which, Perceval was also hurting and tired. He didn't have the energy to go toe to toe with one person let alone the half dozen who currently surrounded him.

He closed his eyes and relaxed. "Tell ye what. Thou canst read, chant, or expound on whatever ye have come to tell me while I lie here. I'm not ignoring you, but I don't have the energy to pretend thou art important."

This statement both perturbed and perplexed the scribes. Each one was insulted, as they were not used to being dismissed by one who was clearly now their inferior.

For a few moments they harrumphed and coughed but when no better course of action presented itself, they finally decided to proceed with their original plan.

The tallest scribe opened up the large book he was holding tightly to his breast. "Reading from the King's Sacred Book of Acquired Wisdom, the letter P. The purpose of pain."

At his pronouncement, the scribes all nodded in unison, as if their agreement somehow added an extra dollop of importance to the reading.

"*And lo, for what purpose doth the King have in allowing his children to suffer so? Let it be said from the valley to the mountaintop that the ultimate measure of man cometh not in moments of comfort and convenience, but rather, where that man stands in times of challenge and controversy.*"

As one, the scribes uttered the refrain, "As it has been said."

The reading scribe continued. "*Even more so! May each man, woman, and child consider it all joy when they encounter various trials and tribulations. For the testing of thy faith, in good measure, doth produce patience, and in turn, charity, and that in turn, character, and then finally, after that, hope doth arrive."*

When the scribes again chanted, "As it has been said," Perceval muttered, "That be me, brimming with faith, hope, and charity!"

The reading scribe scowled but didn't stop. *"And lo, what kind of world wouldst there be, if there be no pain, no discomfort, no challenges, or no suffering?"*

Perceval couldn't help himself. He piped in, "A damn sight better one!"

The scribe ignored the reclining man's rude retort and continued. *"We would, in all likelihood, be shallow, self-absorbed creatures. For pain, in small doses, can be a welcome friend. It can help thee avoid much larger pains down the road."*

When the other scribes threw in another, "As it has been said," it was all Perceval could do to not scream out at the insensitive idiots invading his privacy.

He desperately wanted to dress them down. He took the fact that he had the energy to want to rail against such inconsequential idiots to be a good sign.

The endless droning continued. *"For whom among us doth not need to sleep when our bones be weary? And what man doth need to be reminded to put not his hand over a flame once he hath been scorched? And what knave doth not forever protect his tender heart after once foolishly asking the beauty queen to the spring dance?"*

This last statement seemed to resonate with the scribes. Their echo of, "As it has been said," sounded more like a rallying cry than a simple agreement.

In what he hoped would be a clear signal for the scribes to wrap it up, Perceval struggled to his feet, walked over to the corner of the stall, and relieved himself.

The man was a disheveled mess. Clumps and strands of hay were matted to his body and sticking out of his hair. His red bulbous boils were a sight to behold. But no one in recent memory had ever had the audacity to pee during a reading of the King's Sacred Book of Acquired Wisdom. On top of which, it appeared the lost soul was using his valuable copy of the sacred book as a pillow!

The reading scribe stuttered a bit, scanned the book and skipped down to the bottom of the page. "Uh, *and from all these lessons, may the hearer have both a restoration of hope and great relief from their various and sundry ailments, knowing the King walks with thee through all of thy pain and suffering.*"

When he closed the book, his brothers in arms emphatically stated, as they always did, "As it has been said."

Perceval walked back to face the shocked and sullen scribes. "Well, wasn't that a complete waste of time. Please let me know when one of you has any kind of infirmity or setback so that I may come over to thy home and vent my spleen on thee when thou art down."

The leader took umbrage. "Sir, ye would do well to keep a civil tongue. I dare say thy unfortunate circumstances have brought out a shamefully distasteful side."

Perceval's civility had officially run out. "At least I have an excuse! Out of the whole lot of thee, ye couldn't fill a thimble full of compassion! Ye think I'm in pain? No, that's where thou art wrong. I passed pain the moment I was told my first child was dead!

"I be not in pain, gentlemen, I be in agony! I am being burned alive in the trash heaps of the Outskirts! Ye do not bring comfort today! Ye mock my pain and callously kick at the scabs of my heart. Shame on ye! A pox on every one of you! May ye not live to see or feel the hand I have been dealt, for I fear ye would not survive the comfort of your friends!"

Perceval was now itching for a fight, but the scribes were cowards. They bowed their heads, turned, and hurriedly made their exit, clucking like hens as they shuffled off, incoherently mumbling about their mistreatment at the hand of the man formerly known as Altruistic.

Perceval followed them out into the sunshine and waved his arms as they tripped over each other cramming into their carriage. "Thank ye for stopping by! Great talking to you! Mayhaps I can make it into town for Hypocrite Sunday so I can see all of ye again! Or Selfish People Pretending to Care Day! I may be busy for Screw the Rest of the World month, but I'll see if I can drop by for a bit to bow down before one of thy tiny statues! At the very least I'm sure I can make it to your weekly narcissist luncheon! Assuming there be any seats left!"

He kept going on like that, giggling to himself, shouting at the top of his lungs, until the grumbling scribes left his property and were well on down the road.

Passing the scribes, coming from the opposite direction, were two dark figures on a horse drawn cart.

They reverently bowed to the gaggle of religious elders and, from the look of it, seemed to be taken aback when they were summarily ignored.

As the wooden cart drew closer, Perceval could see Brother Bob holding onto the cart's reins and a smaller figure sitting next to him.

Perceval waved the monk on. "Keep going, brother! No more visitors today! I've had my fill of compassion!"

The kindly brother took no mind of Perceval's request and, instead, turned his cart directly onto what used to be Perceval's property.

This was the last straw for the downtrodden man. His temper flared. "Art thou both deaf and dumb? Go away! I cannot tolerate another human! Leave me be!"

Like a child throwing a tantrum, Perceval jumped up and down in a puddle left over from the night before, splashing mud all over his legs and torso.

"Please! I beg of thee! Leave me be!" Having exhausted himself, Percy fell back on his haunches, smack dab in the middle of the puddle, and hung his head in his hands.

Ignoring the spectacle sitting before him, Brother Bob helped the other figure out of the cart, walked around to the back, unfastened, and then rolled out a rather substantial barrel of ale, giving a slight heave as he maneuvered it onto the ground. "Hail thee well, my good friend! And how are we on this fine day?"

With his head down, Percy raised one arm over his head and put his thumb and forefinger together in a circle, indicating with all the sarcastic body language he could muster, that all was well.

Brother Bob rolled the barrel over in Perceval's direction. "You're looking much better than I would have expected! There was no need to trouble yourself by putting on such airs for the likes of me!"

Despite himself, Perceval could only laugh. "I hate thee! Do ye hear me? Hate, I say! Ye and every other do-gooder in the land! I hate thee and thy cheerfulness and the horse ye rode in on. Begone! Before I infect you with my curse!"

Closing in, Brother Bob could see the extent of his friend's physical ailments. He held in his shock and did his best to retain his sunny disposition. "Before we intrude any further, may I introduce, from the King's order, Sister Mary Angel."

Perceval raised his head, ready to snarl out a long list of nasty invectives, but he was stopped short by the sister's face.

In all his days he had not seen such a vision of rapturous beauty. And this came from the man who was married to Gwendolyn the Exquisitely Beautiful! The young woman literally took his breath away.

He stared at her piercing blue eyes and marveled at the rose color in both her cheeks and pouting lips.

The rest of the woman, from head to toe, was completely covered in black cloth, the garment of choice for the sisters of the King's order. But it didn't matter. Her face was all she needed to open any door, or to have her way with any man who possessed at least one good working eye.

Perceval suddenly felt embarrassed at his appearance for he

knew he was meeting the most divine creature on the planet in his most deplorable state.

He vainly crossed his arms over his chest and midsection in an attempt to cover himself, but all he succeeded in doing was rubbing his limbs over his boils. He grimaced in pain.

Sister Mary Angel ignored Perceval's dumbfounded expression. There is no doubt the woman well knew of her beauty's effect on everyone she met. To her credit, she moved on as quickly as possible.

This impressed Perceval all the more because he knew of his wife's insatiable need to be fawned over.

Sister Mary walked back to the cart, stood on her toes to reach and then roll out a large cauldron. The diminutive woman comically waddled as she carried it over to the fire pit. She called over to Brother Bob. "It is as we heard. Boils." She turned to her new patient. "Tea and olive oil compresses will lessen the pain."

Brother Bob uncorked his sloshing barrel of ale and poured a healthy portion into a pewter mug. "As will this!"

Perceval wanted to protest both, but he was mesmerized by the speed and efficiency at which the sister worked.

She returned to the cart several times to bring over dry firewood and kindling to the pit. She arranged the logs into a circle and set the iron cauldron upon them.

Once the blaze was going, she opened a knapsack, uncorked two large bottles of oil, and poured them into the large pot. After which she began to methodically lay out dozens of pieces of cut cloth. She looked at Perceval once or twice, redid some calculations in her head, poured in more oil and brought out more bandages.

Perceval accepted another mug of ale from the monk and said under his breath, "Wouldn't happen to have a skinned rabbit hiding in the back of that cart, would you? Seems a waste to boil all of that oil with no rabbit."

Brother Bob merely nodded and said, "Drink."

When the sister was satisfied with the heat of her concoction, she dropped in several pieces of cloth and used a stick to stir them around and draw them out.

Walking over, she waved the dripping material in the afternoon air to cool it off a bit.

Perceval raised his hands in protest. "Please, no! I am beyond—" He instinctively winced when the sister laid the first compress over the most egregious sore on his arm then abruptly did an about face. "Oh, say, that is nice. Oh, it is. Thank you!"

When the sister looked up at him and smiled, Perceval felt a part of his heart melt away. He held out one arm for her to continue her ministrations and the other to Brother Bob to refill his mug.

He took a long swallow and felt immediate relief when she put another compress on a second sore. Draining the cup, Perceval raised the mug to the heavens. "At long last, a blessed reprieve! May I have another?"

Percy was perplexed when his angel of mercy stood up and shook her head. She looked over at her companion. "He's caked in mud and filth. It all needs to be washed off if I'm to continue."

Percy needed no more convincing. "To the river! And then back to relief!"

Chapter Six
On The Road

By the time Perceval left his old homestead, he was covered from head to toe in bandages. To anyone passing by it appeared as if the monk and the sister were transporting a living corpse to its own burial.

Percy was aware he was dressed in a makeshift funeral shroud, but he didn't care. As a result of the sister's miraculous hot oil compresses and copious amounts of alcohol, he was finally feeling no pain.

Which was the monk's intention as the back of the cart was about as uncomfortable a ride as one could imagine. Doubly so when one's hindquarters were covered in sores.

Brother Bob tried to steer the horse around the larger divots in the road, but there was only so much any man could do.

He called back to their inebriated passenger, "How doth it go?"

At that particular moment, Perceval was doing his best to retain his balance on a bed of straw sandwiched between the cask of ale, his family's sacred book, and Sister Mary's still too-hot-to-touch cauldron.

He was also the victim of what some might call a loose tongue. "What? Oh, as well as can be expected, I suppose! I am being driven by a goodly man of the King and the most beautiful woman I have ever set eyes upon. Did you know that? Of course, you did! You have to look at yerself every day. But maybe you don't! Maybe you just roll out of bed looking like that! In which case, ye be even more amazing! Could you imagine being that beautiful and not even trying? My wife be beautiful, to be sure, but she tries, I can tell you that."

The cart hit a rather severe bump, sending Perceval up in the air and back down on a variety of still tender bumps and boils.

"Ow! For the love of the King! Me blistered bum! Where was I? Right, my currently absent wife. It be a secret, but she tries. With the beauty thing, I mean. She wakes up Gwendolyn the Sort of Haggard and Tired with Puffy Cheeks. But then, somehow, she works her magic, and she comes out exquisitely beautiful! It be a skill that I admire. But, oh, it can take forever and a day!

"Do you take forever? I bet you don't. I bet you wake up as fresh as the morning dew. What does that mean, anyway? You wake up with your face all wet? What a stupid saying! I'm never going to say it again! Brother Bob!"

"What, Perceval?"

"Remind me to never say 'as fresh as the morning dew' ever again! Promise me!"

Brother Bob was enjoying his friend's drunken diatribe immensely. As was Sister Mary Angel. She could hardly keep from bursting out in laughter.

Brother Bob raised his right hand. "I swear by all that is holy I shall never again let you utter such a ridiculous phrase!"

Perceval continued on unabated. "Good! I'm glad we settled that! Oh, you know what? I bet all the other sisters in the order hate thy guts! Not you, Brother Bob, I'm talking about the pretty one. I'll bet the second ye come down, or up, or from whatever location ye come from to break your fast, they look at ye and think, 'Oh, here comes Sister Mary Rub it In Your Face with Her Face!' You know they do! Women secretly hate every woman who be prettier than them. 'Tis true! Gwendolyn tells me that every time I ask her why she has such a dearth of friends. Which means every woman on the planet clearly hates thee! That's got to be rough. Brother Bob!"

"Yes, my friend."

"We should pray for Sister Mary Angel Face. She's hated! For something she hath no control over! She didn't ask to be the most beautiful person on the planet! She just is! And that's just her face! The rest of her be all covered up! Either her hidden sections be altogether hideous or she's even more beautiful! By the King's grace, I don't even want to think about it. We should change the subject before she gets embarrassed! Brother Bob!"

"I'm still here."

"Quick, change the subject before she notices!"

Sister Mary patiently smiled and said, "In fact, if you must know, the sisters of my order are all lovely women with nothing but love for me and every other person in the kingdom."

Perceval whispered in his loudest voice. "Brother Bob! Too late! She noticed! And Sister Mary Angel Face, if you must know, you're wrong. To a person, they all hate you."

"They don't."

"Sorry to say, they do. They smile to thy face, your unbelievably gorgeous face, and lie like a bunch of rugs. It be so sad!"

"They don't."

"They do, do, do, do, do, do, diddily do! There! I won! Brother Bob!"

"What may I help you with, my friend?"

"Not that I don't appreciate the ride, but should I know where we art going?"

Brother Bob wasn't entirely sure how his old friend was going to take the news. "I'm afraid, for the time being, it appears the best place for you to stay is out at the Outskirts."

As a man who had made peace with the fact that he had little left to lose, Perceval was surprisingly nonplussed with the new information. "And why be that?"

Sister Mary turned around to face Percy. "We asked around town, and there's a general uneasiness surrounding your circumstances."

Perceval let this sink in, then cut to the chase. "Everyone thinks I'm cursed, be that it?"

The monk chimed in. "That be pretty much the long and the short of it."

"Dost thou think I'm cursed?"

Brother Bob shook his head. "Wouldn't be here if I did."

Perceval disagreed. "Yes, ye would. You're a good man. And since everyone hates Sister Mary Angel Face, she has nowhere else to go."

Sister Mary smacked her palm down on the buckboard. "No one hates me!"

Perceval shrugged. "It pains me to say it, but they do."

The sister nudged Brother Bob. "Tell him no one hates me!"

Brother Bob laughed. "Well, I don't, but I can speak not for anyone else."

The sister crossed her arms and turned away. "You're both horrible."

Perceval returned to his loud whisper. "Brother Bob. Change the subject before she notices."

"I believe that bridge has been crossed."

"Then I shall sing to distract the fair maiden from her sad lot in life!"

Percy spread his arms out wide and lifted his voice to the heavens. "*Oh, hear me out, dear people, for I've boils from me head to me bum! And though they be disgusting, turn not yer hide and run. But here's a first, I may be cursed, for I fear the worst's to come. But shed no tear and gather near to count the boils on me bum! It be fun! Let's all count the boils on me bum!*"

And that was how Perceval was introduced to the fine people of the Outskirts, as a drunken man covered with boils, sitting in the back of a monk's horse drawn cart, singing at the top of his lungs.

Whenever she looked back on their fateful meeting, Sister Mary Angel was often heard to remark that in all her days, she was quite certain she never had the pleasure of making the acquaintance of anyone quite like Perceval the Altruistic.

Chapter Seven
The Outskirts

The first week passed by in a medicinal drunken haze. Which was just as well, because Perceval's new home was little more than what could politely be called a hovel.

Along with the ale, Brother Bob had brought along a rather large tarp. He secured one end to the top of the remaining standing wall of an abandoned dilapidated structure, pulled the cloth out as far as it would go and hammered the bottom down with wooden pegs. Several discarded robes from the monastery provided the privacy flaps on either end of the jury-rigged tent, while another pile of cloaks made a semi comfortable covering on the dirt floor.

The King's book was rewrapped in Percy's tunic and was used as both a makeshift seat and, at night, a rather stiff pillow.

For the first six days, Perceval was vaguely aware of the monk and the sister as they attended to his needs, be they drink, nourishment, or hot compresses.

Upon coming out of a deep slumber on the seventh day, Perceval shoved the offered ale away. "Enough! I will have no more deadening of my pain! Let me face it. And let me take in my new home."

He looked around at his dismal surroundings with clear eyes for the first time since he had arrived. "I doth love what thou hast done with the place. Unless I be mistaken, its decor be early leper colony."

Perceval sniffed his underarms and recoiled. "Nay, I smell like early leper colony! If I've been this ripe all along, I beg thy forgiveness. Point me to the nearest river."

With that, Perceval willed himself up to a standing position, wobbled for a moment, gingerly held his pounding head, then pushed aside the monk's privacy flaps and stepped outside.

Taking in all that is the Outskirts, from the mishmash of lean-tos to the liberally scattered garbage, to the ever-present pungent aroma of smoke, feces, and decay, he rightly declared, "What a dump."

The man dressed as a disheveled mummy then turned to Brother Bob and smiled. "But it be my dump."

The monk pointed the way to the river, and with a spring in his step not seen for several weeks, Perceval side stepped a decrepit man sleeping off a bender in the middle of what passed for a street and began to make his way through town to what he hoped would be a brisk, refreshing bath.

Sister Mary Angel called after the wobbling man. "I wouldst gladly guide thee to—"

Percy emphatically pointed to the skies and shouted back, saying, "Nay, good woman! I shall not sully thy fine reputation by being seen with the likes of me. But if I not return by nightfall, send out the monk. His reputation I can tarnish."

Turning toward his new place of residence, Perceval got an eyeful. To a person, all the inhabitants of the Outskirts were dirty, unkempt, and foul smelling. As proof, not a single soul seemed to either notice, comment, or be put off by Perceval's body covering of flapping bandages.

An angry woman of undetermined age with one good tooth kicked a wooly bear of a man out of her dilapidated shelter. The muffled cries of a newborn could be heard coming from inside her dwelling.

The woman pointed a bony finger at the man on the ground and shouted, "And stay out until I get what's due me!" She then looked up at Perceval and thrust her hips his way, lifting her skirt up to her knees. "Looking to wet yer whistle, Captain? I'll throw ye one for no more than a song."

Perceval bowed and hurriedly took his leave. "Thank ye, no, my good lady."

As he scampered off over the hill the woman laughed. "Good lady? Not from around these parts, be ye?" She turned, squatted, and crawled under the flapping threadbare walls of her residence, mumbling to herself, "Good lady. Ain't that rich!"

The further Perceval moved into town, the more depressed he became. The entire city seemed to be devoid of color. Everywhere he looked all he saw were dark hues of mud brown.

Two bloodied men appeared to have knocked each other out mid-swing and collapsed where they stood in front of some kind of pub. Or it may have been a brothel. Or both. It was hard to tell.

On another corner, unattended urchins picked through a pile of garbage, apparently looking for something to eat.

Wild dogs ran free, barking, growling, and fighting over whatever scrap of food they managed to steal from local vendors selling fly infested brown, moldy vegetables.

But Percy's heart truly sank when he crested the hill and saw the river.

It matched the color scheme of the town in that it was brown, stagnant, and full of ash. Looking downriver, Perceval saw much of the same. A few people were washing in it, others beating their dirty nappies on the rocks.

Upriver was worse. That's where the burning trash heap rested. It was originally placed adjacent to a bend in the river, but over the years it had grown so large and unmanageable it now rested on the bank. The refuse was piled so high that mounds of it had tumbled down into the river, infecting it as well as damning up a good part of what used to be fresh spring water.

Seeing that as his only option, Perceval headed for the mound of trash about half a furlong away.

Walking along the side of the river, on the back side of the Outskirts, Perceval could see many of the cramped and crammed houses along the bank had dug sewage trenches emptying into the river. He stepped over what he could and maneuvered around the rest until he came within a stone's throw of the mountain of smoldering trash.

At the bottom of the river, he made out what appeared to be a cracked chamber pot. He waded into the water, pulled it out, and tossed the ceramic piece onto the shore. He stubbed his toe against another piece of trash and did the same thing with that.

Over and over again, Perceval would walk out into the waist deep darkened water, feel around, grab hold of some unwieldy refuse, waddle over to the shore, and make a deposit.

As he continued this strange quest, Percy began to attract an audience. A few of the gawkers started sorting through the items tossed onto the shore, looking for anything of value.

More critical onlookers stood back and laughed while others openly mocked him.

"Did yer lose somethin' mister?"

"I dropped me gold ring in there last night. If'n ye find it, it be mine!"

"An' I lost me mother's silver tiara! I claim that if'n it turns up!"

Another yelled, "Yer wasting yer time, mister! Nothing beats the mountain!"

Hearing the laughter while searching for their missing friend, Brother Bob and Sister Mary Angel came upon the scene.

The first thing they noticed was that Perceval's compresses had come off in the water and that, other than some vaguely red splotches, his sores were nearly healed. The second was that he was wearing himself out dredging the river by hand.

Brother Bob walked up to the water's edge. "Have a plan, do ye?"

Perceval stood up, pushed the wet hair out of his eyes and caught his breath. "No plan exactly, but I noticed the trash has damned up the river, and it be polluting the water the town is drinking and bathing in. If'n I can push the trash back, the water mayhaps be clear again."

Brother Bob ignored the howls of laughter behind him. "Figure on doing that all by yerself, are ye?"

"Nay, I was hoping for some help, but that seems to be in short supply today."

Brother Bob pulled up the hem of his robe and tucked it under the rope tied around his waist. "Two hands be better than one, I always say!"

Sister Mary Angel did the same with her long, black tunic. "Make that three!"

Perceval tried to stop her. "No, Sister Mary. I can't let ye do it."

The determined woman waded out into the murky water. "I don't recall asking for thy permission."

The petite sister reached down, struck gold on her first try and pulled up a wooden beam bigger than she was. She struggled mightily to free it from its watery grave.

She grunted as she shouted, "I've got it!" Upon which the sister lost her footing and fell bottom first in the river. Perceval and Brother Bob splashed their way to her side and pulled her up out of the drink. She spit water out of her mouth and laughed. "Methinks I don't got it!"

As a team, the three of them managed to pull the massive beam onto the shore. After letting it drop, Perceval looked up at the crowd and goaded them. "'Tis a shame that the sister here be a bigger man than everyone else in this town!"

And that was the official introduction of Perceval the Altruistic to the Outskirts. Only a few remembered the drunken singing man who was carted into town the week before, but no one forgot the idiot optimist who single-handily inspired over half the population to dive into the river and pull out a literal mountain of trash.

It was hard messy work, to be sure, but with Perceval's direction, by the end of the afternoon progress had been made.

Teams were formed and assigned different parts of the river. Slowly but surely, after a prolonged effort, the people of the Outskirts managed to clear out their most valuable resource and push back the encroaching refuse.

Sister Mary was the first to notice it. She looked down and yelled, "It's clear!" Others along the river echoed her refrain.

People could not only see the bottom of the river for the first time in recent memory, but the current was strong! And it went higher up the banks than it had in years.

Hearing the siren call of their friends, the town went wild! It appeared that the whole population of the Outskirts ran down to the river and dove in, splashing and laughing like giddy schoolchildren.

Old men floated on their backs, women dunked their hair in the fresh water and washed out weeks of debris. Perceval saw more than a few bare bottoms jumping into the refreshing bath.

Percy, Brother Bob, and Sister Mary Angel dunked one another down into the water time and time again, until Perceval and Sister Mary both broke the surface in unison, mere inches from each other's faces.

He was taken aback, yet again, at her natural beauty, but she, for the first time, saw up close how ruggedly handsome Perceval was. Not to mention he possessed the kindest eyes she'd ever seen, save one.

That's when the strangest feeling passed over Percy. From out of the blue, he was struck by an overwhelming urge to kiss the sister. Fortunately, before he could act on it, the woman turned away in a flash and swam off in another direction.

He quickly repressed his desire to swim after her, to at least tear away her head covering so he could see her entire face, or perhaps the color of her hair, but her wrap was bolted down so tightly even a roaring stream couldn't dislodge it. Returning to his senses, Perceval quickly did an about face, flipped around in the water and reminded himself that, regardless of his current circumstances, he was a married man.

Swimming away from his lustful near miss, Perceval made his way to the shore and called everyone in. He dropped his soggy arse onto the shore and looked around.

They had done it. The dam had been broken. The river was cleared out. The bottom of the mountain of trash had been shored up in hopes of preventing the problem from happening again any time soon.

To be sure, there were more than enough problems to deal with on another day, but at that moment Perceval felt a sense of accomplishment he hadn't felt for longer than he cared to remember.

Many a man and woman dragged themselves out of the water and slapped him on the back as they passed by, praising him for a job well done.

Each slap caused pain to radiate from his healing sores, but Perceval never let on. He merely gritted his teeth and repeated the phrase, "We all did it!" over and over again.

When Brother Bob and Mary Angel came up out of the river, Perceval instinctively cast his eyes downward lest they linger on the sister's heretofore unseen legs and how the wet cloth clung to her shapely figure.

Aware of his reaction, the woman quickly adjusted her modest attire by untucking the hem of her garment from her belt and pulling the wet cloth away from her midsection.

She and Brother Bob sat down on either side of Perceval, admiring their handiwork, watching the rushing river as it cascaded over their toes.

Brother Bob exhaled and broke the silence. "I can't believe we did that!"

Perceval agreed, "Nor can I."

Sister Mary put her hand on Perceval's knee. "Ye did that."

"No, it be all of us."

Sister Mary patted his leg and said, "'Tis true. But it was you. It wouldn't have happened without thee."

Perceval had never learned to accept praise, so he deflected. "The good news is these people have clean water again! I can only imagine how their health shall improve, let alone the smell of the place!"

As the words came out of his mouth, they all heard a low rumble. Then the ground around them began to tremble. What happened next can only be described as a trash avalanche.

Debris from the top of the mountain began to give way until a huge section broke off and tumbled down directly toward Perceval and his friends.

The three jumped up and ran to safety just moments before the boulder of refuse crashed down with a terrific force, bounced past where they were sitting, and landed smack dab in the middle of the river, damming it up worse than it was before.

Surprised and shocked, the three looked at the newest obstacle that had just erased all of their hard work. After a few seconds of stunned silence, they all burst out laughing.

They threw their arms around each other, turned, and made their way up the trash strewn bank. Brother Bob said, "Who said the mountain always wins?"

Sister Mary muttered under her breath, "Some idiot."

Perceval laughed as he shook his head and said, "Well, methinks I know what we be doing tomorrow!"

Chapter Eight
One Bite at a Time

There's an old, oft repeated phrase Perceval had heard ever since he was knee high to a gopher's eye.

Whenever someone faced an insurmountable problem, and was complaining about the impossibility of said task, inevitably some wise old coot would speak up and ask, "How does one eat an entire whale? One bite at a time, my boy, one bite at a time."

That was the saying he had to repeatedly remind himself of over the next few months, as the whale that was the Outskirts certainly seemed both insurmountable and indigestible.

Ready to eat his fill after a long day of physical labor, Perceval walked through the town square and over to the long nearly empty serving table supplied by the sisters of the King.

Concerned, he glanced at the long line of waiting hungry people, then back at the extremely limited offerings of bread and watered down stew. Under his breath, he asked Brother Bob, "Art we waiting for the rest of the food to arrive?"

The monk shook his head. "Nay, this be all we have."

"What happened to all the money and supplies I've been sending here over the years?"

The monk shrugged. "Think, perchance, of how bad all of this would be without thy kind support!"

Perceval was too wise to accept sarcasm as an acceptable answer. "Doest not thou have a commandment or two about lying?"

Brother Bob spoke in hushed tones. "We work with what we've got. Sad to say, the system here be broken. But better that a few get a lot and the rest get scraps than everyone getting less than nothing."

Perceval understood the ways of the world better than most. "So, the Outskirts be run on graft."

Brother Bob gestured to the food line. "See for thyself."

The sisters of the King, perhaps ironically, set up their food line in front of the brothel. Or pub; Percy still didn't have the lay of the land down. What he witnessed, however, was unmistakable.

The large crowd of scrawny, obviously hungry residents of the Outskirts stood a fair distance away from the table of food, while a noticeably large man filled his mouth, plate, and pockets with as much stew and bread as he could carry.

Sister Mary Angel gathered a few of the bread pieces in her apron before the big man stopped her. He said, "I like the ends. Good for soppin' up stew. Put 'em back!"

Assuming good manners would always carry the day, Perceval walked right up to the public glutton and said, "I say, my good man, it appears thou art taking the lion's share while the good people of—"

That was as far as Percy got.

The town brute known to all as the Hammer turned with surprising speed and threw one of his ham hock fists directly into Percy's gut, causing the well-intentioned man to double over.

The Hammer then clenched his bread-holding fist, swung it straight up, connected with Percy's left cheek, and lifted the winded man completely off his feet, if only for a second.

The crowd sucked in the air as they watched their failed savior crumple to the ground. Several people from the river project moved to Perceval's aid but were quickly warned off by the Hammer's bellow. "Don't nobody touch 'im! First person who aids this idjit don't eat for a week!"

Brother Bob bravely ignored the man's threats and knelt down next to his friend, helping him up to a sitting position. After a few moments of impotent wheezing, Perceval's lungs opened up and he was able to breathe again.

Brother Bob gestured with his thumb back at the Hammer.

"That be the guy I was telling you about."

Perceval wanted to laugh, but his head was throbbing. He winced in pain. "Thank ye for the heads up." He put his palm gingerly on the side of his face. "Be my eye still there?"

The monk nodded. "For now."

Perceval pushed off of Brother Bob's arm and staggered to his feet. The bully glanced over his shoulder at him and spoke with his mouth full, spraying bits of stew across the table. "Ready for lesson number two?"

When Perceval turned and ran off, the big man bellowed, "That be right, man. Run, ya coward! The Hammer owns the Outskirts, and no amount of trash haulin' and tidying up is gunna change that!" He turned to the watching and waiting crowd. "And now all of you is gunna hafta put a cork in it whilst I fills me belly."

About ten minutes later, the Hammer was more than a little surprised to see Perceval walk back into the town square. His gait was unsteady, and one side of his face was red and puffy, but returned he had.

Brother Bob shook his head.

Sister Mary mouthed a silent, "No!"

A hush fell over the crowd.

The hooligan smiled, licked each of his fingers and balled his hands into fists. "Ye got guts, I'll give ye that."

Perceval tried again to reason with the man as he walked up to face him. "I believe if we all share what we have, equally, there shalt be more than enough for—"

The moment Perceval was within striking distance, the Hammer swung his huge fists at the newcomer's head.

Ready for him this time, Perceval managed to pull back so that the bully's knuckles barely grazed his chin. But the Hammer's second punch landed a direct hit in Percy's midsection with a force that, again, lifted the older combatant up into the air.

The second it happened, everyone standing nearby heard an odd crunching sound and then were treated to a surprise when the Hammer screamed out in pain. Shocked, he held up a severely mangled hand.

Landing back on the ground, and quickly regaining his balance, Perceval reached behind his neck in order to untie the iron fireplace grate that was secretly sequestered underneath his tunic. Letting it fall into the dirt, he then placed both hands upon the iron weapon, swung it around to build up a healthy amount of momentum and smashed the Hammer directly upside his head, connecting squarely with the bully's jaw.

The big man's eyes rolled up into their sockets, and he collapsed like a sack of potatoes into the dirt. A cheer of amazement went up from the crowd, the likes of which hasn't been heard since.

Perceval tossed the iron grate aside and said, "Amazing what one can find at the bottom of a river. Anyone have any rope? I be hungry, and I believe this man has had his fill."

This declaration was immediately greeted by yet another cheer.

✝✝✝

The Hammer woke up the next morning courtesy of a refreshing bucket of cold water to the face. He sputtered and tried to move but soon discovered he was trussed up and hanging upside down from a tree, with a broken jaw and a throbbing broken fist. He cried out, "What be this? Let me down!"

As his rope slowly turned his body around, he saw well over a hundred people gathered outside of town. Even hanging upside down, he instantly recognized Perceval, and it sent him into a rage.

The victor of the previous night's fight said, "Oh, good, ye be up!"

The Hammer used all of his anger and might to uselessly swing from side to side. "I swear, when I get down from 'ere—"

And that was as far as he got.

"I'm afraid you leave me with no choice," said Perceval as he wadded up one of the sister's compress cloths and stuffed it into the big man's big mouth, which instantly shot a bolt of pain to the man's brain, as if he were jabbed by a red-hot poker.

Perceval turned to the crowd and projected so those in the very back could hear. "The man you see hanging before you hast been accused of various crimes against humanity. Who here can testify before the King and country that the aforementioned Hammer didst willfully steal something from your person and, or place of residence?"

Over half of the hands in the crowd went up.

Percy leaned down to the swinging bully. "Just so thee know, we went through thy house last night when thou wast napping like a baby and found a wide assortment of items thou art accused of pilfering."

The bully impotently screamed his muffled protest and wiggled his belly from side to side.

Percy turned back to the crowd. "And who here hast been physically assaulted by yon Hammer?"

Even more hands from the group shot up to the sky.

"And finally, who among us is generally tired of the Hammer treating the Outskirts as if it be his own personal fiefdom?"

At that, every hand was raised.

Percy looked down at the subdued prisoner. "Congratulations! Thou didst hit one hundred percent with that one!"

The hatred in the Hammer's eyes told Perceval he need not prolong the man's humiliation any longer. Perceval raised a hand and Brother Bob steered his waiting horse and cart over to pick up the dangling hostage.

A few men picked up the wiggling bully and deposited him in the back of the wagon. Perceval untied the rope from the tree, secured the man to both sideboards, double-checked the knots, and for good measure tied him down a second time.

He gave a rolled-up parchment to the monk. "Here be a list of all the crimes the Hammer hath been accused of. Tell the sheriff all the good citizens of the Outskirts will gladly come and testify, if need be."

Perceval then gave the monk a small pile of papers. "And if

ye would be so kind, please post these throughout the town. They tell Gwendolyn where I'm staying. If she ever decides to return."

Brother Bob nodded, patted his friend gently on the back, and began his one-day journey. Perceval shouted out a last request. "And at the end of the Hammer's sentence, if there ever be one, kindly implore that he be escorted out of the kingdom of Kingston!"

As Brother Bob waved goodbye, a shout of relief went up from the crowd.

The feeling of euphoria didn't last very long.

The very moment Perceval turned back to the waiting throng, one old woman shouted out, "So, what now?"

Perceval smiled to himself and thought, *One bite at a time, one bite at a time...*

He looked around at the hopelessly lost people and said, "I've been thinking about that, but what say ye? What dost thou want done? What bothers thee?"

A voice in the back yelled out, "Everything!"

Everyone laughed as Perceval nodded. "Duly noted. Anything more specific?"

Since no one had ever asked for their opinions before, it took a while for the groundswell to begin. But once it started, there was no stopping it.

A lone voice stuttered, "Th-th-the r-r-r-rats."

A murmur of agreement immediately answered the comment.

"Sewage."

"The endless smoke from the dump."

"It's not safe for me kids."

"Robbers."

"Rapists."

"Having to beg for our food."

"Sick all the time."

"No privacy."

"So cold at night."

One man stepped to the middle of the gathering. Perceval remembered him as one of the first to help out in the river. "Good sir, we know who ye be. And while we appreciate thy help getting rid of the Hammer, dare ye not give us hope. Dare ye not give us hope if thou art not going to be here to follow through."

Perceval smiled. "What be your namesake, my good man?"

That simple question rocked the fellow back on his heels. He appeared to be flustered. "My namesake? No one hast asked me that for years. Around here I'm known as Big Bud. But my namesake be Bartholomew the Valiant."

At that the man looked to the ground and shook his head, doing his best to hold back the tears.

Perceval answered him. "Well, Bartholomew the Valiant, I have no home. I be not even sure if I have a wife anymore. Like most of you, I have lost everything."

Now it was Perceval's turn to look at the ground in a futile attempt to stem his tide of emotions.

When he looked up again, his gaze was met by people who understood his pain. "But I haven't given up. I still believe in the King and his directive for all good people to help one another."

The old woman piped up again. "So, what art thou going to do about the rats?"

Perceval smiled at the matriarch. "Good mother, can ye give me until dinner?"

The old woman huffed and turned back to the village. "Dinner? I've been in this hell hole for nigh on twenty years! Ye can have until the morrow's break fast."

The tension broken, the majority of people laughed and slowly returned to their dwellings.

As Perceval watched the outcasts of the Outskirts walk away, he was struck by how much his opinion of them had changed in just a single day. Then he wondered how long he truly would be there and vowed to himself that he wouldn't be the one to let down Bartholomew and his friends.

Percy spent the rest of the day walking around the countryside deep in thought.

Through the woods, the fields, and over the hills, he explored as much of the Outskirts as time would allow.

When he made it back into town, it was nearly dark. Exhausted, he was sorely tempted to crawl into his tent and escape the problems of the day by sleeping them off, but he was famished, and the thought of seeing Sister Mary Angel gave him enough reason to put off a good night's slumber for at least another hour.

When he wandered into the public square, he was met by the collective stares of the entire community. He saw the soup line hadn't been touched. The sisters and apparently the entire town had been waiting for him to arrive.

"I'm so sorry I be late. Why didn't thee start?"

Sister Mary ran over to her friend. "Since ye defeated the Hammer, by all rights, thou needs to go first."

Perceval realized he had much to learn about this community. He walked over to that morning's outspoken old woman, took her calloused hands in his and asked, "Mother, wouldst thee do us the honor?"

What should have been a commonplace courtesy seemed to totally surprise the matriarch. She slowly made her way to the waiting table of food, picked up a tin tray, and looked over the pile of bread.

After a moment, her shoulders began to heave, and tears dropped down her cheeks. She wiped her face with her sleeve and mumbled. "Beggin' yer pardon. Ain't never been first in line before."

Taking her cue from Percy, Sister Mary followed him out into the crowd and began urging the smallest and the weakest to the table.

Grinning from ear to ear, Perceval stood at the back of the line and, one by one, insisted that every living soul take their fill before him.

After a time, Bartholomew walked over. He put his hand on

Perceval's shoulder, looked him in the eye, and nodded. "Lead on, good man, and we shall follow."

That was one test Perceval the Altruistic never forgot. One can read the King's Sacred Book of Accumulated Wisdom until one's face turns many shades of blue, but it's not until you actually put one of its lessons into practice that it truly sinks in.

Today Perceval the Altruistic learned the best way to be first is to put yourself last.

By the time Percy reached the food, he was pleasantly surprised to see there was enough left over to not only feed him, but the sisters as well. Naturally, he insisted they go before him.

Assuming they'd go away hungry, as they normally did, the women refused his offer, but at Sister Mary Angel's urging, they eventually partook.

When Perceval was able to fill his plate, he plopped down on an open space of dirt and was immediately overrun by children wanting to sit on his lap and climb on his shoulders.

When the parents of the rambunctious ragamuffins tried to call them back, Perceval insisted he was perfectly fine with their elbows in his ears and their feet in his food.

The newest resident of the Outskirts didn't get to eat much of his meal that night, and the side of his face smarted each time an errant elbow smacked it, but he didn't care. The smattering of joy breaking through the dark abyss of his soul was overwhelming and more than made up for any lack of comfort.

Across the way, sitting with her sisters, Mary Angel saw all of this and held it closely in her heart.

Chapter Nine
A Change Be Upon Us!

The next day's dawn came entirely too soon. Perceval was awake most of the night, planning, scheming, and fretting over the immensity of the plan he was about to present to the people of the Outskirts.

He didn't want to come in with such a long list of actions but felt down to his toes that each one was necessary.

Uncharacteristically, walking into the middle of the gathered group of eager faces, his resolve weakened. He began to second guess himself. He wondered if it would be best to start small, concentrate all their efforts on one task and work their way up to his ultimate end goal.

Before he was done processing, the old woman prodded him with an accusatory, "Well? We be waiting!"

Perceval nodded, then looked down to the ground and up into the heavens, hoping one or the other would hold the answer for him.

He stammered, "Uh, as it says in the King's Sacred Book of Acquired Wisdom, somewhere in either the pain or the perseverance section, I think I have this right, that the only way to truly effect change, is if the pain of thy staying the same be greater than thy pain in that of making the change."

Percy was met by a wall of blank stares, so he clarified. "Staying like this, as ye are now, has got to hurt worse than the immense amount of work we have before us needed to climb out of the abyss."

A few began to understand, but he still wasn't getting through to them. He blurted out, "How many of ye are sick and tired of living in sickness and squalor?" At that, everyone's hand went up. "Good! Then remember this! Remember the rats and the smoke and the hunger and the cold! I need every last one of thee to remember how much ye hate this!"

Bartholomew chuckled as he said, "Good Perceval, thou art preaching to the converted."

Percy sighed with relief. "Thank ye. That helps. I've gone over this a hundred times in my mind, and I keep coming back to the same point."

Perceval looked around at the dirty, expectant faces. He finally came out with it. "Nothing here works! You're downstream from the trash. Trash that will never stop burning! You have no crops, no animals, you live in filth! It all needs to be burned down to the ground so we can start over!"

The old woman grunted out, "Ye be telling us what we already know! Art thou slow, because ye don't seem to be catching on?"

With that, the matriarch slowed her speech down so that even an apparent imbecile like Perceval could understand. "What... Be... Your... Plan?"

Perceval took her gentle ribbing and jumped into his prepared remarks. "We need four things to survive: water, food, fire, and shelter. We have water. We can make fire. And we get the rest by having an income. Which means we need animals, crops, and a trade besides consumption of ale and prostitution."

At that he got more than a few grumbles from those who enjoyed both trades. Undeterred, he kept going. He laid out everything and then some.

He told them a new city had to be built on the other side of the trash heap. Upriver. The trash heap had to be broken down and moved away from the water. The fine citizens of Kingston would have to pay for the right to dump their trash here in the future. The Outskirts needed to sort the trash, burn what could be burned in small, confined areas and salvage the rest. The raw sewage needed to be gathered into compost heaps and spread on fields to fertilize their soon-to-be planted crops. They needed to acquire chickens, cows, and borrow some oxen. A wall had to be built around their new dwellings. Guards would have to be posted to protect their citizens. They needed to start a trade school. Maybe two or three.

He went on like that until more than a few stomachs were rumbling and most bladders were in sore need of relief. By the time he was done, he had not only beaten the fine folks of the Outskirts into submission but had also given them a workable plan.

When he came up for air, the old woman (known only, Percy later found out, as Hazel the Harrumpher) put her hands on her knees and pushed herself up into a standing position. All eyes were upon her as she winked at Perceval. "I asked ye for a plan. Ye read us a tall tale worthy of the King's grandest theater! After all that, I need to take care of my necessaries and indulge myself with a nap!"

When she shuffled past Bartholomew, the big man laughed along with the rest of the crowd, then asked, "And which part of thy plan do we start first?"

Perceval rubbed his chin, "I've narrowed it down to all of it."

Not getting much of a reaction, he continued. "Who here be skilled in masonry and stonework?" A few men grunted as their hands went up.

Percy nodded and continued down his list. "Carpentry? Farming? Animal husbandry?" Anywhere from one to half a dozen hands went up after each question.

One of the workers from the brothel stood up, smoothed her skirt, pushed her thick black hair away from her face and said, "I know my way around chickens and such. Where do ye plan on getting them?"

He felt himself smiling an impish grin and said, "Good woman, I know of a place where we can gather a few chickens and one particularly vexing rooster. And if one particular chicken coop disappeared from one particular barn, who's to say where it ran off to? Would not the new owners think some desperate vagrants took it before they had moved in?"

From the sea of confused looks staring back at him, Perceval became aware he was rambling. He stopped short and forced himself to get to the point. "We need a cart, one or two men along with thyself, and I shall take you to the chickens."

Seeing Perceval was preparing to leave, Bartholomew asked, "What shalt we conquer first?"

This gave Perceval pause. He pointed beyond the smoldering trash heap. "See the raised area upriver? That be our new home. We need a group to clear out all the trees and stones. After we mark out the city, we'll use the stones to build a wall around it. Another group needs to clear the river, then attack the trash heap one section at a time."

He pointed to the woods bordering their town. "We also need to clear that entire forest, for that be where we shall plant our crops."

A burly man shouted out from the back, "I kin raise the trees and make ye planks for building, but we'll need an ox or two if'n' we're to pull out the stumps."

Perceval could only nod. "I be working on that."

Bartholomew followed Percy's gaze around the land surrounding their homes, taking in the enormity of his plan. He nodded and said, "And how shall we keep ourselves busy if we manage to finish all thy tasks before dinner?"

It took a moment before Perceval realized his new friend was joshing him. He said, "Aha, humor! Very good. We'll need that in abundance if we are to rise up from the ash heap. Very good."

What Perceval didn't tell the citizens of the Outskirts was the second part of his plan.

He started writing to the King.

Beyond his own burning questions about his overwhelming calamities, he quickly came to see that his rag-tag group of outsiders needed more help than they could muster from their own community.

Each week he would write up a short list of personal questions as well as a longer list of needed supplies and then send them off with sister Mary Angel and her sisters of mercy.

Here, he got two surprises. The first was that the King of Goodania totally ignored any query Perceval had concerning his current situation. That was troubling enough, but the second surprise compounded the first.

In short order, supplies began showing up. Cart after cart of wood, stone, seeds, and various beasts of burden were dropped off at the Outskirts entrance. Nary an order or a decree accompanied these apparent gifts from the King.

More often than not the delivered items matched Perceval's requests to the letter. Which made the King's screaming silence regarding Perceval's more pressing personal problems all the more perplexing.

When he discussed this with Brother Bob, all he could get from the monk was a curt, "The King's ways be higher than our ways."

His other comment was even worse. The brother would say, "Ye have the King's Sacred Book of Acquired Wisdom. Need ye more than that?"

To which Perceval would mumble, "If I were married to thee, I'd be sorely tempted to murder thee in thy sleep."

Brother Bob only smiled and said, "Indeed, if I were married to thee, I'd help thee murder me!"

And so it went, week after week. Perceval would ask straightforward questions of the King, and in reply, he would get nothing but indifference and a hefty load of supplies.

More out of frustration than any desire to learn, Perceval began to spend every night searching through chapter and verse of the King's sacred book.

No small part of this was inspired by Sister Mary, who met him nearly every day to quiz him on what he had learned the night before.

The man knew his heart was steadily drifting away from his estranged wife and moving closer to the beautiful sister, but he also knew his blossoming love was doomed to be unrequited.

He rationalized his infatuation, telling himself he was just happy to feel anything but pain at this point. Yet he was too wise of a man to be blind to the fact that he was playing a dangerous game with his heart, one that was most likely going to end very badly.

Because of his schoolboy crush, Perceval scoured the scriptures, searching for any wiggle room when it came to the subject of divorce or infidelity.

Sadly, he found nothing that would bolster his position. Everything he read only reaffirmed the King's current unrealistic position that each man should be married to one woman, until death do them part, and nothing should ever tear them asunder.

While he did find quite a few passages warning of the snares of loose women, comparing them to various bejeweled farm animals, he came up short concerning women who stole your heart just by virtue of their virtue.

That frustration aside, one of Perceval's serendipitous surprises was discovering how much joy he gained by going through the scriptures.

In contrast to his previous life where he could go months without even glancing at the sacred pages, now he would spend an entire evening reading through the bloated Book of Pithy Sayings and found himself giggling as he read Stories of People Much Dimmer Than Thee for the umpteenth time.

That particular section was one of his children's favorites, and when he found two signatures at the end of the final verse, it brought a tear to his eye.

Despite these highlights, little of what Perceval read answered his secret longing. But as a bonus, the wisdom he gleaned from the endless advice contained within the pages was invaluable in his dealings with the inhabitants of the Outskirts.

Invariably, disagreements arose between workers, and Perceval often surprised himself by quoting the King's wisdom almost verbatim.

Getting in the middle of one such disagreement earned him the undying respect of the female population of the village.

Claudius the Strong came calling one morning practically frothing at the mouth. He sputtered and stuttered and gesticulated every which way until Perceval finally stuffed a pomegranate in his mouth.

Using his most soothing voice, the elder statesman urged, "Calm thyself, good brother. Enjoy the fruit, relax, and explain thy problem in words a person as dim as I can understand."

Claudius wiped the red juice from his cheek, spit out a few seeds, and pointed behind him. "Her!"

Percy looked up to see a very tiny woman whom he knew to be called Tammy the Timid standing a few feet away.

Perceval got up and bowed before the woman. "Ah, good woman, Tammy. To what do I owe the pleasure?"

Tammy lowered her eyes, gave a quick indication of a courtesy, and began a tirade that left little doubt she had long outgrown her namesake and conclusively proved who currently wore the girded loins in this family.

"Claudius the Strong and I have been put in charge of planting the first crops of both wheat and corn. We was chosen as I come from generations of farmers. Me an' me mother an' me mother's mother were born in the dirt an' have it in our blood. I know when to detassel the corn as well as how to separate the wheat from the chaff at harvest time. But Claudius the Strong here, who couldn't raise a weed in a pile of shite, fer some reason has got it in his thick head that he be the one who should be leading us straight to starvation!"

Seeing the seriousness of the situation, Perceval bit his lip to keep from grinning. He turned to the man who towered over his wife. "And what say ye, good Claudius?"

The big man's tone changed a bit, but he refused to back down. "I'll not disagree with her on those points. She be wise in the ways of farming while I be a stonecutter by trade."

"I see. But despite ye both agreeing with yer wife, thou art still of the mind that ye should be in charge?"

At that, Claudius stretched out to his full height and puffed out his chest. "Aye. For I be the man!"

Perceval had been on this King's earth long enough to realize there was a great difference between knowing the right way and actually accepting it. He then remembered the King's admonition about a gentle word turning away wrath, and he came upon a tactic.

"Say ye had an apprentice who saw a way to save ye both from having to redo an entire wall. Would ye listen to him?"

Claudius was quick to answer. "Aye. I've seen too many builders who have wasted weeks of back breaking labor because their heads were made of prideful stone."

Perceval continued, "And when the time comes to add support beams to a stone wall, do ye take it upon yerself?"

Claudius was beginning to catch on. "Nay, I'd let the carpenters take over."

"Pray, say thee why?"

"Me daddy always said, 'Tis better to have a house built by cooperation than a pile of rubble built by experts.'"

Perceval shot a glance over to Tammy. "Your father sounds like he be a wise man."

Claudius was not so dim as to miss Perceval's point. He sputtered one last time. "But, but, I be the man!"

Perceval nodded. "Aye. A man, who, I have no doubt, be strong enough to know in what areas he be weak and with enough power an' influence to convince everyone else to listen to the expert in these matters."

At that, Tammy subtly raised her hand, indicating to Perceval he should go no further. They both waited for the big man's brain to put all the pieces together. Eventually he arrived at the exact spot where his wife, the better named "Tammy of Hidden Strength," knew he'd land eventually.

Claudius spoke softly now. "So, sometimes, being a man be knowing when yer partner has the better idea."

Seeing Perceval nod with approval, the strong man hit one

fist in the palm of his other. "An idea I can force other people to listen to if'n they're too headstrong to know what be good for 'em!"

Perceval finally let go of the laugh he'd been holding onto. "Something like that!"

Tammy walked up to her husband, gently slid her arm around his thick middle, turned him around, and headed back to their home.

Watching the tenderness between the couple was akin to a splash of cold water on Perceval's heart. He couldn't remember the last time he and Gwendolyn shared such a moment.

Barely a second after that, he was saddened by the brutal realization that he honestly didn't care if they ever did again.

Chapter Ten
The New Outskirts

As the weeks and months slipped by, Perceval found himself in great demand as a judge presiding over both petty and life-threatening squabbles at his new address.

This led to a greater degree of delegating more of his duties than he was comfortable with. But it had the side benefit of entrusting the future of the Outskirts to those who had found this area to be their home.

Sadly, more than once he fell victim to the axiom, "no good deed goes unpunished," but the end result was that Percy was pleased to discover his area managers rising to their individual potential.

He knew in his heart that, if left to his own desires, he'd be the one barking out the orders and finding himself stretched to his breaking point. After a time, he began to see this new system of delegation worked much better than his old way.

One of the best examples was the former prostitute, Belle the Bodacious, who was now known more for her ability to run the animal husbandry side of their operation than for her impressive décolletage.

But hands down, the true hero of the new building operation was Bartholomew the Valiant. He took to leadership like a duck takes to water. The man who was once so downcast he had given up all hope of any kind of future, now latched on to Perceval's rudimentary vision and turned it into an impressive reality.

With the help of a local artist, Barth laid out the new city. After living in less-than-desirable conditions for so long, he knew exactly what each dwelling should have in order to give the residents a measure of dignity and safety as well as to ensure a relatively stress-free environment.

The streets of New Outskirts were laid out on a grid, with several common areas in the center set aside for shops, public gardens, eating, and congregating.

In the interest of simplicity and an attempt to keep envy at bay, all of the homes were exactly the same. Each one had a fireplace with a stone chimney, two windows, and a front door with a locking latch. Row after row of the two room huts spread out from the center of town and filled the streets.

Inside every dwelling, either bunk beds or a single bed frame was built into the wall next to the hearth. Opposite the straw mattresses rested a roughhewn wooden dining table with a generous selection of stools courtesy of the monks.

The city wall was knee high at the moment, but in a few months, a tall fortification would surround their new city. Here, at Claudius the Strong's suggestion, Bartholomew slyly installed a secret. He put footholds up the wall about every two feet. That way, if there was ever a need, such as a fire or a wild boar on the loose, the people inside the city could easily lift themselves up and climb over the top of the wall.

The outside, however, was smooth from the bottom to the top, increasing the difficulty of nefarious strangers who might attempt to sneak into their fair enclave.

One particular occasion stood out from all the others. That was the day the city charter was established. After a hearty debate, it was agreed upon by all that every man and woman who was of age would be allowed exactly one vote on every issue. And the issues were plentiful.

After a long day of wrangling, cajoling, yelling, filibustering, and occasionally laughing, it was decided that there would be no house of gambling nor one of ill repute within the city walls.

It was of particular note that, as all of the former ladies of the evening had moved on to more respectable trades, each of them vehemently voted to end that nefarious phase of their gainful employment.

When one of the regular customers shouted out, "But what about our manly needs?" Belle stood up and yelled right back, "Then I'd suggest courtin' and marrying us!"

Another of her former sisters chimed in with, "And why not? We already know what ye like!"

That issue settled with a raucous laugh; the fledgling town moved on to other pressing matters.

The only other mildly controversial item to pass was the rather strict ordinance outlawing all trash and sewage within the city walls. Evidently the fine people of the Outskirts had lived in their own filth for long enough.

Day by day, the progress continued. Perceval would gather with the town's leaders, send off their wish lists to the King and include shorter and shorter requests of his own personal, unanswered needs.

In what felt like no time at all, the wall was completed, Tammy the (formerly) Timid's first crop of wheat and corn came in, and the village gardens were overflowing with ripe, succulent vegetables.

One crisp dusk in the late fall, early winter, the entire town left their old rodent infested dwellings, kicked the dust off of their sandals, and with a collective glee not seen or felt in years, burned their former ramshackle shacks to the ground.

Such a bonfire has not been seen before or since in the whole of Goodania.

Before night fell, everyone was officially given their own home in New Outskirts. Each resident entered their cabin with a sense of awe. Even the men who had helped build the structures were overcome with emotion.

The sisters of mercy lovingly placed fresh flowers in the many cracked pots and pewter mugs they salvaged from the trash heap and placed them on the mantles of each dwelling.

The homey, personalized touches would come later, but tonight, hearts were full, and many a person was heard to exclaim as they entered their new residence, "An actual door! With a window! And a fireplace! And flowers!"

It became a night of jubilation.

Everyone was torn between wanting to dance around the rising ashes of their old shanties and settling into their new homes. More than a few opted to do both, as well as imbibe in Brother Bob's free-flowing celebratory ale.

In great contrast to their previous village, when the last person stumbled into their new home, not a speck of trash was to be found on the grounds.

Of course, it was not all a bed of roses. Perceval anticipated a few other shoes to drop, and a rather large one did, directly into his lap.

More accurately, what happened was that a rather stubborn thorn developed in his side, and no one was quite sure how to remove it.

One of the Hammer's former associates, a scrawny little man by the name of Horace the Hoarder, began clamoring for Perceval's time close to every day with a long litany of complaints; some real, most imagined.

He claimed he wasn't getting enough food. The clothes he was given were old and threadbare. No one in town gave him the respect he deserved. His home was purposely drafty (as if the builders knew which hut was going to house him). His bad back was exacerbated by the work he was assigned (which, from all reports, he never did) and the bratty children of the town insisted on mocking him behind his back.

Based on the sheer volume of the little weasel's complaints, one had to be impressed by his imagined list of grievances.

At the start, Perceval was sorely tempted to throttle the man and give him a piece of his mind, saying something along the lines of, "Thou art getting more than ye deserve! Thou didst aid and abet a long-standing criminal enterprise! Thou shouldst thank thy lucky stars that ye weren't run out of town alongside the Hammer!"

Instead, Perceval patiently listened to a bitter, twisted man who was seriously untethered to reality.

Each day just after the crack of dawn, well before the leadership committee could even get their bearings, Horace would rush in and commence with his long and loud declarations.

Unprepared for such a force of nature, Percy would grimace, mentally check out, and attempt to deal with the complaining rabble rouser as if he were talking to a rational man. After a few weeks that strategy was dropped entirely.

What Perceval discovered was that regardless of what was said to placate Horace, no matter how much time or empathy was poured down the bottomless pit of the Hoarder's cold, black heart, the man would twist everything he heard until it fit into his own personal narrative of persecution.

Word got back to Perceval that the bane of his existence would walk around town complaining about everything under the sun, but mainly about Percy. Horace would spread lies about the leaders and their projects and then cry he was unfairly persecuted when he was threatened with bodily harm for the very malicious rumors he manufactured.

The end result was that very little of the daily agendas were being addressed. Horace the Hoarder was gumming up the works.

The momentum the Outskirts previously experienced had ground to a halt.

Various suggestions of recourse ranged from banishing the little man to pulling out his fingernails, one by one.

Finally, Perceval consulted the King's Book of Acquired Wisdom and against the advice of all, implemented what he called, "the uncomfortable good."

Horace the Hoarder was given grace.

He was also given several handlers, but grace was the overarching theme.

Each day Horace came in to complain, he was sent off with his own personal liaison to the ruling committee. That personal emissary (who had drawn the short straw that morning) would walk around the Outskirts with the Hoarder, writing down every single presumed slight as well as his innumerable suggested ways to improve life for the inhabitants.

After a few hours Horace would eventually tire, require a nap, and the long list of complaints would make their way back to the committee who would then look them over and actually act on them!

Obviously not every single one, but if an idea had even the slightest merit, the ruling board would swallow their pride and do their best to implement the tiny man's desires.

These ever-so-slight modifications to life in the Outskirts became known as the Horaces. In time his name became part of the common language, as in, "This could use some Horacing!" And, "Hey, thou just Horaced me!"

To complete the deluge of grace, each and every Horace was labeled with a sign. After just a week, the New Outskirts were liberally littered with Horace signs. Which pleased the cantankerous old man to no end.

Surprisingly, the daily list of complaints from the Hoarder trailed off to a trickle, while the plethora of suggestions, however slight, made up the bulk of his daily contributions.

In a twist no one expected, after a time people started to compliment Horace for his many improvements and modifications and because of that, eventually, the Hoarder became a reasonably slightly less narcissistic model citizen.

Percy had taken the right path, no matter how difficult, and had come out on the other side not only with most of his sanity intact but also more than a few citywide improvements courtesy of the ministry of Horace.

†††

Some time later, as a new rhythm of life began to emerge, Perceval walked around the ash heap that used to house the shadow of their former selves. He watched with pride as men dug out foundations for their new trade schools.

Making his way over to the chicken coop, now packed with fowl, he encountered the old mother. He smiled and gave Hazel a nod. Surprisingly, instead of her customary waddle-by, she walked up and embraced him.

He patted the shriveled woman's wrinkled hands. "And a hearty good day to you, good mother!"

The old woman slowly pulled herself away and wiped a tear from her cheek. "Wanted to give ye a proper thank ye a'fore I said goodbye."

Perceval was immediately concerned. "Art thou leaving us? After so much—"

The old woman shook her head. "None of that! I be not so dim as to leave of my own accord. Look at me! I've not many more days walking this King's earth. If my end comes sooner than later, I didn't want to leave without a proper 'thank ye, kindly.'"

Percy bowed before the woman. "It has been my honor."

The woman scoffed. "So it has!"

Perceval burst out laughing. "Whenever you do move on, I will greatly miss thee."

"So ye should."

Perceval couldn't help himself. He laughed again.

The old woman's lips crinkled up at the edges, revealing a mouth with nary a tooth. "It does my heart good to see thee laugh. 'Twasn't long ago when your joy was buried alongside ours."

Perceval nodded. "In two months, I will mark my one-year anniversary at the Outskirts. I must admit at the start of my time here, my heart was heavy. And while it is, indeed, lighter by far, even now I wonder."

The old woman looked up at the melancholy man and raised her white, bushy eyebrows.

Perceval continued. "What the King has provided for everyone here is truly a blessing. I know we all put our backs into it, but it seems he provided all that we asked for and more."

The old woman focused her gaze out across the clear, sparkling river. "But—?"

"But never once did he answer my endless queries."

A decent stretch of time passed before the old woman asked, "About—?"

Perceval felt a little foolish as he explained, "Well, about my reversal of fortune. More importantly, about my children. Be there a reason for my overabundance of calamity? I know we all have our own stories of woe, but did the fates merely lash out in such a way as to upend my life? Or be there a purpose behind it? I was hoping the King could clarify, to at least put my mind at ease, but he has remained frustratingly silent on the matter."

It was now the old woman's turn to laugh. Her raspy cackle turned into a deep, wet cough. Perceval realized her time on this earth was indeed coming to a close. The woman shook her head and turned to walk away.

Perceval pleaded with her. "Old mother, say ye not that I be an object of thy folly!"

At that, the woman turned on her heels to face Perceval. She raised the volume of her craggy voice to ensure that he not miss any part of her declaration. "For such a wise man, thou art naught but a fool! Look around! If ye did not experience thy tragedies, would any of this be here now?"

Saying her piece, the woman left, cackling, and shaking her head at the endless stupidity of Perceval and his kind.

Percy was left standing at the entrance to New Outskirts, considerably lighter than he was before, now that the scales had fallen from his eyes.

Chapter Eleven
Out of the Outskirts

At the one-year mark, the dilapidated town Perceval first encountered at the Outskirts had been most radically transformed. Sickness was down to the most run of the mill coughs and colds, and the dreaded rats had all but disappeared.

Two trade schools now stood where the original town and trash heap previously commingled.

The first New Outskirts graduate program was run by the sisters of mercy, who taught tailoring and seamstressing. The students soon became experts at taking cast-off clothing the well-to-do sent to their dumps and remaking barely used garments into rudimentary work clothes.

The second trade school was intentionally placed far downwind from the sewing center, as it was dedicated to the pungent brewing of ale and the constant din that accompanied the making of furniture. All courtesy of Brother Bob and his fellow monks.

Some of the townsfolk rightly observed that the quality of the furniture, or rather, the lack thereof, seemed to be directly linked to what the monks liked to call "tasting days." As a result, all quality inspections of the furniture happened during the day, and the ale was only "tested" at night.

Between the schools and the new trash reclamation center stood a thrift store that cleaned and repurposed well over half of what the good people of Kingston seemed to needlessly throw away. The rest of the refuse was used as either compost or fuel, and that which was deemed as irredeemable was gathered in carts and, in a twist of irony, subsequently driven back to Kingston and dumped over the side of a cliff near the city limits.

On what turned out to be his last day of living in New Outskirts, Perceval was making his daily rounds when something buried under a pile of waiting-to-be-reclaimed clothing by the sewing trade school caught his eye.

It was the unmistakable hue of blue that did it. He had not seen a dress of that color before or since.

Looking out of an open window in the school, Sister Mary saw Perceval pivot and make a beeline towards her location. Assuming he was dropping by to pay her a friendly visit, she straightened out her robe, quickly tidied up her workstation, and came out of the building to greet him.

Regardless of Perceval's mercurial mood, the lilt in her voice never failed to change her friend's expression to one of warmth and happiness.

But not today.

Today when she stepped outside to greet him, the man didn't seem to even notice her.

Instead, he walked past the smiling sister and made his way directly to the heap of clothes resting on a table outside of the trade school. He grabbed the sleeve of a bright blue dress and pulled it out from its hiding place.

When he held it out in front of him, Mary Angel could see this was no ordinary dress. In fact, she'd never seen its equal. From the long train to the exquisite beading to the white petticoats sewn into the skirt, Mary could see this dress once belonged to someone special. From Perceval's downcast face, it didn't take her long to figure out who that someone was.

Percy then pulled out another dress, and then another. When he finished his frantic treasure hunt, he'd pulled out at least a dozen gorgeous gowns.

He gathered them all up to his chest, buried his face in their fragrant fabric, and stood still for the longest time. After a bit he relaxed his arms and let the dresses fall back onto the pile, the brilliant blue frock now haphazardly resting on top of all the others.

Perceval then turned around, and without a word, quickly walked past Mary and headed back to his new home.

Sister Mary Angel could have let him go, but instead instinctively ran after him. She caught up in just a few steps, choosing to walk along with her fast friend in silence.

When the two of them reached the stone entrance to the city, Perceval paused. Mary gently put one hand upon his shoulder. Turning to look in her eyes, he saw the very same shade of brilliant blue as his wife's cast-off dress and had to turn away.

He wanted to tell her everything swirling around in his heart but knew it was not only unwise to burden her, but unfair as well. He had managed to fall out of love with his wife and in love with an unattainable woman.

He thought back on the day he met her and wondered which hurt worse: the boils that covered his body or his subsequent never-ending heartache over his unrequited feelings.

Before he fully knew what was happening, a slew of emotions, from regret, to sadness, to guilt washed over him. Then a handful of words spilled out of his mouth in a jumbled rush. "At first, I think I thought it best to let her grieve in her own way…"

When Percy came up short, Sister Mary filled in for him, "You assumed you'd rebuild."

Though lost in his own world, Percy nodded. "Yea, that be it exactly! But, I art sorry to say, I then became angry."

The sister continued, "Which be entirely understandable, as she never came to thee."

"Yea! How could she not care about how I was dealing with our loss? Nor make any effort to find out what I was doing?"

Sister Mary measured her next words very carefully. She spoke in a softer tone than usual when she said, "But ye also neglected to see her."

Perceval nodded, then gestured to the river and the city with his hand. "I think I let all of this distract me." At this point the sister remained silent. Percy sighed. "I suppose I've known for some time that I've lost her along with everything else. I can't blame her when it fully falls on me. In truth, every time I was determined to find her, it just hurt too much."

The sister pursed her lips, exhaled and treaded lightly, "Perhaps instead of working through it together, she instead became the image of your grief."

Percy's failure hit him upside the head. "And now she's done. She's thrown away every remaining memory of our life together. Not that I blame her. I have nothing left to offer."

It was at this point that Perceval the Altruistic came to the stark realization that for all of our accomplishments, humans are a rather stupid lot.

What he once wanted was gone. What he wanted now was standing directly in front of him. But a tangled mess of rules and regulations and shoulds and should nots constrained him from acting on his deepest desires.

He also knew that in short order the seamstresses of the trade school would take all of his wife's dresses and transform them into a wide variety of knickers, skirts, shirts, and perhaps even a coat or two. And then, through no fault of their own, the fine citizens of this new town would be wearing constant reminders to him of his failed life and marriage.

But trumping that melancholy thought was the stark realization that seeing sister Mary Angel and her beautiful blue eyes every day for the rest of his life while holding no hope of ever having her as his own was more than he could take.

He looked down at the compassionate face of the woman whom he thought could well be the love of his life and simply said, "I must take my leave."

As he walked off, the sister called to him, "For now?"

Perceval shook his head and said, "Nay! Forever!"

Mary did her best to cover her concern. "To where?"

Making his way to what had been his temporary home, Perceval tuned to face the sister and said, "I have no idea."

Sister Mary let down her guard long enough to ask, "Be it because of me?"

Perceval wanted to drop his stoic routine, run back, and sweep the woman up into his arms, but lifelong habits die hard. Instead, he merely shrugged his shoulders and gave her a cryptic, "I cannot say."

He hoped that was the end of it and he could walk off into the sunset with his stupid pride intact, but Mary Angel called out again, "Be it because of me?"

Percy stopped. He turned to look at her for what he hoped was the last time. He thought he saw the same longing in her face, but knew she was tied up by even more rules, regulations, and protocols than he was. He closed this chapter in their lives by being brutally honest.

After a long pause spent weighing his options, he emphatically stated, "Pray believe me, I mean not to hurt thee in any way, but of course it is!"

Perceval managed to live most of his life as a man free of regrets. That curt statement, however true, would haunt him for years to come.

When he saw sister Mary's face fall, he immediately regretted what he'd blurted out. When she turned and rushed away, it tripled his resolve to leave and never come back.

Perceval then did something for only the second time since coming to the Outskirts.

He turned and ran.

On this occasion, however, he didn't return ready for a fight. This time Perceval the Altruistic just kept on running.

Chapter Twelve
Friends and Betrayers

After Percy had scribbled out a few goodbye notes, he shoved a stack of tunics, cloaks, and robes into a burlap bag, wrapped up the King's sacred book, and threw it over his shoulder. He took a quick look around at his temporary housing, then left, not even bothering to latch the door behind him.

As he rushed out of town, finding his stride on the main road, who should ride up behind him with a cart full of barrels of ale and stacked chairs, but everyone's favorite monk, Brother Bob.

"Hail thee well, my good man! And where art thou rushing off to on such a fine day?"

In no mood for anything besides grumbling and grousing, Perceval did his best to wave the man on. "To thy errands, good man. I beg of thee!"

Brother Bob nodding, said, "As thee wouldst have it," then proceeded to slow his horse down to a languid trot, matching Perceval's speed exactly.

In response, the runaway sped up. Nonplussed, so did the monk. When Perceval slowed to the pace of a bridal procession in chains, Brother Bob equaled his rhythm.

Perceval yelled at the top of his lungs. "Why must thee vex me at every turn?"

The brother pulled up on his reins, bringing his horse to a stop. "I just left a friend of ours by the river, crying her eyes out. And now I find thee, from all signs, apparently running away. I art not curious, but my mare be dying to know what happened."

Resigned to the inevitable, Perceval threw his worldly

possessions into the back of the cart and swung up into the seat next to his friend. He put his elbows on his knees and his head into his hands.

"Curse thee for bringing her to me that day. Curse thee with pestilence and frogs and painful sores on thy privates."

The monk chuckled. "Pray tell, what hast thy knickers in such a twist?"

Perceval could only shake his head. "I love her, Brother Bob. More than a man has a right to love a woman he can never have. This be all thy fault. None of this would have ever happened if ye had just let me stay in the cesspool of my life. I'd be a farm hand somewhere, telling stories of how I once had it all, but thou brought her to me. You cursed me just as much as the fates cursed me when they robbed me of my former life!"

Brother Bob clicked his tongue, and his horse started trotting down the lane. He nodded and said, "I see. Thou wert perfectly happy wallowing in thy misery."

"Yea!"

"And it be my fault that ye sought out the fair Mary every day, nay, sometimes twice or thrice a day to discuss various and sundry inconsequential bits of business."

"Yea!"

"And it be my fault ye ignored the King's sacred words about guarding thy heart against any who wouldst tear a marriage asunder."

"Yea…"

"Then I be most guilty! I shall immediately turn myself over to the King, confess my litany of sins, and demand to be drawn and quartered."

"Well, that be a tad extreme. Perhaps a year or two in the stocks. But that be in addition to the pestilence and sores on thy privates."

"Nay! Keep thy compassion for the downtrodden. I be the worst offender. I pushed thee out of the depths of depression and helped thee find thy purpose. To the gallows with me."

Perceval sat up and leaned against the back panel of the seat. "I hate thee with the fire of ten thousand suns."

Brother Bob patted his friend on his leg. "So, thou art warming to me."

"And now I've hurt her! Turn thy cart around. Nay, stay that. Clean break. It be the only way."

"Where willst thou go?"

Perceval pointed straight ahead. "As far from the Outskirts and Kingston as possible."

Brother Bob gave his usual nod, which most times meant he was in anything but agreement. "I have found that running from thy problems doth always be the smart bet."

"Make that the hate of twenty thousand suns."

The monk smiled. "And I love thee as well."

The two men settled back and watched the long road unfold before them in silence.

Brother Bob did, in fact, have a subject he needed to broach with Perceval, but before he could find the right way to break it to his friend, the duo saw a group of three riders, one of whom was holding onto a fourth horse, cresting the upcoming hill.

Something about them looked vaguely familiar to Perceval. Squinting to get a better look, Percy said, "I believe I might know these—nay, I do know these men!"

Brother Bob brought his cart to a stop and waited for the trio to reach them. Perceval stood up on the buckboard and waved down his old friends. "Hast thou lost a rider?"

Richard the Conveniently Brave was the first to recognize Perceval. He gave his horse a light kick and galloped over to the monk's cart, shouting, "As I live and breathe. It is you!"

Stephen the Sarcastic and Odd Todd brought up the rear. Stephen was all smiles. "Perceval! Thou art not dead."

"Only nearly. Lo, these many days I have been whiling away at the Outskirts, pining for my long-lost friends for nigh upon a year."

Todd was never a good liar. He tried to smile, but he looked uncomfortable and mumbled to cover. "Hast it been that long?"

Stephen kicked in with, "But how that be possible? Thou hast aged a good decade, at least. Now that I see thee up close, perhaps two."

Each of the men rode up to Percy, heartily shook his hands and enthusiastically slapped him on his back.

All exchanged perfunctory greetings with Brother Bob and settled their horses around the cart. There was a time of silence while the men looked one another over, reveling in the reunion and marveling at how the appearance of each had remarkably remained unchanged (a few more grey hairs here and there notwithstanding).

Perceval got to the point. "To what do I owe the honor? Or wert thee just passing by with an extra horse?"

Stephen laughed. "'Tis true, we have come for thee."

Richard was sheepish in his admission, "Granted, more days have passed than any of us can give a good reason for, but when we last parted ways, we promised to take thee out for a weekend of revelry thou wouldst never forget."

Stephen said, "Unless thou hast already forgotten why thou didst need to be cheered up. In which case we shall save our money and ride straight back to Kingston."

Perceval threw up his hands in protest. "Nay, think not I shalt let thee off the hook, for I am in need of a great diversion. What hast thee in mind?"

As one, the three friends shouted, "Pleasanton!"

Richard continued, "Drink, delicacies, and debauchery!"

Todd couldn't hide his enthusiasm as he lustfully added, "And hopefully all at the same time!"

As if needing to call attention to itself, the extra horse tethered behind Todd seemed to join in the excitement of the planned excursion. His front hooves pawed the ground as he shook his mane.

Perceval glanced over and managed to take a good look at the beast standing not-so-patiently in the rear. At once he jumped off of the cart, ran to the jet-black horse and threw his arms around its neck, exclaiming, "Redeemer!"

Watching the reunion of horse and rider made all the men laugh. While Percy rubbed, slapped, and kissed his horse's hide, causing the animal to rear up in the air with excitement, Stephen said, "I don't seem to recall getting the same kind of greeting."

Perceval turned to Todd, "You found him! I thought he be lost forever."

Todd laid out the story. "You gave him to your servant, but the bank claimed ownership. I was able to convince them that if they returned your prized horse, you might sign away all your legal holdings and at long last they'd be able to put last year's tragedies to bed."

Perceval didn't hesitate. He exclaimed, "I shall gladly exchange what be left of my kingdom for a horse."

Todd pretended to search on either side of his steed for the correct saddlebag. "As it happens, I brought them along with me. Just on the off chance we might—"

"Then, by all means, bring out the bloodsucker's papers! Let us sign away! But only if, after our trip to Pleasanton, I may return my fine stallion to his rightful owner."

Todd shrugged as he dismounted. "By all rights, you can do whatever you like once the property is legally yours." He untied a leather canister fastened to his saddle and looked over to the monk. "Might we use your cart as a signing table?"

Brother Bob looked askance at Todd, but offered no objections, so the odd man moved to the rear of the cart, lowered the back part of the carriage and set up the necessary items.

In truth he wanted to get a few drinks into his old friend before he presented him with all of the documents, but he hoped the sheer number of papers Percy needed to sign and initial would distract him from the true nature of one of the parchments Todd had sequestered near the bottom of the pile.

As soon as the inkwell and pen were unpacked, Todd called

over his friend. He made a bit of a show unrolling the thick stack of papers. "Who could ever have foreseen that mere pieces of paper and parchment would replace a man's handshake?"

Perceval took the quill from Todd the Odd and dipped the instrument of his own sentencing into the inkwell. "Such is done in the name of progress. What be I signing?"

Not knowing what Todd had planned, Richard called out from his horse. "I beg of thee, read every word! Solicitors are a slippery bunch. You'll sign away your soul if ye be not careful."

Stephen piled on. "I agree! Art these articles of dissolution, or art thou indenturing thyself to years of servitude?"

At that, Perceval stopped. "Agreed! What be I signing?"

Todd had rehearsed his answer dozens of times. He did his best to make it seem natural but wasn't quite sure he'd pulled it off. His insides tightened up, and he felt a bead of sweat trickle down from his forehead. He was hopeful no one noticed.

In his most offhand manner he said, "Pray thee, don't impale the messenger. From what I understand, thou and the bank wert partners in over a dozen enterprises. These documents are the dissolution of those partnerships. Ye and the bank have taken a loss. That much ye know all too well. By signing these, thou art free from all financial obligations, so thou wilt not be thrown in debtors' prison. But thou art also signing away any possible profits in the future. Say, from your mines, or the farming. There be also the bill of sale from your house and other stores in town that were sold to cover your losses."

That was good enough for Perceval. He lowered his pen to the first page. "I have had enough of my old life. I wash my hands of it. I know not where I shall land, but let them do their best to squeeze blood from these turnips."

With that, Perceval signed his name and initials in every spot Todd indicated.

As he picked up each page and blew on the ink to dry, Todd's hands began to shake ever so slightly. He covered his tremors by waving the parchments in the air before carefully placing them on top of each other, in theory, to prevent any smearing of the signatures.

Perceval stopped and examined a paper near the bottom of the pile. "How many years didst we live in that house? Dost thou know who purchased it?"

The men shook their heads. Richard spoke up. "Some big family from outside Kingston. I haven't stopped by."

Percy sighed and signed it away. "I hope it brings them as much joy as it brought us."

The next page was the one Todd didn't want Perceval to read. He held his breath.

As fate would have it, Percy was lost in the emotion of the memories of the life he had in his former home, so he didn't give more than a cursory glance to the next document. When he signed the divorce papers and handed them over to Todd, a weight lifted from the man who was secretly betraying his old friend.

Over the past year Todd the Odd aggressively pursued what he had secretly desired for most of his adult life: Gwendolyn the Exquisitely Beautiful.

Feet to the fire, Todd had to admit he was never all that fond of Perceval. Especially after the loser dressed him down when the four of them sat around the campfire the year before. He had gone out of his way to support his old so-called friend, and now people he didn't even know were calling him Todd the Odd. To his mind that sin was unforgivable.

For reasons he couldn't comprehend, Stephen and Richard seemed to actually enjoy the man's company, but Todd merely tolerated him in order to be in close proximity to the man's now former wife.

Todd realized a good majority of his life was spent pretending to be someone he wasn't. But if posing to be Percy's best friend got him even in the same room as his coveted prize, it was well worth it.

After Perceval scampered off into Outskirts, Todd played the understanding friend, listening to Gwen as she mourned the loss of her children, her fortune, and social standing. He then deftly switched to the role of sympathetic protector as she railed against her absent husband.

He bided his time, presenting himself as one who was only there to support the grieving woman in her season of need while he oh-so-patiently waited for the perfect opening to let his true feelings be known.

Some six months ago the opportunity arose, and he *accidentally* let a declaration of affection slip from his lips. Acting his part to the hilt, he immediately chastised himself and ran off, declaring himself an unfit friend to all.

Upon his reluctant return a few weeks later, after a series of notes begging for a meeting, the wolf in sheep's clothing took the fair Gwendolyn in his arms, announced his undying and unrequited love for her, and kissed her with a passion she hadn't felt from her husband in years.

Since that day, the two had become inseparable. In public, Todd played the part of the consoling advisor, but in private, the two were, if the town's wags were to be believed, living as husband and wife.

And now, with his beloved's divorce papers signed, sealed, and soon to be delivered, Todd could relax and devote himself to a few well-earned days of debauchery. He'd break the news to Perceval when and if the time was right.

Todd the Odd didn't really care how his old friend took the news. His long suffering had finally paid off, and to him went the spoils.

"Done and done," announced Perceval. "I, for one, am ready to celebrate my complete lack of worldly possessions. Which brings up a rather delicate point. At the moment, I find myself between fortunes."

Stephen let out a loud put-upon sigh. "Fine! We shalt carry ye yet again."

Richard didn't have it in him to feign a charade. "Fret not, my good man. We have this. It's the least we can do."

Todd rolled up the signed papers, carefully slid them back into the leather cylinder, and carried them over to Brother Bob. "Art thou going to Kingston? It wouldst save me a trip and smooth no small amount of frayed nerves if thou couldst deliver these to the solicitor. He'll make sure each document gets to the rightful parties."

Brother Bob tucked the container into a safe corner of his seat and gave his solemn promise, "It shall be done."

With all skulduggery and legitimate purposes out of the way, Todd was finally able to relax. He turned to Perceval. "Doest thou remember how to ride?"

Percy grinned, walked over to his horse, hiked up his robe, threw one foot into the hanging stirrup, and easily jumped up, swinging his leg over the saddle. Taking a moment to settle into position, he pulled on the reins. Redeemer whinnied and lifted his front legs off of the ground. Perceval shifted his weight and patted the horse's neck when he came back down, once again balancing on all four hooves.

He turned to his friends and laughed. "I believe it mayhaps come back to me."

Looking over at the Monk, Percy implored, "Canst thee look after my many possessions while I be gone?" Brother Bob nodded.

With that, the reunited friends turned their horses around, waved goodbye to the monk, and headed off down the road for Pleasanton, laughing and carrying on as they went.

Suspecting little good would come of their adventure, despite the joyous start, Brother Bob watched the old friends ride away before continuing on his own journey.

Chapter Thirteen
The Song Bird

Many years ago, no one alive can exactly remember when, all of Kingston was united and peaceful. But as everyone knows, cancerous dissension can often simmer for years behind a placid smiling facade.

Such was the case with the King's musical director, Devin the Song Bird. The man was revered by all, far and wide, for his almost supernatural ability to craft the most heavenly music.

His prodigious symphonies and cantatas somehow managed to capture pure emotion. Whether taking the listening audience on an exciting adventure pushed ever onward by pulsating horns and percussive rhythms or making those in attendance uncontrollably weep with the mere use of his soaring strings, Devin was adored by both his King and his public.

Which soon became the problem. Adulation is a powerful elixir few can manage well.

Despite being artistically fulfilled in his job, a dull resentment began to creep in. Devin was given free rein to create whatever he wanted, but there were still restrictions that soon became stifling.

It seems the Song Bird was constantly being asked to write music to commemorate this holiday or that, and almost all of it was intended to praise, worship, and adore the King!

It became abundantly clear to Devin that *his* creativity was what the people were celebrating, regardless of the intended holiday or event.

The King listened to Devin's never-ending concerns and did his best to address them, even going so far as to let the man have several of his own productions every year, but that only served to hasten the eventual burning out of the music director.

It was no secret to everyone who worked with the Song Bird that he believed he was severely overworked, underpaid, and undervalued.

The breaking point came when Devin got it into his head that since the people came to hear *his* glorious music year in and year out, it only made sense that those same people should be celebrating *him.*

From there it was only a short hop over to his final prideful conclusion; that he should be the King.

When he declared that sentiment publicly, the true and good King had no choice but to let him go.

Devin assumed his adoring throngs would follow him wherever he decided to go, and he was quite taken aback when the vast majority of idiots across the kingdom instead threw their lot in with the insipid King!

That was the final blow for the Song Bird. He left the kingdom in a huff, loudly vowing to all within earshot that he would return someday and take his rightful place as the true ruler of Kingston.

His final gift of spite to his King was to gather every copy of every piece of music he had ever written in honor of his lord and master, douse them in oil, and burn them in a huge bonfire.

From that day forward the people referred to Devin in hushed whispers and never again called him the Song Bird. When his name did come up, he was simply referred to as the Dragon.

Sadly, the black-hearted musician never composed another song or symphony. His creativity was applied to other areas.

After he left Kingston, Devin was determined to create a kingdom to rival his former ruler's.

The only land available large enough to accommodate Devin's ambitions was a hot and barren wasteland five hours by horse to the northeast of Kingston.

Armed with several bags of severance gold, the Dragon rode

into the desolate town, pulled up to a dilapidated tavern, and bought it outright for nearly twice what it was worth.

Within a week he had changed the quaint hovel into a brothel. The wenches who worked at the tavern as bar maids were allowed to keep their original jobs just as long as they agreed to the new terms in their contracts.

Most were so desperate for money they couldn't turn down Devin's additional work requirements despite how personally reprehensible they might be.

When they complained, their new boss would laugh and say they should be happy, since, for the majority of their shifts, they were now off their feet! If any of the women balked, they were fired.

A few weeks later the Dragon brought in the gaming tables. When the town's ruling elders pointed out that both prostitution and gambling were against the law in their town, Devin treated them all to a night of raucous revelry wherein they all won hefty sums of money, drank entirely too much, and succumbed to the lurid advances of his wait staff.

After which he blackmailed each and every elder until the town's statesmen reluctantly gave the original tavern and all of Devin's subsequent properties perpetual exemptions to the prohibitively strict morality laws currently crippling the town.

In the days and months following, Devin either bought or leveraged all the property on either side of the town's main strip. He used his profits to build more taverns, houses of ill repute, gaming houses, and entertainment venues.

Thus, Pleasanton was born.

Devin's philosophy was simple. While the King urged his people to rise above their basic natures, the Dragon was happy to indulge his customers most animalistic, selfish desires, all while covering it up with a high sheen of respectability.

Pleasanton was wall to wall distraction. Be it food, sex, gambling, or entertainment, the whole town throbbed with an insatiable curiosity of *what's next?*

But the real key to Pleasanton was its ability to satisfy almost every person's addiction in the most nonjudgmental way possible. That's how the Dragon got his hooks into so many poor souls who ended up wasting their lives away in the bowels of his city.

Within a year Pleasanton was Kingston's number one vacation spot.

Chapter Fourteen
A Night in Pleasanton

When Perceval and his companions arrived late that afternoon, they were all tired, thirsty, and famished. They found lodging at a tavern and checked in, two to a room. Stephen bunked with Percy, and Richard was saddled with Todd.

Meeting downstairs after throwing their belongings onto the beds, the foursome ordered up a meal fit for, if not a king, then at least high-ranking members of his court.

An hour later, stuffed to the gills and filled to the brim, none of the men were feeling any pain.

That was when the night's first temptation sauntered over. The name the dark-haired vixen used was Sheba, and her low-cut dress left little to the imagination.

Quite brazen in her approach, she lowered herself onto Perceval's lap, leaned over, and licked his ear. Whatever invitation she softly whispered was lost to the other gentlemen, but her intent was clear.

Richard burst out laughing. "Why, Percy, old friend, I do believe thou art blushing!"

Perceval had indeed turned a deep shade of crimson. He laughed along with his friend. "If thou had heard what she just offered, thy skin wouldst burn as well!"

He then turned to the woman, helped her off of his lap and gently let her down. "And while I be sorely tempted by thy offer, I be not only a married man but also without a penny to my name. Thou art very attractive and I suspect ye wilt have no trouble getting most every other man in this room to succumb to thy charms."

Either the woman was under pressure from the management, or she liked a challenge, as the tart redoubled her efforts. She slowly raised her skirt higher and higher, leaned over and purred, "But my charms be the least of my skills."

This is where Percy would take no more. He slammed his fist down on the table, startling both the woman, his friends, and most of the patrons in the tavern.

"Woman! What part of *nay* doth thee not understand?! Thou shalt entice me not with thy feline wiles to betray my vows. I have already broken them in my heart, that be enough. Away with thee!"

Before the shocked woman of the night could slide back under whatever stone she crawled out from, Todd stood up and offered his hand. "Fair maiden, I have a room at the ready. Richard, join us if thou doth so desire, but otherwise our room be occupied for the foreseeable future."

After the Odd and his rentable tramp scampered away, the remaining friends looked at each other. Stephen threw back the remnants of his ale, wiped his beard with his forearm, and said, "I understand there be a jester playing across the street. What say ye?"

The other men stood up. Richard was all for it. "Hopefully that wilt be a sight more entertaining that what's going on in my room. Let us be off!"

†††

Perceval had seen his share of court jesters before. In most cases they came out to distract the audience when various performers or stages had to be reset during some program, but he'd never been to a show dedicated solely to the art of tomfoolery.

Cushioned chairs and couches surrounded a small stage in a dank tent which was illuminated by a semi-circle of torches. Percy thought that if the entertainment involved an uncoordinated juggler, things could get dangerously interesting very quickly.

The men had barely sat down when the show began. The first jester was young and obviously inexperienced. He stammered when he spoke, and his attempts at humor through the use of various props fell flat.

In short order the young jester became so flustered by the audience's total lack of response that he turned and ran back into the wings.

Moments later, a surprised second jester stumbled out onto the stage. He asked for the nonexistent applause to continue for his inept friend and got only the barest smattering in return.

This performer was older, a bit more frayed around the edges, and possessed the demeanor of one who was confident in his craft.

The headliner showed no fear as he looked out at the crowd. He then bowed and began, diving with relish into what was apparently his favorite topic: all things in and surrounding the crotch.

Despite his obsession with making one's privates quite public, this jester piqued Perceval's interest much more than the opening sacrificial lamb. This experienced performer was, indeed, funny, in that he was able to hold a crowd and move them to laughter through his exaggerated stories and a wide array of voices.

What was both surprising and off-putting was his entire reliance on vulgarity. The man was more unabashedly crass than anyone Percy had ever heard. He knew of the salty reputation attributed to sailors and other men of low class, but out of respect for his station, no one had ever dared to utter in his presence the sheer volume of curse words that were currently rolling off of the jester's tongue.

Perceval looked around at the crowd and saw an equal mix of both sexes. What shocked him was that the majority of women were not only laughing but some were busting a gut at tales no gentlemen would ever tell in mixed company.

After a goodly portion of his act had passed, the jester evidently couldn't take Perceval's stone-faced expression any longer.

He turned to the patron he couldn't crack. "If I may be so bold, what be thy problem? The rest of the crowd doth laugh, but not thee!"

Though positively brimming with opinions, Perceval bit his lip to avoid a confrontation. He looked at his friends, shrugged and turned back to the performer. "Thou art amusing, I give thee that."

The comic sarcastically bowed low to the ground. "High praise indeed, kind sir! Me thinks ye shouldst telleth thy face!"

Accepting the laugh at his expense, a slightly peeved Perceval did his level best to accept defeat. Still, being only human, one word did manage to slip out. He said, "Although..."

Mistakenly thinking he'd have the upper hand in a one-sided battle of wits, the jester egged Perceval on. He acted as if he were excessively put out and declared, "Oh, by all means, please, express thy bountiful displeasure!"

"Only if thou doth insist."

In anticipation of an easy kill, the jester bowed low a second time. "Oh, but I do!"

With permission given, Perceval didn't hold back. "It doth seem to me that thou art doing little more than engaging in rough shipyard banter where thou doth use vulgarity and curse words to not only prop up, but, if truth be told, to distract an eager audience from thy string of weak premises."

The jester was dumbfounded. On a nightly basis he dealt with drunken rabble-rousers and had a slew of comebacks to fit almost every occasion, but facing an actual competent come-uppance caused him to stand slack jawed in silence.

Perceval took the lack of a retort as a sign he should continue. "Surely thou canst mine the immeasurable depths of the human experience and find fodder in subjects other than excrement and our reproductive systems! It be clear thou dost know there be people in the crowd who laugh out of embarrassment at coarse talk, so methinks thou hast taken the easy road. As the merest of suggestions, perhaps intertwine a few stories of daring, or love, or the differences betwixt dogs and cats."

At this point Richard the Conveniently Brave was so mortified he slid down in his seat to the point where he was nearly horizontal to the ground. Stephen, however, was enraptured by his friend's ability to dissect, discern, and get to the heart of what was truly being said. He also loved to watch a good fight.

After a long moment of silence, the jester swallowed hard and coaxed out the only line he could think of resembling a retort. "Oh, thou art done! I appreciate thy long-winded observations and wish to thank the sisters of mercy for allowing thee to get out tonight."

The audience laughed, and Perceval joined them. "Yea! That be more like it! Thou dost have a wit after all!"

Richard tugged on Percy's tunic, urging him to stand down. The combatant saw the pleading request in his friend's eyes and whispered, "I see not the problem. He started it!"

Sensing the upper hand, the jester took Perceval's advice and did indeed change course. But he switched to an area that made the first subject seem tame by comparison. He began to insult the King.

In a flash Percy saw the method to the comic's madness. The bawdy performer's apparent intent was to lower the crowd's defenses with a barrage of vulgarity in order to condition them to accept his ultimate goal: that of disparaging the King.

At first, though the subject made him uncomfortable, out of deference to his companions, Perceval suffered through it until he could take no more. When the jester accused the good King of a particularly heinous act (of which I shall not darken these pages by repeating here), Percy stood up and called out at the top of his lungs, "Nay! Nay I say! I'll not hear it!"

Not surprised by the outburst, the jester rolled his eyes and said, "I be taken aback! Who wouldst have guessed that thou art a King's man!"

Indignant, Percy refused to back down. "Hast thou no decency? In Kingston, thou wouldst be brought up on charges of treason for speaking such lies!"

"Ah, but be they lies?" Now the jester had Perceval and the crowd exactly where he wanted them. "Hast thou proof of our

King's supposed purity? And if not, then who's to say what be a lie and what be the truth?"

Perceval practically spit out his reply. "The King be only goodness and mercy, and thou art devious in thy manipulation of the truth. You, sir, art of the lowest character, and I have no recourse but to challenge thee to a duel to defend my good King's honor!"

A hushed murmur swept through the crowd. The jester tried to laugh it off, but seeing how serious Perceval was, the comic's self-preservation kicked in with, "Hey, canst thee not take a joke?"

Already on his feet, Perceval made his way towards the stage. "Not when it be insurrection disguised as humor! Dost thou accept my challenge, or art thee a coward?"

On the jester's signal, a trio of burley men burst in from the back, ran to the front row and forcibly grabbed Perceval. He struggled against them but was easily overpowered. "What miscarriage of justice be this? Didst thee not hear this man drag our good King's name through the mud? I demand satisfaction!"

Perceval continued on like that as the men dragged him kicking and screaming out of the tent, roughly throwing him to the ground, and barring any thoughts he might have had of returning to the fray.

Seeing their time was up as well, Stephen and Richard meekly followed their friend out. After their exit, the jester called out to the crowd, "Just another typical night in Pleasanton, folks!"

As he picked himself up and dusted himself off, Perceval could hear the crowd laugh and applaud the comic's final line before the tent flaps closed behind his friends and muffled the sound.

His fury knew no bounds. "The unmitigated gall of that man! Didst thou hear him disparage our King? He leaves me no recourse but to stalk him after the conclusion of this so-called show and rain down the King's justice on his head!"

Wanting to avoid a fight at all costs, Richard said, "Or, or, or... understanding the jester doth speak the words of a fool, we could all just let it go, and then perhaps we might seek a way to salvage this night without the loss of life or limb!"

Perceval stared at his friend and asked, "Tell me, good sir, when art thou actually brave?"

Richard said it plainly, "As my namesake suggests, whenever it be convenient."

That comment made Perceval roar with laughter. He grabbed his compatriot by the shoulders and enveloped him in a hug. "Ah, my dear friend, thou art a balm for my troubled soul."

Releasing him and adjusting his skewed clothing, Percy added, "Let us waste not another minute of our lives with that fool! What other attractions doth Pleasanton have to offer?"

A cursory examination revealed the entire strip was jam packed with various barkers doing their best to entice people to come into their one-of-a-kind tents in order to see freaks of nature, buy miracle elixirs, or have their fortunes told.

Urging his friends to hurry up, Richard stopped outside of Madame Futura's tent long enough for the human eel outside to sink his fangs in him.

The hired man slithered out of the shadows, pushed up his sleeves, then whipped his long greasy hair away from his face to get a good look at the rube standing before him. "Hello, my good man! Come to the right place, you have. Madame Futura can predict your future. Love, life, money, conquests, fame, she can unfold all the heretofore hidden secrets life holds for you."

Perceval came up alongside his friend and mocked the shyster. "And how might Madame Futura do that? Doth she possess some kind of magic?"

Unfazed, the beckoning man pulled back the flap to the tent. "Indeed, she does, good sir. Madame was born with an internal third eye. Discovered and trained by masters in the far east she was. Uses the stars, bones, cards, and her mystical crystals."

Percy shook his head. "Sounds to me as if the woman can't rely on her own mind."

The barker smiled, showing stained teeth hiding behind a sparse beard and thin lips. "The answers to all your questions lie within."

105

Wanting to salvage the night, Perceval practically ran through the opening. "All my questions? That settles it. Gentlemen, indulge me! Madame Futura is the elixir I have been seeking."

Richard shook his head, Stephen paid the entrance fee for the three of them, and they followed Perceval into the dark enclave.

Madame Futura was already seated, nestled in between two large flickering candelabras, patiently waiting for her next mark. She wore a turban over her long snow-white hair and was adorned with enough jewels, necklaces, and rings to outfit an entire harem.

When the men seated themselves around her purple velvet covered table, the self-proclaimed spiritual vessel dramatically looked up to the heavens, as if her very soul was cast into turmoil by the appearance of her latest customers.

The old woman raised and waved a wrinkled hand to silence any attempt at conversation. With her eyes closed and her lips tightly clenched, she let out an almost imperceptible moan.

Richard was just about to speak when he saw Perceval shake his head. Taking his friend's lead, the conveniently brave man acquiesced and settled back into his chair.

Finally, because time was money, Madame Futura spoke with a wobbly vibrato. "I sense trouble in the room. One of thee be not happy. Not satisfied with the cards life has dealt thee. Ye have come to Madame Futura for answers."

Perceval couldn't help but smirk. "I see ye do indeed have an amazing gift."

Opening her hooded eyes, the fortune teller looked Perceval up and down. "How may I be of assistance? Nay, tell me not. I sense in thee a man whose fortunes have reversed in love and wealth and health. Nay, not health. Love and wealth."

Richard was amazed. Perceval only nodded.

The charlatan continued, "To manifest wealth, one need only to speak thy desires out into the universe. First name, then claim thy prize. Ye shall be heard, and the universe shall rain down blessings upon thee."

Perceval looked around at their less-than-stellar surroundings. "From the looks of things, ye and the universe don't seem to be on very good speaking terms."

Undaunted by the skeptic, the woman waved him off. "Madame Futura cares not about material things. I find all the solace I desire communing with the spirits from beyond."

Percy nodded. "Still, ye might consider having those spirits come in once a week to spruce up the place a bit."

"I see thou art an unbeliever."

Perceval shook his head. "Nay, I believe in many things. Just not that the grand creation cares a whit about my financial holdings."

Madame Futura leaned forward with a dead serious look in her eye. "If thou wouldst but know of the power of the spiritual realm, thou wouldst not be so cavalier."

Percy acquiesced with a nod. "So say ye."

Richard attempted to be the peacemaker. "We have all seen things of which there be no rational explanation. So, if ye be the woman to pull back the curtain with thy bones and cards, have at it!"

The soothsayer licked her ruby lips. "I neither control nor manipulate. I merely lay out the cards of chance and interpret as the spirit moves."

Percy was wholly unable to let such foolishness continue without debate. He looked up at the astrology chart behind the woman. "I be curious. Wouldst ye or thy spirits have us believe that our lives art controlled by the constellations?"

Madame Futura pursed her lips and nodded, muttering only, "Some wouldst say thy birth be heavily influenced by the conflu-ence of stars."

Hearing that notion was the last straw for Perceval. "So ye wouldst have us believe that the stars in the sky have somehow divided all of humanity into groups according to the days of our birth? And regardless of my own volition, where I go, whom I love, or who loves me depends on the mood of some unreachable light?

Accurately predicting the future, Madame Futura could easily see where this conversation was headed. She leaned over and rang a small cymbal next to her chair.

Moments later the roadside barker slid into the tent behind the trio. In his fist he held a rather sizable club.

Perceval held up his hands in surrender. "I have not the gift of a third eye, but somehow I feel the spirits telling me our time be over."

The woman nodded. As the three men got up to leave, Richard turned back. Pleading, he said, "Madame Futura, before we go, I beg of thee, throw thy bones, or cards, or ask the stars, I care not. Will our friend's question ever be answered?"

Perceval and Stephen stopped. They and the barker turned back. The old woman gave Percy the once over again, reluctantly shrugged her bony shoulders, then slowly filled a ceramic cup with a variety of small dry bones. She closed her eyes, shook the cup and spilled the contents over the velvet covering.

When her eyes cracked open, she looked down and chuckled to herself. Exhaling a long, low breath, she raised her eyebrows, stared for a moment at the three men then finally said, "At the end of thy journey, thy burning question shall finally be answered. But yet, at the same time, it shall not be."

After uttering her final decree, the old woman let out a loud cackle and sent out the three unbelievers with a curt, "Madame Futura has spoken!"

Years later, thinking back on that night, Perceval the Altruistic was amazed at how right the old woman was.

Chapter Fifteen
Torn Asunder

After a restless night where a good deal of the evening was spent with one eye on the door, fearful that an unscrupulous wench would attempt to slip in, and the rest of the night fitfully dreaming of Sister Mary, Perceval and his friends used the next day to lie low and recuperate.

Todd was in a particularly foul mood. He was uncharacteristically tight lipped about his previous night's exploits, but when Percy and his cohorts stumbled downstairs at the crack of noon to break their fast, the brazen bar maid from the night before glanced over at her conquest from across the room and stifled a laugh. Todd's reputation for being odd continued unabated.

After their lazy start and a restful afternoon, the evening began as well as could be expected. Sadly, by the end of the night, secrets were revealed, and friendships were forever shattered.

First up on the night's agenda was Max the Mysterious. He was a magician of particular skill and dexterity, and Perceval was enraptured from the very start.

Other than his tendency to shout out how he thought each trick might be accomplished, Perceval was on his best behavior, and the four men actually made it through an entire show without being kicked out.

Next, the friends went to see the Circus of the Sun. This elaborate show under a yellow and blue striped tent offered impossibly limber acrobatics, jugglers, clowns, and amazing feats of derring-do. Perceval was completely enthralled.

After the show, Percy couldn't say enough about the experience.

He babbled on and on, recounting every moment of the show as he wandered through a side tent featuring endless rows of merchandise. Eventually he borrowed enough money from Stephen to buy a robe with the name of the circus embroidered on each sleeve.

Standing outside the huge tent, Perceval smiled, carefully tucked his recent purchase into a burlap bag, then raised his shoulders. "What be next, gentlemen? I could call it a night or attend one more show. What say ye?"

Richard stuck his toe in the water. "We have yet to try a house of chance."

Stephen nodded, but Perceval was less than enthusiastic. "As I currently have no funds, I should have to borrow from all of thee in order to double thy losses in a fraction of the time. I am close to giving up the ghost. The three of thee could certainly go after I check out for the evening. Be there another option?"

Todd spoke for the first time that evening. "Friends, for the love of the King, we be in Pleasanton!"

Not quite catching his drift, the other men nodded, urging him to continue.

A little frustrated, Todd continued. "Art all of thee so dim? What doth this city be known for?"

Stephen caught on first. "Ah, noblemen's clubs."

Todd bowed his head in his friend's direction. "'Tis something we cannot see back in Kingston."

Not as worldly as his friends, Percy inquired, "Noblemen's... clubs?"

Richard put the best face on it. "'Tis the latest. They be like the Circus of the Sun, an endless array of dancers who art highly skilled. But, from what I understand, all be exclusively of the female persuasion."

Perceval was intrigued. "I loved the Circus of the Sun. But tell me true, what kind of dancers? I shall not tempt my eyes or darken my soul with impropriety."

Before his old friend could completely squelch the idea, Todd did his best to sell it. "Canst thou step off thy high moral horse for just the briefest of moments? It be much like what we just saw, save this entertainment be designed purely for the artistic appreciation of the feminine form! It be my understanding the belly dancers are not to be believed! I have heard tell they can move every part of their body in a different direction at the same time. Hips from side to side, chest in and out, arms akimbo. Their skill be beyond compare."

Perceval was waffling. "And it be made for *noblemen*?"

Stephen smirked as he said, "Not for noblemen exclusively, but yea."

Curiosity and the desire to be with his friends for one last show overcame his reluctance. "Then let us throw caution to the wind! Dancing girls it is!"

After the friends found the home of the nobleman's club residing in the center of the entertainment district, Todd generously paid their exorbitant entrance fee. Immediately after, an attractive young girl dressed as a harem concubine used a candle to lead the men through the pitch-black packed house of rowdy drunkards to a table adjacent to the stage.

Looking around, dimly observing the room full of rough, unkempt men, Perceval failed to spy anyone of noble heritage. He leaned over to Stephen and Richard. "It doth appear all men of high birth have been given the night off."

Wanting to at least see part of the show, Stephen gave a cursory look around. "Judge not so hastily, my friend. Perhaps all such men are seated in the back in the dark!"

Perceval scoffed. "Darker than this? I can barely see my own hand!"

As if to answer Percy's query, a man several seats behind them jumped up, rushed to the tent wall, and apparently dove to the ground in order to shove his head underneath the canvas. Seconds later, all in the tent heard the familiar sound of a man regurgitating the entire contents of his stomach. After a few violent spasms, the man pulled his head back in, wiped his beard with his forearm, and headed back to his table, yelling, "Ah, 'tis much better. Time to fill me up ag'in. More ale, wench!"

All the men around the drunken reprobate laughed heartily.

While Perceval waited for his eyes to gradually adjust to the dim light, he muttered to his friends, "Methinks we've eliminated the back section for the noblemen."

Before Stephen could answer, a tired, worldly woman dressed as a gypsy sauntered up to the table. She wore ribbons in her hair and a low-cut vest with a frilly skirt. Her lace up top was cinched tight to enhance her bosom.

Her perfunctory, "What'll ye have?" was spoken as if she had given the same greeting for most of her adult life and cared not a whit for a single customer's response.

Before Todd could even finish saying, "Four ales," the woman slid away from their table and disappeared into the darkness.

The show started with all the flourish of a drenched blaze. The main tattered curtain unceremoniously parted, two men with percussive instruments entered, seated themselves on their respective stools, and commenced to drumming.

An acolyte with a torch ran to the front of the stage and lit a row of lanterns.

A disembodied voice from the back yelled out, "Noblemen, prepare to drool like fools and welcome to the stage, the temptress from Toulan, Esmerelda!"

A shout of lustful glee and rowdy applause erupted from the audience.

A few moments later the first dancer of the night poked one leg out from behind the curtain, then seductively slipped out onto the stage.

Esmerelda wore a faint smile, colored paint to accentuate her lips, cheeks and eyes and yards of gossamer fabric flowing over form-fitting undergarments made of some sort of chain mail.

The dancer whipped her long auburn locks back and forth as

she pranced from one side of the stage to the other in a well-re-hearsed rhythmic dance whose sole purpose appeared to be the systematic discarding of any excess material that was only tempo-rarily covering up her toned and well-muscled physique.

Soon clad in little more than her shimmering protective demi-armor, the undeniably attractive woman found her mark center stage and began to undulate to the staccato beat of the drums.

As Todd had testified, the belly dancer had the uncanny ability to isolate various parts of her body. She rolled her stomach as if it were a wave on the beach, then popped her rib cage in and out, followed by her hips shaking from side to side, all while her arms caressed her body like a pair of slithering snakes.

Perceval was transfixed. He had to admit he enjoyed the long-forgotten feeling of yearning currently washing over him, but at the same time, he began to experience an overwhelming sense of guilt.

His burgeoning sense of pleasure quickly turned to concern as the men in the crowd began pelting the young woman with coins, demanding the removal of her bustier with cries of, "Take it off!"

The talented performer forced a smile, teased the crowd by reaching down to unfasten the top clasp holding her top together, then whipped her arms aside and continued her dance.

A roar went up from the house and more coins were tossed toward the stage, some landing harmlessly at her feet, others smack-ing the dancer on various parts of her body, many of which struck her neck and head.

One of her hands went up to protect her face, the other undid the second of her three clasps.

At this point Perceval ascertained he had been hoodwinked by his friends. Indignant, he stood up at his table and shouted at the top of his lungs, "Nay, I say, goodly daughter! Keep it on!"

Surprised, the dancer stayed her hand.

Perceval continued. "Thou art fine in both form and skill. Ye need not debase thyself. For if these truly be noblemen—"

In an unmistakable sign Percy had angered someone in the tent, a coin flew out of the darkness and hit him directly between the eyes, momentarily cutting off his impassioned speech and causing no small amount of pain. A high pitched "Ow!" escaped from his lips.

He stepped back to regain his balance and managed to croak out another, "Nay, I say, keep it on!"

In answer to his virtuous plea, a virtual hailstorm of coins descended upon him, his table, and his friends.

Covering his head with his arms in an attempt to protect himself, Perceval stumbled his way through tables, chairs, and arms shoving him to the entryway. He continued to be pelted until he managed to reach the exit.

His parting words went unheard. His accusatory cry of, "This be no tent of noble—," was silenced by a final barrage of coins and a cheer from the crowd as he tumbled out into the night. A heartbeat later, the crowd returned to their previous chant of, "Take it off!"

Reluctantly following their pal outside, Stephen and Richard found Percy pacing back and forth muttering to himself.

He turned and lambasted his friends. "Thou hast both lied to me! This be no Circus of the Sun. Circus of the full moon, perhaps."

Shrugging, the two men walked over to the most moral man they knew and offered the lamest of excuses. Stephen said, "It was worth a shot," while Richard immediately fell on his sword. "Guilty as charged. But in my defense, I was hoping they'd start with the dancing girls and build up to the stripping. I'm as surprised as you they started right out of the gate."

Percy turned to them, his face full not of anger, but that of compassion. "What these girls must have experienced to lower themselves to such debasement, I can only imagine."

Stephen nodded. "I must admit that thought n'er entered my mind."

Percy started pacing again. "That could be one of my daughters! They be of the same age. And when I thought of their sweet faces,

I just couldn't take it. I beg of thee, go, enjoy thyselves. I be fine waiting out here."

Stephen chuckled, "Me thinks thou hast managed to ruin it for us as well." Richard added, "These places be not made for men with compassion or a conscience."

Perceval waved his arms around. "One could say the same for this whole festering cistern of a city. It all be designed to leave the King's teachings of temperance and moderation in thy knapsack and shoved under thy bed. Every waking moment encourages excess and promises big dreams, but I have seen not where it delivers. Save the magician and the Circus of the Sun. Both of those shows were highly enjoyable."

Stephen and Richard could only nod. Perceval stopped in front of them and tried his best to help them understand. "If thou art wondering, for this past year I have practically consumed the King's Sacred Book of Accumulated Wisdom."

Stephen said, "And it hast ruined thee."

Perceval threw his head back and laughed. "That it has, my good friend, that it has. But it hast also opened my eyes. Everything the Dragon offers here be but an empty imitation. It be thinner than that dancer's costume."

Richard looked wistfully back at the noblemen's club. "Which most likely be completely off by now."

Perceval shook his friend. "Hast she anything thou hast not seen before?"

Richard emphatically said, "I know not. We left before I couldst find out!"

Perceval gave the flimsiest of apologies. "For that, I take the blame. But this city's lures of money, lust, and crude mocking laughter all be little more than perverse counterfeits of the King's good gifts."

Stephen the Sarcastic couldn't resist the temptation to goad his friend. "Oh, by all means, please tickle our ears with the King's morality. I know of no better time or place."

This stopped Percy. He exhaled. "Tell me true. Was I ever any fun?"

The men exchanged glances. Their delay in answering was all the confirmation Perceval needed.

Stephen grimaced a little. "Define *fun*."

Perceval truly loved his friends. "Why be I so consumed by doing the right thing? I hear my father's voice reading from the King's sacred writings, and it strangles any impulse of recklessness."

Richard chimed in. "That not necessarily be a bad thing."

Stephen agreed. "We shouldest all thank whatever voice be in thy head, Percy, for it has kept thee on the straight and narrow and saved us all more times than I can count."

Percy brought his friends in for a hug. "Thank thee. Though I also know ye wouldst have had a lot more revelry without me around to prick thy conscience."

Stephen weakly protested. "Nay."

Richard joined in. "Nay."

Percy laughed. "Thou art both bad liars."

The men nodded and said in unison, "Aye."

Perceval was wistful. "'Tis sad, really. At the start, I thought of my daughters nearly every day. But of late, their faces be growing dim in my memory. Perhaps that be why it was such a shock to have this remind me..."

Stephen asked, "Still no answer from the King?"

Percy shook his head. "His ways be higher than mine. After such a time, methinks any answer he could have given in the midst of my pain would have rung most hollow."

Richard put his hand on his friend's shoulder. "To thy scars. Thou hast born them well. I suspect far better than I would have."

Stephen put his hand on Perceval's other shoulder. "Aye. I beg thy forgiveness for dragging thee to see a show of iniquity, but, more importantly, leaving thee to heal on thy own."

Perceval nodded. "What could ye say or do? I was inconsolable. But methinks 'tis time to discover my new life."

Before Richard or Stephen could agree, Todd burst out of the noblemen's tent, spitting fire. "Ye three art unbelievable!"

The men shot knowing glances at each other as the Odd man crossed over to them, grumbling with every step.

"There be beautiful girls inside doing things no woman I be acquainted with knows how to do! And ye three windbags art outside pontificating about who knows what. Let me guess. Thou virgin sensibilities art offended? I didst not ride five hours on a horse's ass to be lectured on morality and goodness by the likes of thee. There be naked flesh inside, and I for one want to see it!"

Perceval threw up his hands, "Then by all means, return to yonder tent teeming with lustful noblemen. We be not stopping thee!"

"But thou dost think it be wrong!"

Percy nodded. "Verily, but for me, not for thee."

As his face turned a bright shade of crimson, Todd commenced to vigorously wag his finger at Perceval. "There it be. There it be!"

Perceval looked over at Stephen and Richard. "There be what?"

Todd continued his tirade. "That be the problem with all ye insipid disciples of the King! Thou art all so high and mighty. Thou dost stay awake at night, endlessly scheming on how to control everyone else."

Perceval realized he was dealing with a seriously unhinged man. He knew silence was probably the best defense against such an emotional outburst, but where wa's the fun in that?

He smirked as he said, "I believe thou dost overestimate thy importance in both my waking and sleeping hours. Thou art free, brother, to do whatever thou wilt with no condemnation from me."

His anger unabated, and no acceptable insulting retort coming to mind, Todd yelled in frustration up to the skies, whipped around and headed for the club entrance.

Seconds before he entered, he slowed to complete stop. The three men stared at him, wondering what he was doing. After a long suspenseful wait, Todd the Odd slowly turned to face his new nemesis.

His demeanor was much different now. The frustration was gone. In its place was a haughty confidence. He began to retrace his steps towards Perceval, wanting to see his false friend's reaction when he lowered his boom. He said, "Ye shouldst know, thou hast lost everything."

Perplexed, Perceval quickly agreed. "I be well aware."

Todd shook his head. "Nay, I mean everything! Ye had a treasure, and thou didst throw her away."

"Doth thou speak of Gwendolyn? What have ye to do—"

"She be mine, foolish man! Thou didst always have everything. And I hated ye for it. Money, power, prestige, her. But now I have won. She be mine!"

Perceval couldn't entirely process what he was hearing. "I do believe she be gone. She has cast aside her dresses and I fear—"

"Ye signed the divorce papers on Brother Bob's cart. Now I can legally take her as my wife! She be my prize as a reward for all the years I suffered, tolerating thee just so I could be near the light of my life."

Perceval turned to his friends. "Didst thee know of this?"

Richard instinctively threw up his hands in self-defense. "I heard wild stories in town based on rumor and conjecture. I paid them no mind."

Stephen chimed in. "Not I! Todd, what hast thou done?"

Todd laughed. "What I have wanted to do from the beginning. I have taken her and made her mine. She wants nothing to do with thee!"

Perceval stood aghast. For the first time in recent memory, he was speechless.

Todd continued to kick the man while he was down. "Act not shocked, ye hypocrite. What man leaves his better half for an entire year? Not to mention the whole of Kingston knows of thy infatuation with the King's whore, Sister Mary Ang—"

Pressing that hot nerve was as far as Todd got. In a flash, Perceval ran across the dirt patch and practically leapt into his betrayer's chest before Mary's entire name could leave his mouth.

Todd may have thought his revelation and cocky attitude gave him the upper hand, but he was no match for the pent-up fury of Perceval.

Stephen and Richard's mouths were agape. This was not just uncharacteristic of Percy; they had never seen him strike anyone before. Ever. He more than made up for it here.

Throwing Todd to the ground, Perceval the Altruistic sat on his back-stabber's chest and began to whale on his face. Percy's fists were flying. Todd's arms were pinned down under the weight of his assailant's knees.

When their shock subsided, and Todd's blood made him unrecognizable, Stephen and Richard came to their senses. They rushed over, grabbed Perceval, and dragged him off of their near-unconscious friend.

Doing his best to avoid being on the receiving end of Percy's anger, Stephen yelled above the fray, "Hold, dear friend, hold! Methinks he hast learned his lesson."

Richard looked down at Todd. "Methinks his nose wilt remember this lesson for the rest of his life."

Perceval shook off his friends, reared his foot back and kicked Todd in the stomach. He stood over the moaning man trying to suck in air and yelled, "I break with thee! Thou art the lowest of men. Thou mayest have Gwendolyn, but if I ever hear of thee disparaging sweet Sister Mary, I wilt finish what I have only started tonight."

Perceval stepped away and tried to shake out the pain in his hands. "The man's skull be made of rock."

Stephen looked down at Todd, who had rolled over on his side and was curled up in a ball. "Yea, clearly, ye got the worst of it."

Richard looked at Percy and Stephen while indicating the moaning man at his feet. "Shall we help him?"

Stephen shook his head. "Nay, I think this be the bed he made. Let him lie in it."

Throwing his arm over Perceval's shoulder, Stephen led the victor away. "So, thou dost have a short fuse."

Richard followed behind. "And a mean left hook."

Perceval resisted the impulse to go back and beat a man while he was down. "Fine, let us go at first light. I can't wait to shake the filth of this town off of my garments."

Chapter Sixteen
Gwendolyn

The three men rode in silence for the majority of their journey back to Kingston. Perceval was lost in thought, and his longtime friends knew it was best to leave him be.

About a furlong from his old home Perceval veered his horse off the path and made his way through the bramble to the river.

Sliding off of his saddle to get a drink next to his stallion, the man looked back at his approaching friends. He wiped the sweat off of his brow and squinted up at the sun overhead. Loudly sighing, he asked, "Be I an idiot?"

Stephen was the first to answer. Jumping down to solid ground, he stretched his legs, arched his back, and led his horse to the river. Shrugging, he said, "I have always thought so."

Remembering the Altruistic's previous night's fury, Richard was a touch more cautious. "That be not a title I wouldst give to thee. Why doth thee ask?"

"I spent a year in the Outskirts."

Stephen countered with, "And from all accounts, ye transformed it."

Perceval shook his head. "But at what cost?"

Richard shifted in his saddle, adjusting his balance as his horse waded into the water to sate his thirst. "Over this past year, I have often thought of how I would have reacted to thy calamities. Who can explain grief? We all slog through it at our own pace."

Stephen cupped his hands to take a long drink, then rubbed his palms together to wash off some of the grime from the trip before wiping them on his tunic.

He dropped his normal sarcastic tone, turned, and held his friend in his gaze. "Art thou an idiot? Yea. Most certainly. But we all be idiots. Pushing through our days doing our best with what we have been given. Hast thou made mistakes? I cannot say, for I be a bigger idiot than thee. But I love thee, my friend, for the man we know ye to be. And if thy wife loves thee not and left thee for Todd the Odd, of all people, she be the biggest idiot of us all. No matter how long she had to wait."

Richard answered with a hearty, "Hear, hear!"

Perceval took his friends words and held them closely to his heart before speaking. "I thank thee. She threw away all of her dresses, ye know. I assume to rid herself of everything that reminded her of me."

Percy continued. "Was it wrong from the beginning? Be the fault mine? Hers? I know not. Perhaps I ran myself ragged in my many interests to avoid that very question."

He affectionately rubbed his horse's neck and mane. "Forgive me, friends; I be poking a corpse and asking it to explain to me why it has died."

Perceval put his foot in the stirrup and swung up on his steed. "This be where we part company. I need to find Gwendolyn and ask if our marriage wast already dead, or if I killed it. I thank thee both for our weekend of revelry. It shall not leave my memory for many a day."

With that, Perceval turned Redeemer around and guided his loyal jet-black mass of muscle back to the main road, leaving his friends waving goodbye as he exited.

The next time they saw him was at his trial.

Perceval trotted up the winding overgrown path to his ex-sister-in-law's house. Previously, the cozy tree-lined manse was a welcome sight. Now it filled him with little more than trepidation.

Slipping off of Redeemer, he tied his horse to a fence post

and strode up to the front door, loudly knocking to announce his presence.

A few minutes later the door swung open revealing a petite woman who would be considered the belle of any ball were she not forever cursed and overlooked from having to stand in the shadow of her radiant older sister. Exasperated by the interruption, she pushed a lock of hair away from her forehead with the back of her flour covered hand. "Who be calling at such an odd hour? It be nearly dinner—"

The last word stuck in Meredith the Meek's mouth. Shocked at seeing the man standing before her, the woman stopped stirring the bowl of batter she was holding and simply blankly stared at Perceval, her jaw gaping open and closed like a fish, perhaps hoping that if she moved it up and down enough times the right words might fall out.

Finally, she sputtered, "Perceval, how, how, how good to see you! Sorry to say Gwen's not here. Sadly, ye just missed her. She went into town yesterday. I don't expect her back for at least—"

Perceval pushed past the diminutive woman and entered her home. "Thou art lying, Meredith. I can always tell. Thy cheeks burn the color of crimson."

Shocked and embarrassed, Gwendolyn's sister's free hand flew up to her hot cheek. "Now be not a good time. Perhaps ye could return in a few—"

Perceval made his way down the hall. "I've waited long enough, I'll see her now, thank ye. Last room on the right, be it? No need to announce me, I'll let myself in. Gwendolyn? Your prodigal husband hath returned!"

When Percy barged in the room, he was greeted by a full throttled shriek.

Over the past year he'd completely forgotten Gwendolyn's tendency to scream whenever she was surprised.

The stark abrasive reminder of Gwendolyn's habitual ear-piercing yell was the final nail in the coffin of his affections for his wife.

In that split second Percy flashed over the countless times he had innocently walked into various rooms of their house only to be greeted by her painfully high-pitched banshee cry.

Grimacing through her involuntary salutation, Perceval did his best to contort his face into a smile. "Sorry to interrupt. I be in the neighborhood."

Quite uncharacteristically, Gwen ran to the opposite corner of the room, curled up in the corner chair, hid her face, and tried to wave Perceval off. "Away with thee! I be not taking visitors today."

Concerned, Perceval made his way into the room. "Art thou hurt? If he hast touched thee in any way, I swear to the King I will—"

Resigned to her fate, Gwendolyn the Exquisitely Beautiful turned to face the man she had known and loved for most of her adult life.

Her shoulders slumped as she admitted, "Nay, I be not hurt. Well, I am, but it be of my own design."

Looking at the grotesque vision sitting before him, Perceval had to bite his lip to keep his reaction in check.

Her bottom lip was three times its normal size. That abnormality was accompanied by a trio of large welts on either side of her nose and another immense blister resting directly in the middle of her forehead.

It took all Percy had to calmly ask, "What on earth happened?"

Gwendolyn sighed, "Bee stings."

Not comprehending, Perceval shook his head. "Didst thou walk head first into a hive?"

Irritated she was being forced to explain her humiliation in detail, Gwen pointed to her face. "Nay! 'Tis a beauty treatment! They make your lips look full and attractive!"

"Methinks ye overshot the mark a bit."

Gwendolyn tried to smile, but she couldn't. She sighed, "It's not an exact science. Little bugger stung my hand as well. Then he finished me off with a stinger in me bum."

That was all Perceval could take. Despite his best intentions, he threw his head back and howled with laughter. Seeing the humor, Gwendolyn tried to join him, but her lips hurt too much.

"Oh, my dear Gwendolyn, the lengths thee go to retain your namesake art beyond my comprehension."

"I'm glad I still amuse thee!"

Perceval plopped down on the side of bed nearest her chair. "What possessed you?"

Sensing no anger or malice in her old partner, Gwendolyn let it all out.

Instinctively, both partners seemed to understand they had long passed the point of reconciliation and were meeting again as long-lost friends.

"When we first met, I fell in love with thee because ye ignored my beauty. It didn't affect you the way it did all the others. Thou wast the only one who saw me."

Perceval nodded his head. "And I fell in love with thee because I finally found a woman who didn't have to worry about her outward beauty. I was attracted to the woman I knew thee could be."

Gwendolyn's eyes glistened as she admitted, "But a girl still wants to be noticed. Especially by her husband."

Now it was Percy's turn to sigh. "That be on me. I admit I was not enamored by thy pride, or need to be praised, whatever it was. I couldn't understand thy desire to be puffed up, so I erred on the side of silence. Thou wert always beautiful, my Gwendolyn, and I be sorry I didn't say it enough."

A tear dropped down Gwen's cheek as she softly said, "I thank thee."

"I assume Todd feeds that particular appetite."

Gwendolyn nodded. "And then some. He treats me like a queen. Although I fear how he'll react when he sees this!"

Percy shifted a bit in his seat. "I suspect thy face may well heal before he sees thee."

At that Gwendolyn sat upright. There was concern and no

small amount of accusation in her voice as she asked, "What didst thou do?"

Perceval threw up his hands in self-defense. "Blame me not! He slid the papers of our divorce in betwixt a pile of documents from the bank he requested I sign."

Gwendolyn asked again, "What didst thou do?"

"A year I waited to see thee, only to discover he wast undercutting me and weaseling his way in from the very beginning."

"Perceval! What didst thou do!"

Percy shrugged. "We may have exchanged words."

When he caught his ex-wife's furrowed brow, he expounded. "And fists. All right, my fists. He be more on the receiving end."

"I told him to talk to thee first. How bad is it?"

"Be there a beauty contest between the two of thee, even now, thou wouldst still win, hands down."

Gwendolyn tried to put her head in her hands, but her blisters prevented her. She sat back in her chair and looked at her ex. "What a pair we have become, eh?"

Percy could only smile and nod. He stared at the woman before him for a while. "I have to ask. Didst thy heart leave me before I left?"

Gwendolyn looked out the window. "Mayhaps, mayhaps not. It be hard for me to pin down. Methinks our children were the glue. And when they be gone..."

Percy looked down at the ground. "I miss them, Gwen. I miss thee. I miss us. But things change, I understand. How be thy heart?"

A wave of grief passed over Gwendolyn's face. Several tears dropped from her eyes as she tried to suck in enough air to breathe. All she could do was shake her head and cry.

Percy stood up and walked over to the frail woman in the chair. He took her uninjured hand, held it to his lips and gently kissed it.

Their eyes connected, knowing this was most likely their last truly intimate moment. Perceval softly said, "We shared a truly wonderful journey, did we not?"

Gwendolyn closed her eyes and nodded.

A few heartbeats later, Perceval turned to go.

He stopped at the bedroom door, considered leaving, then realized he'd be remiss if he left before saying what he came to say.

"Thou art free of me, Gwendolyn. Live thy best life with Todd. Or anyone else that pleases thee. I lost thee on that day, I know that now. That was the worst day of my life. Our lives. It seems there be no coming back from that. I wish thee the best. Nothing I can ever say or do can adequately express my admiration for being the mother you were to our children. I will be grateful to thee for that until my dying day."

He looked back at Gwendolyn and asked, "May I do anything for thee? Get anything?"

She could only shake her head as she mouthed the words, "Thank ye."

Perceval exhaled as he let the burden he was carrying in his heart drop to the floor. He nodded. "So be it."

As he left and turned the corner into the hallway, he called out, "Did ye catch all that, Meredith, or shall we repeat everything for thy behalf?"

The flustered woman stepped out from the shadows of her privy across the hall, put her flour-stained fists on her hips and feigned outrage. "Well, I never! I'll have you know I be neither a spy nor a gossip."

Perceval laughed as he closed the front door behind him.

Chapter Seventeen
Entering Kingston

Riding away from the home and woman he once knew and loved, Perceval was relieved when he spied a familiar friend further up the road.

At his master's urging, Redeemer kicked up a cloud of dust and closed the distance in no time.

When he was a stone's throw away, Percy called out, "Hail thee well, old friend!"

Brother Bob glanced over his shoulder, smiled, waved, and waited for the rider to catch up.

Giving Perceval the once over, Brother Bob remarked, "Thou hast returned from thy debauched weekend and are apparently none the worse for the wear. Were thy friends waylaid, or has Pleasanton enticed more victims into its insidious web?"

"Three of us made it out alive. The fourth remains to be seen."

Brother Bob chuckled. "Perceval the Altruistic, nefarious man of mystery."

"Turns out whilst me back be turned, Todd the Odd weaseled his way into Gwendolyn's heart. I repaid his betrayal by slightly rearranging his face."

"Ah, mystery solved. And quite a juicy one at that. Art thou headed to Kingston?"

Perceval nodded. "That I be."

Brother Bob pulled up the reins of his cart, slowing to a stop. He patted the seat next to him. "If it please thee, give thy horse a rest and join me."

Perceval was confused. "Brother Bob?"

"If it please thee, indulge me."

A few moments later Redeemer was tied to the rear of the cart, and Perceval heaved himself onto the buckboard next to his friend. "Now who art a man of mystery?"

The monk shook the reins, clicked his tongue twice, and his sleepy nag resumed her slow, methodic pace.

After a few minutes of silence, Brother Bob found a way to begin what he suspected was going to be a difficult conversation. "Thou hast been gone from Kingston for quite a while."

Perceval nodded. "Yea. Upwards of a year."

"A lot hast changed."

Percy's curiosity was piqued. "Such as?"

Brother Bob laughed. "Thou won't believe it, but performers of the written word art now exceedingly popular."

"Dost thou mean the mindless dullards who call themselves thespians?"

Brother Bob vigorously bobbed his head. "The very same."

"Thou art speaking of the fools who have not an original thought in their collective brains but can only speak lines another has written for them?"

"Again, the same."

This new information was something Perceval couldn't quite process. "I believe it not."

Brother Bob breathlessly elaborated to his kindred spirit. "I can only assume the majority of theater patrons have fallen under a witch's spell of stupidity, but of late, the audiences watching the make-believe couplets presented at the playhouse ascribe the words of romance and derring-do to the performers, not the playwright."

Perceval let out a laugh. "Thou art pulling both of my legs."

Brother Bob was adamant. "Nay, good friend. Somehow watching people pretending to be positively brimming with wit and courage has convinced the gullible viewers into believing the play actors possess those very qualities in real life."

"Define thy term, *exceedingly popular*."

"They be fawned over in public, get the best tables at pubs, and hold endless award ceremonies where they present each other with trophies after casting votes determining who did the best job pretending to be someone else."

Perceval could only shake his head. "As I live and breathe. Thou couldst knock me over with a feather. What other absurd changes have occurred since my abrupt exit?"

"Methinks thee knew this, but the youth of the town have disproportionately grown in both power and influence."

Perceval waved his hand, indicating the monk should continue. "How so?"

"They have a phrase. If any cross or offend them, they call for the errant party's elimination. Their eradication."

"What doth that mean?"

Brother Bob struggled to define Kingston's latest plague. "It be a form of banishment. Ye become a pariah, invisible, shunned, if ye will."

"For what offense?"

"Any! Glance at any entitled teenager the wrong way and thou shouldst prepare for retribution. And by that I mean time in both jail and the stocks for thy crime of hatred."

"Nay!"

"Yea! Hurting a young one's feelings be tantamount to raping and pillaging."

"Nay!"

"Again, I say, yea! I wish I be lying, but these teens art so fragile and excessively vocal about their frailties that the entire town of Kingston bends to their will out of the necessary need for self-preservation, with no little amount of abject fear."

Perceval was incredulous. "Have not these teens parents? Where be their rightful authority's rod and switch?"

Brother Bob laughed again. "Ye have indeed been gone for a goodly time. Corporal punishment currently be considered torture. Any physical chastisement be forbidden across the entire land. Not from an edict from the King, but rather popular opinion. I heard tell of one parent who confined their offspring to their room for a fortnight and they be run out of town."

"Then throw me to the gallows, my goodly monk, for no child of mine wouldst ever rule the roost as ye claim these underlings do."

Brother Bob nodded. "I endorse it not; I be merely the messenger."

Perceval had not even entered the town, and he was already keenly aware he no longer belonged there. He briefly considered riding off before entering his old stomping grounds, but was determined to get some kind of satisfaction from the King, so he asked, "Be there anything else?"

This was the very subject Brother Bob was reticent to discuss. He swallowed, paused, and said, "Naming Day be tomorrow."

Percy shot up in his seat with excitement. "Naming Day? On the morrow? What are the odds? I love Naming Day! Obviously I missed the celebration last year. What were the funny namesakes given? I believe my favorite would have to be when they brought up that shy, skinny child and declared him to be Thomas the Hopefully He'll Become An Accountant Or An Esquire As He Hath No Skill In Farming. The boy's mother was about to faint dead away until they shortened it to Thomas the Hopeful."

The monk did his best to smile at the memory. "That wert indeed amusing."

"I hope he lived up to his name. Say, whatever happened to Sally the Directionally Challenged? I just naturally assumed she wandered off, never again to be found."

Brother Bob thought on that one. "Nay, I believe she married Willard the Dullard. He was hired by the blacksmith and does fine work. They make a goodly pair."

Then it hit Perceval. "Wait, that means tonight be the King's life achievement banquet. Who be awarded the platter this year?"

And so they had come to it. Brother Bob shook his head. "No one. After last year's debacle, it was felt it best to skip a year or two."

Perceval understood. "Ah, of course."

His mood immediately darkened. He put his head in his hands and mumbled, "'Tis one year on the dot, and I choose this day to return to the scene of the crime."

Brother Bob patted his friend's leg. "I'm afraid that be not all."

Perceval peeked at Brother Bob through his webbed fingers. "*What* be not all?"

This was the wound Percy's friend didn't want to pour salt on. His response was slow and deliberate. "It seems that because the King never came out and declared the reason for thy myriad of disasters, the people of Kingston have decided thou wert somehow responsible."

Percy was more stunned by this revelation than by either of the monk's previous assertions. "So, I somehow caused the earthquake? The fire from the sky? Did I contract with mercenaries to rob myself?"

"As I said, of late the entire town be under a witch's spell of stupidity."

"How besmirched be my name?"

"Oh, thou art well beyond besmirchment. Thou art eliminated. Banished! Thou can show thy face not in Kingston. Especially on Naming Day."

"Surely if I but explain my innocence—"

"Nay."

"People be reasonable. They shall see—"

"Nay!"

"Thou art serious?"

Brother Bob left his friend no quarter. "Thou art eradicated! It be as if ye never existed. Thou art not allowed within the city limits under threat of prison time—or worse."

The two men sat side by side as the information slowly sunk in. It suddenly all became clear to Perceval. "Thou hast known of this for quite some time."

"'Tis true, yes."

Perceval turned and looked in the back of the cart. There, in the corner next to his book, was a large package wrapped up tight with rope. "And what be contained in the bundle?"

Brother Bob shrugged. "A few changes of clothes. Enough coins to start over some place new."

"If I be a smarter man, I might begin to believe thou art wishing to get rid of me."

"I am. It pains me to say methinks thou wilt get no satisfaction from the King. If he has yet to answer thee by now, thou art not getting one. I wilt drive thee to the coast. Once there, hire a boat and go. Start a new life somewhere else. Some new land where no one knows of thee and thou hast a clean slate. There be nothing for thee in Kingston but sorrow."

"The Outskirts wouldst welcome me back."

"Yea, as will the unattainable Mary. My friend, thou hast a gift. Ye can name the exact date of the worst day of thy life. Put that behind thee, guard thy heart, and start a new life on another shore. I beg of thee!"

Perceval sat and pondered the good monk's offer. "I thank thee for thy kind consideration."

"That only a fool wouldst refuse."

"Fool I may be, but I cannot go without satisfaction. The stakes be too high. My questions loom too large."

Brother Bob knew he had lost but intended to go down fighting. "Let us say, by some miracle, ye actually get an answer. That still be no guarantee of satisfaction."

Percy agreed. "That be a gamble I be willing to take."

"Listen to reason, man! Thou hast yet to experience elimination. Go away for five, perhaps ten years. In that time, methinks all may be forgiven and forgotten."

"Ten years!"

"Perhaps less. Ye might get away with five."

"How long doth thou really think?"

"Oh, fifteen at least. Twenty be more like it. Hold out for thirty if ye can."

Perceval was about to jump into another rebuttal, but before he opened his mouth, he got an idea.

Percy reached back behind his neck and pulled up the hood of his tunic, pulling it far enough forward to cover the majority of his face.

"I see thy point. Perceval the Altruistic needs to leave and stay away. But if a kindly, generous, and oh-so-thoughtful monk such as, oh, perhaps yerself had, say, an apprentice?"

Seeing where this was going, Brother Bob began to vigorously shake his head. "Nay!"

"One who hast taken a vow of silence and agreed to stay in the shadows."

"Nay, I say!"

"One who would heretofore promise to holdest not a grudge against said kindly monk who knewest of said unjust elimination yet held back that information until just now."

Brother Bob grumbled, "Thy stock and trade be in emotional manipulation."

Perceval nodded. "Good. 'Tis settled. I shall be a monk in training until I find a way to speak to the King."

The monk lowered his head in defeat, saying, "Let it be known far and wide thou hast a brain of wood, art deficient in common sense, and hast insisted on denying perfectly good counsel. Not to mention thou art something of an idiot."

Perceval smiled, clicked his tongue twice, flicked the reins, and on cue the monk's old nag began to clomp forward towards Percy's fate, neither friend knowing whether it was to be his redemption or condemnation.

✝✝✝

At dusk, the monk's cart crept unnoticed into Kingston. Despite the encroaching darkness, the town was alive with a sense of frantic urgency. Other than an occasional perfunctory wave to Brother Bob, the monk and his cloaked companion were summarily ignored.

Naming Day was tomorrow, and a thousand details had yet to be buttoned down.

Passing by the village square, Perceval could see the town fathers had dragged out and erected the temporary stage at the edge of the green. Row after row of benches were being placed in front of it, hoping the weather would cooperate at least until dusk on the morrow.

Percy's own Naming Day was so far back he could hardly remember it, but his own children's were much more vivid in his memory. Their smiling faces rose up through the mist in his mind, causing yet another wave of sadness to wash over the man.

Brother Bob could always tell when Perceval was sinking. He reached over and put his arm around his friend's shoulders. "Thy offspring?"

Perceval nodded. "How did you—?"

"You tend to groan."

The apprentice monk shook it off and sat up a bit. "My apologies."

"Nay, grief hast no set time table."

Perceval exhaled. "If only it did. Sign up for two or three months and be done with it. But this... The slightest nudge of rec-ollection and I'm right back diving into the depths of my despair."

Percy wiped his eyes with back of his hand. "They truly were wonderful."

Now it was Brother Bob's turn to go silent. He hung his head and sighed. Perceval looked over at his friend and raised his eyebrows.

Against his better judgment, Brother Bob exclaimed, "I hope I live not long enough to regret this, but methinks ye should mayhaps ignore what I said earlier. Get thee to the King. Find thy closure. Surely he won't rebuff thee if thou doth make thy appeal in person."

Percy looked at his friend. "Dost thou truly believe that?"

"Nay, not for a moment. But I thought it best to support thy fantasy."

Perceval nodded. "I thank thee for thy half-hearted support."

Brother Bob loudly exhaled. "I do support thee. But I be of two minds here, and I vacillate betwixt the two. To stand or to flee, I know not which be the wiser course of action. But if it were me, I wouldst flee."

Pondering his fate, Perceval sat back in silence.

Brother Bob's horse knew the way to the monk's shelter with little need of assistance from anyone attempting to guide the cart.

Along the way Perceval took in a dozen familiar sights: the bakery, the blacksmith's barn, the cursed bank, and the theater—all standing in and alongside the local pubs and eateries.

To Perceval's eye, the newest development in Kingston had apparently sprung up virtually overnight on nearly every street corner like an outcropping of huge obnoxious weeds.

Just a few years ago, before the advent of the printing press, word of important events got around at a fairly nice pace in the village. The town squires were the primary source of information, with the ever-ready gossip chain coming in a close second.

But with the advent of what have come to be called "social boards" in the town square, and the constant stream of teenagers checking out those boards, information about who was currently courting whom and who was unceremoniously dumped by a scorned suitor soon spread faster than wildfire.

Parents began to notice their children begging to go into town with an irritating frequency. Since the trip would often take up a good part of the day, which would seriously cut into various chores that needed to be done on the farm, the answer, more often than not, was a curt, "No."

After months of tantrums and pouting and mounting anger from their offspring, people began to note more of the community boards popping up all over the countryside.

It got to the point where there were so many social boards scattered across the land that practically any teen could dash off to the nearest board to gather all the latest news and be back home before their parents even noticed they were gone.

With that knowledge came power and no small amount of anxiety for the youths who were not able to get to the gossip centers as quickly as their peers, or worse, discovering that they, themselves, were the unwitting topic of the latest threatening thread of misinformation.

Surprisingly, the ones who found themselves in the most enviable positions of the day were scullery maids.

Historically, the minimally skilled servants were considered at or near the bottom of the social hierarchy.

Interestingly, an invisible subordinate silently dawdling over their work in the background could surreptitiously pick up quite a lot of dirt, listening to the comings and goings of a well-to-do household.

Then, as the maids made their way back home for the evening, they would anonymously post the latest overheard scintillating tales on every board they passed.

Soon, their handwriting and paper of choice became known, and other teens would gravitate to their posts first, regularly reposting the information on the social boards closer to their own homes.

Thus, Kingston had its very first *persuaders*.

More than a little perplexed at this new development, Perceval craned his neck as he passed by several social boards. Each one appeared to be jam packed with various slips of paper pinned to the cork. "More community boards than I remember."

Brother Bob couldn't restrain a gruff cough of disdain. "Those be the bane of my existence. Wouldst that they all could spontaneously combust! It be my observation that people no longer converse. They fritter away hours going from board to board looking at messages from people whom they hardly even know. I swear it be the end of civilization as we know it."

Perceval laughed. "But thou hast no opinion about it."

"Restrain me, dear brother. Get me started not. The latest

debacle be that the town's lonely hearted art using these accursed boards for the purposes of matchmaking. Hast thou ever heard of such a thing?"

"How dost that work? Art parents and relatives who know them best no longer involved?"

"Nay, that be a thing of the past. Perfect matches be based purely on appearances. A lot of good a beautiful face or frame wilt do thee when thy land be ravaged by locusts or famine. Find a mate of hearty stock, I say. I thank the King I had the good fortune to remain single, despite my obvious allure to yon fairer sex."

Perceval turned to look at the community board as they passed it by. He saw several hand drawn likenesses of eager prospective mates pinned liberally throughout.

Brother Bob couldn't hide his disgust. "And the pictures rarely be even a good likeness. The vain suitors instruct the portrait artists to add some heft to a bosom here or straighten out a nose there. It be well reported that when the majority of these witless matches finally meet face to face, most times they do not even recognize one another, for each hath been sold a bill of goods."

The goodly monk was on a roll. "And that be not all. The boards be making the populace mean and critical. Which be what I art doing right now. Forgive me. I be the one in need of a vow of silence."

Perceval was thoroughly enjoyed listening to someone other than himself rant for once. "Stop not on my account, good brother. Spare me not any details."

Brother Bob gulped in a mouthful of air and continued. "If thee insist. It seems to me the problem be anonymity. Before these infernal boards, if I insulted thee, it would be face to face, as our good and wise King hast instructed. But the board posters be cowards of the lowest kind. They put up slips of paper demeaning another's character. Then it be a pile-on whilst other bullies join in the fun, leaving their objects of derision defenseless, out in the cold."

Perceval's blood started to boil. "Such a thing should not be!"

"Thou art preaching to the converted, sir. It hast gotten far out of hand. These entitled teens love to build themselves up by putting others down. They ridicule all not in their special social circle. How the outcasts dress, how they act, what they say. Any slip or deviation from the accepted norm be held up to ridicule and relentless mocking."

"Doth the King know of this?"

Brother Bob shrugged. "I know not. Bring it up when thou doth see him, wouldst ye?"

Perceval looked around as they pulled up to the monk's retreat. "With the King as my witness, if all thee say be true, there doth appear to be trouble in paradise."

"Verily, truer words haft ne'er been spoken." Brother Bob let out a bit of a groan as he struggled out of his seat and onto the ground to untie his horse.

Perceval was riled up with righteous indignation. Ready to take on the world, he looked at the goodly monk. "So, tell me, Brother Bob, how shalt we fix it?"

To Perceval's surprise, the monk merely shrugged. "I say burn it all down to the ground as ye did in the Outskirts and start over. Barring that, I'd still suggest ye leave tonight."

Ignoring his friend, Perceval made his way to the monk's home.

Brother Bob repeated himself. "Walk away from me not. Ye know the advice I give be only for thy benefit."

Turning back for a moment, Percy touched his lips and raised his shoulders. "Even if I knew which of thy two minds I should debate, I fear I cannot. Vow of silence."

Frustrated, the monk yelled at his friend as he made his way through the front door. "Perceval the Altruistic!"

There was no mistaking the brother's deadly serious tone. Perceval stopped and turned back.

Brother Bob looked his friend dead in the eye and stated matter of factly, "Make no mistake. This be thy moment of no return. Take stock of what be at stake, and I pray thee heed my warning!"

Perceval looked at his friend and nodded. "I hear thee. I love thee like a brother. And I thank thee for doing thy best to help. But in the end, I can only do what I believe to be right."

"Even if thou art so very, very wrong?"

Perceval grinned as he nodded and turned to enter the Monk's humble abode. "Even though."

Leading his horse to the stables to be watered and fed, Brother Bob muttered to the mare, "The next time I advise anyone to go against my earlier much sounder advice, give me a good kick in the rear, wouldst thee?"

Chapter Eighteen
Naming Day

Were it a normal day, Perceval would have arrived at the Naming Day festival several hours early in order to get a good seat. But today he was traveling incognito.

The fact that he was planning on attending the naming ceremony at all was in direct violation of Brother Bob's strong advice. The monk stopped sweeping up the sawdust from the floor of his wood shop for a moment and cried out, "Art thou a complete and utter imbecile?"

Perceval took umbrage. "I wouldn't say *complete*."

Brother Bob was growing weary of trying to keep his friend in line. "Have I not adequately explained the danger hanging over thy head?"

"Verily, thou hast expounded endlessly upon it."

"Then apparently, wise counsel be only for thee to offer. For when I dole it out, ye reject it out of hand. I shall say it again, thou hast been eliminated! Eradicated! Done away with! Pushed into oblivion!"

Perceval was determined. "Not a soul shalt even know I be there. All eyes shalt be on the stage. I shall stand back in the shadows. Without speaking. To anyone, be they friend or foe."

Brother Bob shook his head. "'Tis not possible. Ye know it; I know it. Ye shalt forget thyself, or feel an overwhelming need to right a wrong. Ignore Naming Day, go to the King's castle, and make thy petition. It be the only way."

"Then that be what I shalt do."

Brother Bob stopped his rant. He looked askance at his friend.

"What dost thou mean?"

Perceval acquiesced. "I shalt heed thy advice."

The monk didn't know how to respond. "Didst thou just say thou wilt take my advice?"

"Indeed."

"What be thy trick?"

"No trick. I shalt go directly to the King's castle."

"Deceit be not an attractive trait."

Perceval smiled. "Agreed, old friend." He pulled his hood up over his head and stepped over to the door. "To the King's castle. Wish me luck."

Brother Bob did just that. "May good fortune smile upon thee."

"And if, by chance, Naming Day happens to lie in the path of my direct journey to the King's castle, I shalt pay it no mind and continue walking."

Saying his final piece, Perceval quickly slipped out the door and was gone.

Brother Bob yelled after his friend at his highest volume, "Call on me not when thou art arrested!"

Off in the distance, he heard Perceval shout back, "Sorry, can't answer thee! Vow of silence!"

Brother Bob turned back to his chores. "Vow of silence, my elbow…"

Mid-rant he stopped, opened the door, and called out after Perceval. "I shalt hold thy book of the King and thy belongings until thou art kicked out of Kingston forever!"

The monk could barely make out a voice yelling back from far off down the alley, "Thank thee!"

This was a Naming Day unlike any Perceval had ever experienced.

From his earliest memories, the pattern had remained reliably constant. For months, if not years, the naming society would follow children around town observing their habits and discussing their personalities. It should be noted here that regardless of their qualifications, no men were ever invited to be part of the naming committee because, well, it just felt creepy.

After watching the kids for an extended period of time, it became clear which child preferred to hang back, who had leadership tendencies, who was kind, who was a bully, and so on.

Knowing the parents of the children helped as well since more than once it was remarked that the child of so-and-so didn't fall too far from their family tree.

The namers were respected, if not feared, for if they gave someone a negative name, it usually stayed with that person for the rest of their life.

Some could outgrow it, but memories are long, and once a child was labeled as lazy or slow, it was nearly impossible to ever totally erase the original less-than-stellar impression.

As an example, Darius the Dimwitted never managed to entirely shake his namesake, no matter how many books he read or far away universities he attended.

Those kinds of labels were rare indeed, for the namers, at their core, were kindhearted women who felt a great responsibility to both the children and the community at large.

In the past misnaming the occasional child had happened with disastrous results, and those were mistakes no one wanted to repeat.

In the committee's defense, they accurately classified Maurice the Mean Streak for a very specific reason. They wanted to warn everyone he met of his deep-seated sadistic nature.

But when he more than exceeded his namesake and turned into Maurice the Mass Murderer, the namers never lived it down.

That's when the women started giving optimistic names the society believed the children would grow into.

Perceval the Altruistic was one such child.

Once Percy was able to look up the name and understand its meaning, he spent a lifetime doing his best to live up to the namers' lofty proclamation.

All of that was what Perceval was expecting today. Surprisingly, the ceremony turned out to be a far cry from what he and everyone else in Kingston had ever experienced.

As usual, the entire village had gathered on the town square, and each of the two dozen expectant children seated on stage waiting for their namesake were enthusiastically supported and surrounded by their very rowdy onlooking families.

Some broods brought confetti, others had signs and noisemakers, while other clans made their presence known through sheer numbers by taking up the majority of seats on the lawn.

So as not to be noticed, Perceval stood far in the back, which, he had to admit, was exactly to his liking. He was still able to see and hear most everything without having his ear drums shattered by overly enthusiastic relatives banging on celebratory pots and pans.

If one's culture doesn't have something akin to Naming Day, curiosity may abound as to how and why this odd tradition began.

Over the years, it has been rightly observed that most people are innately curious about two things: first, their ultimate purpose in life, and secondly, what others think of them.

Naming Day was Kingston's attempt to give both direction and settle an individual's curiosity once and for all. And in public, no less.

Because, as a rule, children tend to be extremely intimidated by large crowds, at the announcement of their namesake, a great deal of the youngsters would nod, take their certificate, shake the hands of the namers, and circle back to their chair while their parents and siblings cheered them on.

It was usually not until the ceremony was over that the enormity of their name would start to sink in.

Today, as expected, the first few children were well behaved and graciously accepted their namesakes. One sweet little girl was so overcome with emotion she ran from person to person and hugged each of the namers.

It was in the naming of the fourth child, who appeared to be between ten and twelve years old, when everything went to seed.

Her negative reaction was fairly understandable as the sour faced pre-teen was given the moniker Beatrice the Belligerent.

Hearing the name, Perceval was indeed surprised as it was the most negative namesake he'd heard in several years.

But judging from the crowd's reaction, a lot of people totally agreed with Beatrice's given handle.

The young girl and her family, however, did not.

The child balked. After her namesake was revealed, she haltingly walked to the front of the stage, reached for her certificate, but then withdrew her hand before grasping it.

In a sudden rage, she stomped her foot and shouted out, "No! That not be who I am! I be not Beatrice the Belligerent!"

Embarrassed, the namers did their best to shoo her away, but Beatrice was not having it. "I said no! Take it back!"

The head namer attempted to laugh it off and said, "My dear child, that be the namesake thou hast been given. If ye do not care for it, take it as a challenge to become the opposite. Many a model citizen of—"

The child's diminutive fists curled up into balls and her face turned beet red as she yelled, "Perhaps thou art too old and feeble to hear what I said! That be not who I am! I be Beatrice the Princess! Make that my namesake!"

Someone who appeared to be the girl's older sister stood up in the crowd. "Ye tell her, Beatrice! Don't let 'em push ye around! Ye deserve to be whate'er ye want! Refuse any name they give ye until ye get princess!"

That's when her family and a few in the crowd started chanting "princess" over and over again. Partly as an encouragement, but mostly as a threat.

The committee was visibly shaken. They quickly huddled in the middle of the stage, conferred as best they could, considering the volume of the protesting voices, and after attempting to calm the crowd down a bit, they made their announcement.

"The naming committee has heard Beatrice's displeasure with

her namesake, and we promise to revisit this issue at our meeting next month.”

Not accepting their decision, the little girl came out swinging!

She ran over to the committee and started flailing at everyone within striking distance, all the while yelling at the top of her lungs, “I said no! I be a princess! Make me a princess now!”

No one on the committee wanted to be seen hitting a child in public, so they deflected Beatrice’s blows as best they could. Regardless, more than one namer took it on the chin. And stomach. And groin. Though tiny in stature, this kid appeared to pack quite a wallop.

Perceval was sworn to silence, but he desperately wanted to shout out, “Methinks her namesake shouldst be ‘Right Hook’!”

Finally, the naming committee had had enough. As one, they caved. The spokesperson recanted and yelled, “Fine! Thou art henceforth to be known far and wide as Beatrice the Princess!”

The cantankerous child immediately stopped hitting her elders and said, “Good. Write it down.”

Rather than engage the girl in any more debate, a namer took the unruly youngster’s certificate, crossed out the original name, thought about writing “spawn of the Dragon,” but against her better judgment spelled out “princess.”

Oblivious to any negativity she may have caused, the newly crowned princess grabbed her certificate, turned to face her family, curtsied, and skipped back to her seat, happy as she could be.

Sadly, the rest of the ceremony was more of the same. By comparison, when all was said and done, Beatrice the Princess was one of the easy ones.

Taking a cue from the belligerent debacle, parents began to speak up if they didn’t care for the namesake chosen for their precious and precocious offspring.

By the end of the day the harried committee had lost all power. Naming Day officially became a mockery. It was turned into wish fulfillment day.

The namers started giving each child a choice of names, even scuttling those choices if the monikers didn't measure up to the entitled brat's standards.

In the space of a few hours, Perceval was treated to a surprisingly detailed sketch of one of the ills of the current culture in Kingston.

But Naming Day was just a precursor to the true cancer which was eating away at the place he used to call his home town.

Chapter Nineteen
The Crime of Hatred

After the Naming Day farce concluded, Perceval hung back in order to let the throngs filter out and traverse their various treks back home.

Many a tongue was wagging that day, lamenting the annual gathering's sour turn of events.

As the crowd dissipated, Percy made a path up and around the stage, over to the King's statue.

Blocking his way was a huge social board.

Perceval had yet to see one up close, so today he got an eyeful. Looking at the array of different messages, pictures, and advertisements, it was easy to see the attraction.

The biggest surprise was the discovery of the proud sponsor of this board, and most likely the majority of all the other signs blanketing the town. It was none other than Kingston's popular number one vacation destination: Pleasanton.

Percy muttered to himself, "So the Dragon has managed to weasel his way back into Kingston. Why be I not surprised?"

Several of the posts appeared to be fresh, as a few scattered here and there congratulated the latest crop of namesakes. But a surprising majority of the messages appeared to be particularly vicious in tone.

He wasn't sure who the tormented teen Victor the Homely was (surely his namesake was naught but a cruel nickname), but he felt for the youth as post after post insulted the young man's less-than-virile appearance. Adding insult to injury, many was the commentary on his apparent inability to convince any of the young women of the village to enter into a courtship with him.

The most succinct of the messages was a picture of Victor with a literal set of buttocks as a head. The image made Percy laugh, but he immediately felt guilty about it.

What bothered Perceval more than the plethora of gossip pinned to the board was the fact that the edifice itself stood directly in front of what used to be the focal point of the town square.

Stepping around the board, Percy was struck by a stark visual confirmation of his King's currently diminished status.

The once burnished bronze of the inspiring twenty-foot-tall statue had lost its luster and was slowly being taken over by a creeping dull green hue.

In the King's right hand, he held aloft a sharp two-edged sword. Symbolically balancing warcraft with nurture, his left arm cradled a bread basket, which was currently precariously hosting an empty bird's nest.

Weeds grew up and over the entire base, totally obscuring the wise admonishment inscribed at the bottom.

For the life of him, Percy couldn't remember what verse was etched on the plate. He was sure it was something about loving the King, or one another, but the exact scripture escaped him.

Percy attempted to pull away the weeds; however, the task was too much to endeavor without the proper tools or crew. After a few ineffective tugs and pulls, he gave up.

It was at this point that Perceval the Altruistic came to a crossroads.

He knew the wisest choice would be to continue on to the King's castle in order to make his stand, at least until his identity was discovered and the powers that be promptly kicked him out of town.

But over the course of the day, his indignation had gone from a low simmer to a point dangerously close to boiling over.

Curiously, his general sense of irritation didn't have an exact target, but after spending less than a full day in the midst of Kingston's populace, a very specific one was beginning to form.

Almost unconsciously, Perceval put one foot in front of the other and found himself drawn, against his better judgment, to restaurant row on the opposite side of the village.

He rationalized his detour by telling himself he was, indeed, hungry. Further, he thought, as he had taken a vow of silence, he would religiously avoid any confrontation with the terrible teens of the town.

That being said, before he was forced to leave Kingston, he did want to see this illustrious group in action at least once.

He laughed, albeit naively, and said to himself, "It'll be dinner and a show!"

Traversing the thousand steps at a leisurely pace, it was comforting to stroll through once familiar streets, absorbing all the sights and sounds. When Perceval turned a corner, he came upon the large familiar dark wooden building known as the Eagle's Claw, the most popular eatery in the village. Here, he noted two things:

First and foremost, business was apparently booming. Hungry patrons filled the street, anxiously awaiting their turn at a rustic table inside.

Secondly, and more surprisingly, restaurant row was currently defunct. In contrast to the bustling thoroughfare he remembered, the Claw appeared to be the only game in town.

Two of the pubs across the street had, from all indications, recently been shuttered, as the boards nailed to their windows and doors looked to be freshly hewn.

Perceval couldn't hazard a guess as to why. He was acquainted with both families who owned those establishments and, if memory served, their entire livelihoods were derived from the meager profits they managed to squeeze out of their respective taverns.

Percy tapped the shoulder of an older man standing outside the Eagle's Claw, gestured toward the closed inns and raised his eyebrows, silently asking the obvious, "What happened?"

The old man grunted and shook his head with disgust. He spat on the ground and gestured with his chin towards the front window of the Claw, saying, "'Twas the cursed terrible teens that did it!"

Hearing her husband speak such things out loud, the old man's wife whipped around and put a finger up against his mouth, softly whispering, "Hush now, dear, if'n ye don't want us to be eliminated as well."

Not wanting to endanger the man but rabidly curious, Percy leaned in towards the octogenarian and tapped his own ear, indicating he wanted to hear more.

The man ignored the death stare from his wife, lowered his voice, and gladly unburdened himself, saying, "Seems them two taverns upset the terrible teens somethin' awful. So's them prissy pants posted bad reviews of the pubs on every board in town. Gave 'em zero moons, they did! Then they started tellin' tall tales about findin' glass in their food an' such. 'Twasn't long afore both places had to give up an' close up shop. Now the Claw's afeared to rile 'em up, as they cain't afford ta get the same treatment. An' that's why all o' us gets to cool our heels in the street, whilst them half pints get to rule the roost, says I."

When Perceval nodded his thanks, the irascible old man looked at his wife with defiance in his eyes and loudly repeated, "Says I!"

Perceval slipped away from the burgeoning domestic disturbance he managed to stir up and made his way through the crowd. He stopped short of the tavern's open window.

It was there he saw firsthand the end result of a town that was falling headfirst into the wayward paths of enabling and entitlement.

Perceval wondered how it had gotten this far. He also seriously pondered whether or not the societal rot he was witnessing could be reversed. He hoped against hope that all was not lost.

The King's Sacred Book of Accumulated Wisdom clearly delineated how to avoid such pitfalls and snares. But the hearers need eyes to see, ears to listen, and the strength to endure the inevitable firestorm of retaliation.

In many ways it would have been easier for Perceval to walk away, wash his hands of it, and let the chips fall where they may. As one might have surmised by now, when it came to defending his moral indignation, Percy rarely took the easy road.

The first image the disguised apprentice saw didn't make sense to him. A table of teens sitting in the center of the tavern were as still as statues. Not a one of them moved a muscle. Garish fake smiles were frozen on their overly exaggerated faces.

The rest of the restaurant was a flurry of activity, but the self-appointed stars of the moment neither ate any of the delectable dishes placed before them, nor drank from the steins of ale each teen held aloft.

Looking to their side, Perceval understood at once. There, crouched down behind his easel, was an artist furiously sketching the tableau in front of him. His charcoal pencil flew across the canvas while his free hand wiped away beads of sweat dripping down his face.

One of the teens clearly was out of patience. The girl at the far end of the table asked through clenched teeth, "Art thou done yet?"

Another chimed in with, "Yea, this be taking forever."

Yet another said, "My arm ist beginning to shake."

The boy in the middle sighed, "The other painter be so much faster. Why didst we not hire him?"

The artist forced a smile, saying, "Patience, good lords, and ladies. I be going as fast as I can. My partner may spell me after his cramp subsides."

Perceval followed the artist's eyes over to the bar area. There he saw another man, presumably an artist as well, who had immersed his hand in a bucket of water. He raised it up, painfully flexed his fingers and shook his head.

The pressured artist's pencil gave a final flourish to signal he was done. "There. I believe I have captured thy essence." Turning the work of art around, the painter was met by a wall of indifference.

"Is that supposed to be us?"

"My nose be all wrong."

"Ye call thyself an artist?"

Vainly smiling throughout, the artist tried his best to dig his way out. "Nay, kind ladies and gents, this be only the roughest of sketches. I shall work without sustenance nor rest until I have captured thy likenesses perfectly."

The girl leader at the end of the table shrugged her shoulders. "Fine, if ye say so. Bring it around when thou art done. But not a penny of payment until we all art satisfied."

The artist bowed low, signaled his fellow painter to follow him out, grabbed his easel and canvas and maneuvered his way out of the room as quickly as humanly possible.

That is when the show began.

The young girl at the end, whom Perceval soon learned was naught but a scullery maid, took a bite of her chicken and recoiled. "This be stone cold!"

Each of the grown children tasted their food as well and came up with the same reaction.

"I cannot eat this!"

"Nor I!"

"I daresay mine's not even cooked!"

Taking command of the situation, the scullery maid snapped her fingers, and the owner of the tavern practically tripped over himself making his way to her table. "What seems to be the problem, madam?"

"All of our food be cold. Remake it."

The owner of the tavern was near his breaking point. His face was flushed. It was clear the man was struggling to carefully parse his words so as not to insult his powerful guests. "My lady, all the food was hot whenst we didst serve it, some half the hour ago."

The scullery maid wasn't having it. She raised her voice so as to be heard over the din and sternly stated, "And now it be cold! If thou doth want a rating review of more than a waning moon, I wouldst suggest ye remake it."

That simple, selfish request and her table's haughty rebuke of laughter was the final straw that broke Perceval's back. From the window he shouted in a voice loud enough for all to hear, "Nay!"

All sound and motion in the tavern stopped. Every eye whipped over to the front window and watched Perceval cross over and push himself in through the front door.

Once inside, he repeated his comment for effect, "Nay, I say! Thou shalt not remake their food. If it be tepid, they bear full responsibility, not thee."

Not knowing whom she was dealing with, the young woman attempted to brush off the intense man making his way to her table. "Off with thee, old man. Our dinner concerns thee not."

"Nay, I say! Thy dinner concerns us all. There be hungry patrons in the street who cannot get a meal due to thy self-absorption."

Then Perceval turned his ire to the pub owner, "And thee! Why dost thou let these *children* hold sway over the comings and goings of thy tavern? Stand up, man!"

The owner backed up a step or two, stammering, "But their reviews..."

Perceval was having none of it. "Art naught but the tantrums of spoiled brats!"

The tallest of the teens naively assumed an assured victory and stood up to challenge Perceval. "See here, my good man. If thou art famished, take these coins and find a goodly street vendor." Smirking at his friends, he tossed a few pennies on the ground.

Before the last coin rolled to a stop, Perceval grabbed the young man by the scruff of his neck, lifted him up in the air and threw him down on his knees. "You'll not find me groveling before thee, sprout. Pick up thy pittance and pay them to the owner for thy surly attitude."

As one the teens jumped to their feet, ready to attack Perceval. He turned, pointed his finger at them and in his most threatening parental voice, commanded them to sit. Unaccustomed to such power, every bottom hit their chairs at the same moment.

As the scene unfolded, several patrons of the tavern began to recognize Perceval. A murmur of awareness spread like wildfire around the establishment.

Left with no recourse, the scullery maid went into her act. She screamed at the top of her voice, shocking everyone in the room.

After her painful cry, she shouted "I feel unsafe! This man art attacking us! I pray someone run for the sheriff! We art assaulted! This be a crime of hatred!"

Another girl jumped on the bandwagon. "He raped me with his eyes!"

The young boy on the ground found his seat and shouted as he rubbed his knees, "Me kneecaps be broken! This indeed be a crime of hatred!"

To say Perceval was dumbfounded would be an understatement. As he had never encountered such foolishness, it took him a few moments to get his bearings.

When he did, he made the mistake of mocking the teens. "Art thou serious? On what orb dost thou live? Art ye all so fragile ye cannot take correction? Stand down, pay the owner what he is owed, eat thy cold food and depart!"

At this, the scullery maid and her female friends started crying. "Why dost no one believe us? Ye all saw it! He hast assaulted us!"

Percy shook his head. "Ah, tears! The last vestige of a desperate child. Your fakery holds no sway over me."

It was here the table turned. The terrible teens put their hands over their ears, increased their waterworks and began to cry in unison, "Crime of hatred! Crime of hatred! Crime of hatred!"

Perplexed, Percy looked over at the cowering owner. "What be a crime of hatred?"

The harried owner shook his head, "Oh, the worst offense. Thou shouldst apologize before word of this reaches the sheriff or the scribes."

The old man from the street leaned in through the window to clarify. "Now you've stepped in it. Ye have offended them cursed terrible teens. That be a crime of the highest order, fer they have it in their collective noggins they have the right to ne'er hear a contrary word."

Percy was aghast. "Thou canst not be serious!"

Before the old man's wife pulled him out of harm's way, he emphatically nodded, adding, "Says I."

When Percy looked around at the ashen faces in the crowd, he could see the old man spoke true. "Never hear a contrary word. Who among you hast allowed this travesty to take root? It be the parents and society's job to not coddle their offspring but to prepare them for the oncoming difficulties of life. These children hath crumbled at a man saying 'nay?' How shalt they react when they face famine or pestilence?"

Perceval may have spoken true, but his words were in direct competition with the teens continuous chant as well as their vin-dictive reputation.

Eyes around the tavern began to look down and away, each patron seeking only to save their own skin and leave the righteous man alone to hang himself out to dry.

Seeing he needed to go to the source, Perceval turned to the teens. "Ye have no rights. That be yer problem. Our society be built on each man and woman doing what be best for the community, not fer themselves. A world where we banish folks for hurting our feelings be not sustainable! Can none of thee see that?"

Sensing his words had fallen on deaf ears, he attempted one last push to any who would heed his warning. "Love the King with all thy heart, soul, and mind and yer neighbor as thyself. Anything less cannot work. We shouldst all be trying to out serve each other, out give each other. That be the secret. For this, this be madness!"

Having done his best, Perceval was relieved when Augustus the Giant entered the establishment. The sheriff was accompanied by an excited tattling teen outside the current popular circle seated at the table.

Perceval immediately recognized the gangly adolescent from

the social boards. He also understood the young man's motivation and shouted, "Victor! I hope this puts thee in the good graces of thy prickly peers. But be careful what thee doth wish for."

Though Perceval's arrest was a foregone conclusion because of his social elimination, both he and Augustus subtly smiled and nodded at each other, acknowledging their years of respect and admiration.

Bolstered by the sheriff's protection, one of the terrible teens felt his oats and lashed out with the lowest of blows. He said, "Make thy boring proclamations to thine own dead children, old man. For now, thou art going to pay for thy crimes of hatred!"

Chapter Twenty
The Trial

Brother Bob burst in through the jail door with a great sense of urgency. When he saw Perceval casually sitting on the bunk of his unlocked cell playing cards with the sheriff, his ire increased.

The winded monk yelled out, "A vow of silence! Thou art addled in the head. A child of five understands the concept of a vow of silence. But ye! Thy memory be leaking through a sieve. I heard of thy incarceration, feared the worst, and broke a sweat running here!"

The sheriff interjected, "Why didst thou not take thy horse?"

Brother Bob did his best to truncate his excuse. "There's the trouble of saddling, and then my mare's quickest speed be a trot. I thought my friend be in trouble and arriving next week wouldst be too late, and so I didst make the regrettable decision to run! And I be all clammy now. These robes breathe not. All because someone couldst not keep a simple vow of silence."

Perceval could only laugh at his friend's agitated state. "And top of the day to ye as well. The sheriff be teaching me a game of chance. I may return to Pleasanton armed with this knowledge and earn my keep."

Brother Bob entered the small cell, moved aside a small tray of what appeared to be his friend's leftover dinner, and plopped down on the cot opposite Percy and Augustus.

He shook his head. "Thou hast stepped in it this time."

Perceval nodded, "Verily I have. Augustus hast filled me in on what havoc the terrible teens have wrought over the past year. By the King's grace I have returned in the nick of time."

The monk shook his head. "Nay, thou art not holding the spear. Thou art on the receiving end. Ye have been hoisted on the pointy part that doth disembowel."

Perceval politely disagreed. "Nay, my friend. While the charges art overly dramatic to be sure. How doth one even define a crime of hatred? Be there not malice in the heart of all criminals? How does any system of justice parse out which atrocities be based on simple greed or avarice, and which are rooted in a darker depravity? Truth be told, my offense be not a crime at all. I merely chastised a group of rather immature young citizens. In the light of day and upon hearing from a plethora of witnesses, I be certain cooler heads will prevail, and all charges will be subsequently dropped."

It was at this point that Augustus the Giant understood how unencumbered his prisoner was by the facts. His countenance changed to one of grave concern as he said, "Oh, no. No, not at all."

Percy turned to the sheriff. "I be sorry. What?"

The sheriff glanced at Brother Bob for clarification. It pained the monk to say, "The populace of Kingston no longer struggles."

Percy's blinking eyes betrayed no comprehension. "I don't—"

The monk continued. "All their basic needs be met."

It was at that point that the light of understanding began to dawn in Perceval's brain. After only a few moments his worst fears were realized. The words, "Oh, no," dropped from his lips.

Brother Bob nodded. "Sadly, thou wert right all along."

Now it was the sheriff's turn to be in the dark. "Right about—?"

The prisoner filled his captor in. "For years Brother Bob and I have debated this very issue. The question at hand was one of mere conjecture. We never thought such a thing wouldst ever come to pass. Now, verily, it apparently has, and I have run headlong into it."

Frustrated, the sheriff demanded, "Wouldst someone please use the King's English to explain thyself?"

While Perceval's head began to swim with a worrisome list of possible outcomes, Brother Bob took up the mantle. "The King's Sacred Book of Accumulated Wisdom art very clear. It states, that at its core, mankind be depraved. I have always believed that to be a slight exaggeration for dramatic effect. Perceval the Altruistic here, believed just the opposite. He argued, at great length, I might add, that whilst there be the possibility of goodness in all of us, our basic nature be selfish."

That statement received no argument from the man of the law. He knew only too clearly of humanity's base desires and what some are willing to do to satisfy those urges. His past prisoner, the unrepentant, horrible Hammer being the latest example.

The monk took no joy in admitting his error. "So why, if that be our nature, didst we not see a constant parade of wild frivolity and hedonistic acts before now? The answer be the struggle. When life be hard, it takes every ounce of strength just to survive. When thou dost work from sunup to sundown to merely put food on the table and keep a roof over thy head, there be no time for depravity.

"But when thy basic needs be met and one doth find an excess of time and resources at thy beck and call, one's true nature mayest come to the fore."

The silence of understanding was deafening. For the longest stretch, the three men sat in stillness.

Perceval broke the tension. "Every parent wishes to give their offspring a better life than the one they had. But by taking away all obstacles from this generation, they have done them a great disservice. When all of our needs be taken care of through no effort of our own, selfishness doth rule the day. And whatever keeps such entitled creatures from their desired comforts becomes a crime of hatred."

Perceval looked over at this friend and nodded. "Verily, I hast stepped in it this time."

†††

The scribe's stuffy meeting hall was packed to the gills with all manner of folks curious to see the final downfall of Perceval the Altruistic.

160

Percy noted with no small amount of irony that he was seeing many of the very same faces who came to honor him just a year before at the King's lifetime achievement recognition platter award ceremony.

As was his style, the accused was not particularly anxious about the outcome of the trial.

He begrudgingly accepted the King's pessimistic assessment of humanity and understood that left to their own devices, society can easily slide headlong into an abyss of narcissistic behavior. Still, none of that could shake him from his own overly optimistic belief that, given the chance, people can and will rise to the occasion.

In his own life he had seen it time and time again, and he hoped against hope that the level-headed people of Kingston would once more surprise him with their oft suppressed innate goodness.

That hope was short lived.

After he and Brother Bob were seated in the middle of the hall on one side of a long narrow table, he turned to the monk and asked, "So, what be the absolute worst that could happen today?"

"The worst? I would think public humiliation would be the worst, second only to execution."

This statement floored Percy. "Execution! Thou art pulling both my legs."

Brother Bob shook his head. "I be not."

Perceval was incredulous. "For telling teens to eat their food? Art thee mad?"

Knowing every ear in the echoey building was straining to eavesdrop, Brother Bob gave his friend the signal to lower his voice.

He leaned in closer and whispered, "Ye also accosted a young boy and treated the entire table hatefully."

Percy still couldn't quite absorb the information he had just been given. "But execution?! Shall I lose my head for standing up for the rights of others?"

Brother Bob patted his friend on the knee under the table.

"That be what we be here to prevent, my friend. The more likely outcome wilt be a time served in the public stocks. But wilt the very real threat of the gallows help thee keep thy vow of silence?"

Perceval loudly exhaled, nodded and collapsed back in his chair. The life he loved was forfeit, he had already accepted that. But when this charade concluded, he assumed he would aimlessly wander around until he stumbled upon a nice quiet existence on some distant shore where he could find a way to be somewhat useful until the day came when the King called him home.

Now even that dream was fading away under the bright glare of reality.

Perceval could feel every eye in the hall upon him. When Brother Bob leaned in with further instructions, he found he was too depressed to do anything more than acknowledge his friend's sound advice with noncommittal grunts.

"The scribes will enter. Stand when they do. Do not sit until thou art told to do so. Do not speak until thou art told to do so. They shall pontificate endlessly about the heinous nature of thy crime. The longer they go, the worse it be for thee. Then thy accusers shalt have their day. Expect them to be overly dramatic in their effort to sway the court. Then, and only then, wilt thou have a chance to rebuke their charges. Do so kindly. Any vehemence wilt only show more hatred."

Perceval had enough energy to mutter a question. "What about our witnesses?"

"Alas, we have none. All art too intimidated by the terrible teens to declare thy innocence for fear of retribution. I fear thou art on thy own."

This information hit Percy hard. He only saw one glimmer of hope. "Except for thee, my goodly friend."

Brother Bob feigned surprise. "Nay, I shall not sully my reputation by siding with thee."

The monk defiantly stood up, looked around for a few moments, shrugged, then sat back down suppressing a chuckle.

"It appears all the chairs be taken. This be the best seat in the house. I shall stay, but only as a disinterested spectator."

Percy smiled and put his arm around Brother Bob. The Monk bristled. "Touch me not. Or they'll throw me to the gallows after thee."

Percy started to laugh but it was cut short by the solemn entrance of the scribes.

The large, round stained-glass window at the top of the domed roof allowed the filtered sun to softly light up the center of the room where the judgment table rested.

This effect caused the oncoming scribes to be cloaked in darkness until they entered the circle of light illuminating both themselves and the team for the defense seated on the opposite side.

A voice from the back demanded, "All rise!"

As Brother Bob and Perceval scrambled to their feet, the accused's heart sank. To a man, these scribes were the very ones who visited and then were forced to retreat from his home the previous year while Perceval shouted after them with belligerent accusations of their ineptitude.

The six self-important men with short fuses and long memories silently stood behind their high-backed chairs, each one glaring at their captured prey.

When the voice from the back shouted out, "Be seated," the religious leaders pulled out their ornately carved seats, stately stood in front of them until all were in place, and proceeded to sit down in solidarity.

The unified body of clerics stared at Perceval for what seemed like an eternity before the tallest one nodded and mumbled, "Be seated. Unless thou doth need to first relieve thyself in the nearest corner."

That confirmed it. Perceval was sunk.

Concerned and confused, Brother Bob shot a look at his client. Percy bit his lip, shook his head and sank down into what, if things went well, could possibly be the last comfortable thing he would sit on for the foreseeable future.

And thus, the circus began.

An ancient, ornate, leather-bound copy of the King's Sacred Book of Acquired Wisdom was placed on the far-right end of the table. Each scribe reverently bowed his head before it, air kissed the cover, mumbled something unintelligible under his breath, then passed the tome on to the fellow keeper of the law on his left until it reached the other end, now, presumably, properly blessed and kissed.

The last scribe in line was now in first position. The short, serious man cracked open the collection of sacrosanct sayings, cleared his throat, and began to read. And read. And then read some more.

Finally, after a good King's age of rock-solid wisdom about love and gratitude and the evils of pride, he closed the book, air kissed it again, and waited for the entire crowd to say, "As it has been said."

Only then did he pass it back to the scribe who had only recently passed it over to him.

Now that scribe did exactly what the first scribe did, only, so as to not be outdone, he carried on even longer. And with more emotion in his voice.

The trial had turned into a one-up-man-ship contest.

Percy figured that at this rate, the final scribe had better have his selected verses set to music with a few back-up belly dancers, or he was going to appear pale by comparison.

He leaned over to Brother Bob and whispered, "Doth this trial count as time served?"

The second scribe stopped reciting his verse, shot a look over at the defender, and when he was confident the monk would properly chastise his client, he continued on with his thinly veiled lecture.

When the second judge finally wrapped up his portion of the preamble, he closed the book, puckered up for his perfunctory near-miss kiss, and signaled it was time for the crowd to validate him with a hearty, "As it has been said."

Seeing his opportunity with the oncoming transfer, Brother

Bob sprang into action. When the scribe slid the King's book down the row to the next waiting reader, the monk whipped around in his chair in order to get up in Perceval's face.

Gesticulating wildly, he whispered in his friend's ear, "Don't ye dare do that again! This be serious. Now cast your face down in abject shame, look at the scribes with puppy dog eyes and slam a cork in thy attitude."

Seeing several of the scribes break into smiles at Perceval's unintelligible dressing down, the monk righted himself in his chair and apologized to the tribunal. "Our deepest apologies, goodly scribes. My client hath forgotten his place. Far be it from me to influence thy excellent readings in any way, but if perhaps one of ye couldst impart a few of the good King's scriptures on humility and knowing thy station, it mayhaps do these proceedings a world of good."

Before the third scribe began his readings, there were a great many *harrumphs* of agreement heard around the table.

Percy took his chastisement in stride. While he had determined some time ago to no longer suffer fools, he, himself was not an idiot. There's a time and place for everything, but when your head is on the chopping block, it's no time to mock the executioner.

The pompous trial preamble pontifications continued unabated for the next two hours. By the end Percy was pinching himself to stay awake.

The final scribe did indeed use his rich baritone voice to sing-song most of his verses, but alas, his impromptu one-man-show had a dearth of back-up dancers. Something to improve upon at the next public lynching, perhaps.

Immediately after the audience shouted out their last, "As it has been said," two junior scribes dragged out another high-backed chair and placed it at the end of the table.

After which the scribes called the young scullery maid to the witness chair.

Walking up with great effort, as if life itself was too great a burden to bear, the girl's eyes were puffy, making it appear she'd been crying herself to sleep for days, if not weeks. The more likely scenario was that she'd tossed in some coal dust for the same effect. Either way, Perceval was impressed.

At the scribe's prompting, the overwrought girl recounted the events at the Eagle's Claw. To hear her tell it, she and her friends were but innocent babes in the woods hatefully accosted by a terrifying ferocious marauder whom they feared had many knives and swords hidden on his person.

By the time she was done, Perceval was sorely tempted to give the young thespian a standing ovation for her stellar emotionally compelling performance and suggest she was wasting her time cleaning up after others as her true talent was obviously in the theatre.

The next witness was the young girl who claimed that Perceval somehow raped her with his eyes. She stated quite emphatically that he was a danger to society at large. And did she mention he viciously raped her with his eyes?

The parade of egregiously damaged children continued until the final flourish. Here the young man who tossed coins at Percy's feet valiantly fought his way through the crowd to the judgment table.

Both his legs were tightly wrapped, as if he'd just returned from war. He leaned heavily upon two crutches and struggled to lower himself down into the witness chair.

Taking a moment to catch his breath, the boy played the martyr to the hilt. He was the innocent victim, while Perceval was, without a doubt, the most hate-filled hater in all of haterdom.

His accusations left no stone unturned save the fact that Percy seemed to have neglected to sexually assault him with his eyes.

Throughout his character assassination, Perceval wondered if there could ever be such a thing as a fair and impartial trial? One would need the wisdom of the King to ferret out the truth from so many convoluted tall tales. The current tribunal of scribes, he was quite sure, did not possess such mental acuity.

The final death knell in his mockery of a trial was one that totally blindsided both Percy and Brother Bob.

When the scribes called for their final surprise witness, a hooded man stepped over to the table, helped the broken knee-cap boy find his balance on his crutches, and then took his seat in the chair.

Removing his cloak, an audible gasp emanated from the crowd. The mystery man's face had recently been beaten to a pulp. His purple and black eyes were nearly swollen shut. His lips were twice their normal size; his nose was most definitely out of joint.

Perceval gripped Brother Bob's arm and whispered, "Todd the Odd!"

The scribe in the middle looked directly at Perceval and asked, "Dost thou know this man?"

Percy nodded, "I do."

The scribe continued, "And art thee solely responsible for the cruel and unusual pummeling of this man?"

Reluctantly, Perceval nodded again, "I am."

At that admission, a loud murmur erupted from the gallery.

The sergeant at arms in the back would have none of it. "Quiet in the hall! Quiet! Be silent or be gone!"

Without saying a word, Todd pulled his hood back up over his head, grunted as he pushed himself out of the chair, and then left the meeting hall. Perceval's eyes followed him out but did not spy Gwendolyn.

Brother Bob rose to his feet. "If it please the scribes, may we inquire as to why my client meted out such a drastic punishment upon the face of Todd the Odd?"

To a person, all the clerics shook their heads.

The apparent leader strongly stated, "Nay! This trial concerns itself only with the character of Perceval the so-called Altruistic."

Another scribe continued, "While he successfully hid behind a cloak of respectability for lo these many years, it be shocking to see the man for who he truly be."

Another piled on with, "A man of reprehensible ugly violence with a propensity towards hatred."

The last scribe truly lowered the boom. "For his status be much on our minds this past year. What didst cause the many calamities that befell the town's friend Perceval? We all know the King to be full of grace and goodness, and no wickedness be in him, so the fault cannot lie with our sovereign. As such, we be of the opinion that this day's investigation doth prove conclusively that the full weight of the catastrophes that fell upon this man doth lie entirely on the shoulders of the deficient character of the accused."

As one, the scribes signaled that the proceedings were now concluded with a decisive, "Judgment hast been found!"

Brother Bob didn't wait to be called upon. He jumped to his feet and said, "This trial be a travesty! Thy collective minds were made up before a one of ye even entered these hallowed halls."

The scribes ignored the monk's outburst. Without another word, the men of the cloth rose as one.

From the back, the lone voice rang out, "All rise!"

Everyone in the meeting place was relieved they were finally able to stand. More than a few joints cracked as the people got up and stretched.

All Perceval could do was hang his head. To be thrown under the carriage for his actions at the tavern was bad enough, but to lay the blame on him for the deaths of his children was more than he could bear.

Brother Bob urged him to his feet. "Stand for the sentencing, my good man."

His entire body felt as if it were made of lead. Still, loyal and obedient to the end, Perceval managed to lift his trembling body to an erect position.

Silence and tension reigned in the hall as everyone anxiously waited for the final pronouncement.

After what seemed like an eternity of mumbling debate in the dark, the lone voice rang out from the back. "The accused has been found guilty of hate crimes against humanity. He shall be sent to the stocks for a period of no less than 20 days and be then forevermore banished from the kingdom of Kingston!"

The reaction from the crowd was mixed. A few booed the decision, but the vast majority approvingly applauded. Most were just relieved they were free to go feed their bellies and empty their bladders.

Percy didn't register their reaction at all. Any sound felt as if it was coming from a hundred furlongs away.

It took Brother Bob shaking him before the man finally came out of his fog. "We'll appeal to the King, as is our right. Perceval, can you hear me? All is not lost."

Percy looked at his old friend, shook his head, and merely said, "It be finished."

Chapter Twenty-One
In Stocks

At first light Augustus the Giant swung open the door to Perceval's jail cell. It wasn't locked because the sheriff trusted his inmate more than the people who accused him of the crime of hatred.

He gently knocked on the metal door and cleared his throat to rouse his guest.

Perceval opened one eye, propped himself up on his elbow, then swung his feet out until he was in a sitting position on the edge of the bed. He stretched and spoke through his yawn. "Hast the day of my humiliation arrived?"

The sheriff nodded. "You'll be in the stocks for the good part of the day. I can bring ye in for a bite to eat and to do your necessaries, though, sadly, I can't protect ye from the people. I'll keep me eye out for the terrible teens, but it be what it be."

Perceval stood and shook the Giant's hand. "I appreciate thy kindness. This be my final gauntlet. In twenty days, I shall wrap up my business with the King, and ye'll never see nor hear from me again."

Augustus nodded, saying, "And that be a shame, good sir."

The stocks were situated directly next to the jail. One instrument of humiliation had three separate openings for one's head and hands carved out of a split wooden beam. It stood some five feet off the ground, so most prisoners were forced to stand hunched over. Its companion on the ground had four openings, one for each limb, which necessitated a sitting position.

The sheriff gave Percy his choice. "The tall one be hard on

thy legs and neck. The short one doth look to be more pleasant, as ye get to sit, but with thy hands and feet locked down in front of thee, it doth kill thy back. Not to mention it be sheer torture if ye have an itch. We can go from one to the other if'n it pleases thee."

Perceval raised the top portion of the taller of the two and said, "Let us start with this." He put his neck in the center groove and placed his wrists in the holes on either side as the sheriff lowered the heavy lid into its place.

The lawman's tone was somber as he said, "I'm afraid I have to lock ye in."

"Do what ye need to do." Perceval tried to nod but found his head had very little room to move. "Oh, this is... going to be a long three weeks."

The sheriff put the padlock through the opening of the latch, turned the bolt until he heard it snap shut, then slipped the key into his side pocket.

He squinted as he looked up into the sky. "Not a horrible day. A bit overcast. Methinks the heat shouldn't be too bad. I'll bring out water when I can."

As a force of habit Perceval tried to nod again, but the wooden constraint reminded him he could barely move his head. He said, "That be fine."

Augustus gave one last piece of advice. "Unless ye want splinters in thy neck, try to not move thy head."

Perceval could only agree. "Sage advice."

When the sheriff walked away and Perceval was alone with his thoughts, all he could do was laugh, thinking, *How far the mighty have fallen!*

Here Percy had an advantage over a great deal of the populace. While some people holding the crap stick get stuck in an obtuse malaise that can take years to shake off, as Brother Bob reminded him, he could definitively point to the exact date when his whole life fell apart.

After the initial explosion at his award ceremony one year

past, Perceval mistakenly thought he was on the road to recovery, but it now appeared that his experience in the Outskirts was just a temporary tick upwards on his doomed downward trajectory.

There was no sugar coating it any longer. Perceval the Altruistic had fallen to the lowest rung of his life's ladder. Along with all of his fortune, save a grand total of three remaining friends, all of his loves had been lost.

In the plus column, he retained his health. As far as he could tell, he was currently boil-free, but the thought passed through his mind that this would be the perfect time to break out in leprosy.

Exempting the outside chance of either fire, flood, or an invading horde of locusts, try as he might, the man couldn't imagine how he could sink any lower.

Which is exactly when the terrible teens showed up.

The group silently slipped into position, making a semi-circle before their conquest. A few snickered as they settled in front of Perceval.

Holding court in the middle was their leader, the scullery maid. The handle of a large wicker basket nestled in the crook of her arm.

She acted surprised as she said, "Why, what doth we have here? Be this the man convicted and banished from the kingdom of Kingston for committing crimes of hatred against an innocent group of teens?"

The tall boy, whose legs had made a miraculous recovery, leaned in for a closer look. "Why, I do believe thou art correct!"

From the corner of his eye, Percy could see a rather homely looking boy on the outside of the mini mob. The youth wore a nervous smile, looking more than a little uncomfortable. Perceval made eye contact with Victor but didn't say a word.

The ringleader grinned as she opened the lid of her basket. "We didn't want thee to suffer under the hot sun without sustenance, so we brought thee some food..."

The sound of buzzing flies reached Perceval's ears first, then the putrid smell.

Each of the teens reached in and pulled out a handful of rotten fruit.

The one-sided melee commenced as a barrage of sticky garbage rained down on Perceval's head. He recoiled and shut his eyes, but he was defenseless against the dripping juice and the accompanying flying insects.

Squinting, he noted Victor lobbed his handfuls of rotting peaches and melons either wide or low to the ground.

As Percy could only shake his head so much, most of the produce remained stuck in his hair.

When their ammunition ran out, the laughing teens ran up, wiped their hands on the prisoner's back and shoulders, and gathered around him as if posing for a portrait. That's when Percy saw the artist from the Claw.

The nervous man set up his easel in front of Perceval and, once he was given the go-ahead, began to furiously sketch.

Suddenly the scullery maid called out for the painter to stop. She directed her friends to gather several of the rinds from the ground and formed them into a makeshift crown on Percy's head.

Finished, she stepped back and admired her artistry. "Perfect! A crown fit for a king!"

Rather than shake off the precariously balanced concoction, Percy stayed as still as possible, hoping to truncate the whole ordeal.

The teens laughed and quickly reassembled next to their prey. The scullery maid commanded the artist to resume.

As usual, their patience was at a low ebb.

"Canst thee hurry?"

"These flies!"

"Thou art so slow!"

The put-upon artist only nodded and continued in his craft.

Perceval spit out a few seeds from his mouth and softly muttered, "Thou art all better than this. Though not ye, scullery maid. This be the peak of thy life. But the rest of thee need not be dragged down to the gutter with this foul wench."

The young woman was incensed. "What didst thou call me? I'll show thee who be a foul wench!"

In a fit of anger, the girl bent down, picked up a rotten pomegranate, rose up and began to stuff it in Perceval's mouth, choking him.

As Percy struggled, coughed, and spit, Victor stepped up and grabbed the maid's arm. He shook his head and firmly said, "Nay!"

He then pushed her hand away, reached in Perceval's mouth and cleared out the mush as best he could.

This sent the young girl over the edge. "How dare ye! Who dost ye think ye are!"

Victor had apparently found his humanity. He knocked the crown of rinds off of Perceval's head, then used his sleeve to wipe off the man's face. He laughed and agreed with Perceval. "He art right. Thou art a foul wench. Why I ever wanted to throw my lot in with thee art beyond me."

The young girl screeched at the top of her lungs. "I allowed thee in my group! Thou art nothing!"

The tall boy sheepishly shrugged, "Choking the man doth seem a bit much. We agreed—"

The maid's second scream of indignation was even louder than the first. "I canst not believe my ears. Thou art all cowards. He sinned against us! *He* be the criminal."

The loud ruckus finally alerted the sheriff inside the jail. He dashed outside and ran the teens off. "What in the King's name? Off with ye! Off!"

All scattered but Victor and the artist. When Augustus gave him the signal to shoo, the painter picked up his easel and scampered away.

Percy called out after him. "I'll take yon portrait if they don't want it. It be a reminder I'll cherish to the end of my days."

The sheriff kicked his way through the trash to his prisoner. He glared at Victor. "What be all this?"

Perceval came to the young boy's defense. "Blame him not, sheriff. Victor here be my savior."

The teen hung his head in shame. "Nay, I bear the brunt of it. I be the one who brought the sheriff to the Claw! This all be my doing."

Perceval shook his head as best he could. "Nay, good sir. I hold no grudge against thee. But rise above this. Thou art a leader, I can see it. Pay the scullery maid and her kind no mind. Be thy own man, and make thy father proud."

Victor nodded, turned, and walked off alone into the morning sun.

The Giant fumbled for his key and unlatched the lock. "What a mess! And such a stench! Let us get thee to a bath."

Perceval stood, stretched, and picked several pieces of fruit out of his hair and beard. "I wouldst not argue with thee on that."

Chapter Twenty-Two
Proper Good Byes

ater that day, after Perceval had bathed, changed, and eaten, he accompanied the sheriff back outside to continue his sentence. There he saw a slightly different set up.

The rotten fruit droppings had been cleared away, and in their place, mats and pillows were placed on the ground.

Brother Bob, Stephen, and Richard busied themselves tying fabric between four upright poles over the stocks. The rickety canopy was intended to provide a modicum of shade and shelter.

Upon seeing his faithful friends, Perceval declared, "What in the King's name? Be off with thee. Off!"

Stephen smiled as he said, "I thought I be the sarcastic one."

Richard walked over to give Percy a mighty bear hug. "The trial be a travesty. I be so sorry."

Stephen got his shot in. "That being said, methinks Todd the Odd looked especially well."

All the men laughed, and Brother Bob addressed the situation. "Good Augustus here got word to us of this morning's debacle. We thought it might be a good idea to keep thee company until thy sentence be commuted."

Perceval shook his head. "I can't have thee wasting thy time on me."

Brother Bob clarified. "Not all three at once, mind ye. We'll take shifts. When thou doth become unbearably boring, endlessly waxing on and on about the state of mankind, we'll trade out."

The sheriff added, "And I'll not be locking thee in. When thou doth need a break, either trade stocks, or come inside. The scribes be damned. When thy time be done, it wouldn't surprise me if, in the dead of night, an axe found its way to these infernal contraptions!"

Perceval couldn't help but smile from ear to ear as he looked at each of his friends. "Thank thee, one and all. I appreciate thy efforts. However, if I might clarify one point, I don't think I endlessly wax on and on about the state of—"

Richard rolled his eyes, saying, "Oh, for the love of the King, to the gallows with this one."

Brother Bob looked at the other two men. "Who drew the short straw?"

Stephen said, "If memory serves, 'twas thee."

Brother Bob protested, "I believe someone didst say, 'best two out of three.'"

Richard agreed. "Aye, ye did. And ye lost."

The monk put on his best fake smile, saying, "My cup doth runneth over."

Percy took the ribbing, sat on the short stock, and maneuvered his legs and arms through the holes. "I wonder if someone couldst call back the terrible teens. Methinks they might be better company."

The men laughed, patted Perceval on his shoulders, gave their salutation, and went on their way, leaving him with Brother Bob.

After the shortest period of time had passed, the monk asked, "Well?"

Perceval was practically brimming with ideas and thoughts, but he was hesitant. "I wouldn't want to bore thee."

Brother Bob laid down on a nearby mat, putting his hands behind his head. "A nap couldst do me a world of good. Fire when ready."

Over the next few weeks, Perceval the Altruistic did, indeed, endlessly wax eloquent about the state of mankind. As he pontificated, each of his friends did their best to interject an occasional "Uh huh," or "I doth agree," so as to make it appear they were listening, when the truth was none of them fully appreciated the insights their friend espoused.

Not that it mattered. Percy had nothing but time on his hands, so he tried to engage his companions with his thoughts.

Naturally, he started with the terrible teens. "Strange as it may sound, I truly bear the young hooligans no ill will. As I see it, they all be compensating for their various hurts and shortcomings. Some be better at hiding it than others, but are we not all the walking wounded?"

Brother Bob interjected with, "Go on..."

He refined his thoughts somewhat when it was Stephen's turn. "Some know and have accepted the depth of our ugliness, and it incapacitates them. Others are seemingly totally oblivious to the fact that they're metaphorically missing a limb."

Percy was on such a roll he completely missed his friend's sarcastic reply, "Oh, please continue."

Oblivious, he did. "Some people try to cover up their wounds with a myriad of salves, be it drink, or business, or the endless pursuit of pleasure. But at our core, each of us be missing something. The only question be, how doth ye choose to either rise above or live with it?"

When Richard's turn came around, he couldn't help but be wonderfully dense. "Wait, we each have a hole? Where?"

If Percy could have risen to his full height, he would have. "That be my point exactly! Our life's pursuit should be to discover what be missing and do our best to fill that void! Or better yet, find a mate or best mates who know yer strengths and weaknesses and as ye come to know theirs, together we strive to make a whole."

Richard was unfailingly honest. "I love ye like a brother, but think I be missing the part that understands what thou art talking about."

That made Percy laugh. He clarified with the best example he could think of. "Take Gwendolyn as an example."

When his turn came around again, Brother Bob raised both

of his hands in protest. "Nay, I shall not! I saw what happens when one doth try to steal thy wife."

Percy continued unabated, "The woman didst put up a good front before we were wed, but soon after the honeymoon, her wounds became clear. She based her life and worth not on internal fortitude, but on her external trappings. And fight against the ravages of time for as long as ye can, we all know who be destined to win that battle."

As if to prove his point, two weeks into his punishment, Gwendolyn made an appearance.

At first Percy mistakenly assumed she dropped by to comfort him in his plight, but moments into the conversation, it became all too clear her only objective was to complain about how difficult her life was.

The woman ran up to her ex-husband with tears in her eyes, sobbing, "Oh, Perceval! Ye wouldn't believe what happened to me."

Knowing all too well who she was, Percy played along. He looked up from his stooped position and innocently asked, "Pray tell. I hope it not be anything too dire."

Not catching his ironically intended meaning, Gwen continued with her lament. "The other day I met someone new in town. In an effort to compliment me, the man tried to guess my namesake by saying, 'I'll wager thou art known far and wide as Gwendolyn the Fair.'"

Percy did his best to look shocked.

His performance left much to be desired, so the mother of his children stomped her foot down for emphasis. "Didst ye not hear me? The Fair?!"

Considering his circumstances, Perceval was as charitable as one could possibly be. "I'm sure that came as quite a shock. Perhaps their eyes be dull, or a rival, jealous of thy beauty, wert playing a prank on thee through thy new acquaintance."

Gwendolyn touched Percy's hand, seemingly oblivious to the fact it was currently imprisoned between two planks of wood. She shook her head and said, "Thou art sweet, but nay. The man had no guile or ulterior motive in his eyes. He took one look at me and deemed me—*fair*. My life be over! How much longer until I be known as Gwendolyn the Not As Beautiful As She Once Was?"

Looking off to the road, Perceval saw Todd the Odd sitting in a cart laden with furniture and housing supplies.

Surprised, Percy queried, "Art thee moving?"

Gwendolyn threw up her hands, "What choice do I have? It be only a matter of months before my namesake be Gwendolyn the Hag! I need to go to a land where no one knows of my previous beauty and the heights from which I have fallen."

Perceval was at a loss. "Doth that not seem a tad extreme?"

Gwendolyn couldn't believe what she was hearing. How could someone she was with for so long be so dense? "Extreme? I say it again, the Fair! Canst thou imagine anything worse?"

Perceval merely stared at her and flatly said, "Surely, I cannot."

Gwendolyn paced in front of the prisoner. "The bee swellings hast gone down, but I pulled out another grey hair today. That be four this week alone! At this rate in a year I'll be Gwendolyn the Bald."

Percy knew his next statement would be met with resistance, but he tried anyway. "My dearest Gwendolyn, thou art so much more than the sum total of thy—"

She stopped him cold. "Say it not! I be Gwendolyn the Exquisitely Beautiful from before my namesake ceremony, and I shall live out the remainder of my days as the very same."

"And Todd be fine with leaving?"

Gwendolyn waved that thought aside. "Oh, the man wilt do whatever or go wherever I command. He be an adorable lap dog who be satisfied with the crumbs from my table. Now ye, ye gave it back as good as I gave it to thee. Those were good times. I thank thee."

Gwendolyn patted Percy's hand one last time as she turned to leave. "And Todd hast forgiven thee. He can see out of both eyes now and only lost one tooth. He considers thee even." She looked down at her old flame with a twinkle in her eye. "As for me, I would have thought defending my honor would have been worth at least two teeth."

Perceval tried to be gracious in his final words addressed to the woman with whom he spent the better part of his life. "Be there a return engagement, I shall do my utmost to loosen at least three. My dear Gwendolyn, I wish for thee only the best. May thy life be filled with joy and happiness."

Those words stopped Gwen in her tracks for the briefest of moments. Her shoulders slumped. She looked back at her ex-husband with longing in her eyes, saying, "If only thy kindly words could make it so."

Then she shook off the sentiment and slipped away, calling out, "Joy and happiness? Nay, they be for the exquisitely beautiful. Never for the fair. But I shall make do. Perhaps we can find a country where the people be hideous."

Perceval shouted out after her, "That be the spirit! May ye find a land of buck teeth and perpetual homeliness!"

Gwendolyn laughed, pulled herself up onto the cart, Todd the Odd gave an almost imperceptible nod, and the strange pair drove off out of Perceval's life forever.

Standing off to the side, Stephen shook his head in disbelief. "Thou wert married to that for how long?"

Percy couldn't help but smile. "Her empathy tended to wax and wane."

Brother Bob sauntered up for the shift change. "From low ebb to nonexistent."

Percy's chastisement was mild. "Charity, ye two. Which one of us be perfect?"

Stephen would have none of it. "I be a far sight closer than she. I wert standing right here the entire time. It be as if I didn't exist."

Changing the subject, Brother Bob asked, "Other than a visit from vanity herself, any trouble from the townsfolk?"

Stephen shook his head. "Fewer gawkers every day. Methinks our friend art becoming old news."

And so it continued through the final week. Each day Percy's friends would drop by to insure no one threw anything at the prisoner, and each night around dusk Perceval would stare off at the hill of the King's castle where the sisters of mercy would call out at the gate, the drawbridge would drop, the massive doors would open, and the women would make their way inside.

As the sun set on Perceval's final night in the stocks, Brother Bob asked his friend a question. "Doth thou miss her?"

Knowing full well Brother Bob wasn't speaking of his ex-wife, Percy looked down at the ground and admitted, "More than I can possibly express."

The monk stood up, stretched, and said, "Then methinks ye ought to tell her."

Perceval looked over at his closest companion and caught the small frame of a cloaked woman slowly walking up out of the dark.

Brother Bob nodded and said, "Sister Mary."

The woman nodded back as the monk gathered his things and made himself scarce.

After his exit, the two estranged friends stared at each other for the longest time.

Perceval's heart melted as he took in her soft features. He knew he missed her, but the magnitude of his longing wasn't something he was prepared for.

He practically spat out, "Thou doth always seem to catch me at my worst. At least there be no boils to speak of this time around. However, if it pleases thee, I couldst sing thy praises at the top of my lungs!"

The sister shook her head.

Perceval dropped all pretense. "As it seems thou hast taken a vow of silence, I pray thee let me speak. I hurt thee, and for that I wilt forever be sorry. I handled our parting horribly, but I pray thou dost let me explain."

Percy drew in a long breath and closed his eyes. Over the past month he had made this speech a hundred times in his head although now that he had the opportunity to say it out loud he wasn't sure of the wisdom of being totally forthcoming.

Regardless, he let it fly. "Sister Mary Angel Face, the long and the short of it be, I hast fallen hopelessly in love with thee. There, I said it."

Perceval swallowed hard and barreled through. "I have been in such a state, methinks, from the moment I set eyes on thee. At the time, I wert married to Gwendolyn, and I knew I couldn't have thee. Then, when I found she had let me go, the pain be worse. For I was finally free to pursue a woman who was married to her vows, and again, I knew I couldn't have thee."

Sister Mary turned away, obscuring her eyes, allowing only her silhouette to be visible in the bright moonlight.

Perceval continued, "That be why I wert so curt when I left the Outskirts. Brother Bob said I made thee cry, and it doth kill me. I be so sorry. But the truth be that my love for thee causes me so much anguish I can barely stand to be around thee. Yet that be all I long for. I know thou can do nothing, and my words are but for naught, but I beg thy patience as I unburden myself. When I am free of these stocks, I shall ask for an audience with the King, after which ye shalt never see me again. I know not of thy feelings toward me, although I suspect if we both were free of our constraints, thou might find me only slightly reprehensible."

A small smile crossed the sister's face as she nodded ever so slightly.

"And if I may, I need to clarify. Which, according to my friends, I seem to do to excess. My love for thee be not because of thy beauty. Thy overly abundant outer beauty, I mean. I know most men confuse attraction and lust with love, but I have had outward beauty, and it canst not hold a candle to the purity and goodness I have seen in thy heart. You serve the poor and the downtrodden, yet ye have no need to be noticed for it. I didn't think that existed in the world anymore. So, as I end my declaration of undying love and admiration, I have but one question for thee."

Sister Mary stood perfectly still. Finally, she nodded and softly asked, "What be thy burning question?"

"Why in the King's name art thou celibate? Ye art the only perfect woman on the planet and thou hast taken thyself off the market!"

The audacity of this question finally got to the sister. She let loose with a burst of laughter, covering her mouth as she did so.

After she calmed down she turned to Percy and said, "I come to thee this evening with a question of my own."

Percy lifted the top piece of wood off of his neck. He removed his head and hands, rubbed them, and sat down on the edge of the shorter stock.

Mary was more than a little shocked. "How can thee free thyself? Hast thou a key? And if thou art not locked in, why dost thou stay?"

Perceval laughed. "For some reason, the sheriff trusts that I shall serve out my sentence. And in so doing, hopefully garner some sympathy from a particular sister of mercy."

Mary Angel looked away.

Perceval continued. "So, we be ignoring the whole 'Percy doth love thee with an undying love the strength of a thousand suns' part of the conversation?"

Sister Mary nodded, "For now."

Percy shrugged. "Ask thy burning question."

Mary Angel stepped closer to Perceval. "Wouldst thou consider not asking for an audience with thy King?"

Percy was put off by her question. "May I say, no. I have waited to be heard for an entire year. I shall not be dissuaded."

"Regardless of the consequences?"

This gave Percy pause. He asked, "What consequences?"

Sister Mary laid it out for him. "From old there be a steadfast law. If one requests an audience with the King and he be displeased with thee in any way, he doth have the right to punish the offender."

"Punish, how?"

The sister continued, "In any manner he doth please, from banishment to imprisonment to death."

"To what?"

Mary nodded. "The King doth have the right to execute all who displease him."

Perceval was beside himself. "What be with this town and its fondness for executions? Why doth this be the first time I have ever heard of this?"

Sister Mary didn't hold back. "From what I understand, thou art the first man in memory who be foolish enough to request an audience!"

Percy cocked his head. "Art thou speaking true, or art thou just trying to scare me away?"

"I speak true. Now and always."

"Then what say ye about my declaration of love? The undying kind I just spoke of. Remember just a few moments ago when I poured out my heart to thee? Speak ye true about that."

Sister Mary shook her head. "I fear I cannot. I have only come to beg thee to not request an audience with thy King."

Perceval was in a quandary. He pondered his choices for the longest time, stood up, knocked on the jail wall to call for the sheriff, and answered his true love.

"As I see it, the choice be simple. I already be banished. If I displease the King and he imprisons me, that be a step up from my current circumstances. And if he doth choose to take my head, it will finally stop my heart from aching for thee once and for all."

Sister Mary was insistent. "Be not so cavalier! Treat not thy life with such disdain."

Perceval was equally intransigent. "And what kind of life wouldst I have if I chose to compromise my values? My love for thee be true, but more highly doth I prize my integrity! I must do what I believe to be right. My entire life wert taken from me. I deserve to know why. But more importantly, the King doth need to know what be happening in his kingdom under his very nose. For these reasons I shall risk both life and limb by requesting an audience with the one who doth hold my life in his hands."

A tear dropped from sister Mary's eye. "And there be nothing I can do to dissuade thee?"

This time Perceval was silent. When the sheriff came outside to escort Percy in for the night, his prisoner looked at the sister one last time, shook his head and walked away, resigned to a very questionable fate.

Before he entered the jail, he turned back and said, "I could be dissuaded if thou didst decide to renounce thy vows and run away with me."

Now it was sister Mary's turn to be silent. She looked away, then slowly turned back to face Perceval. Tears welled up in her eyes as she whispered, "Ye know that I cannot."

Perceval nodded and stepped inside the jail.

Chapter Twenty-Three
The King's Castle

The next morning Perceval strolled outside of the sheriff's jail unaccompanied by the Giant for the first time in three weeks.

While his slap on the wrist was comparatively minor as jail sentences go, filling his lungs with fresh, free air felt surprisingly breathtaking.

This rare moment of blissful satisfaction was interrupted by a horse whinny. The freed prisoner squinted into the sun and brought his hand up over his eyes to shield them.

Laughing, Perceval exclaimed, "Redeemer, my faithful friend!" The horse stomped his front hoof into the dusty ground as Percy ran over to hug his mighty steed.

Looking up, he spied Brother Bob sitting in his cart just a few yards away. "And what dumb beast of burden doth accompany ye this fine morning?"

Brother Bob ignored the friendly jab and got straight to the point. "I've brought thy horse, the King's book, several change of clothes, and enough money to buy passage to any place other than here. I can ride with thee as far as the nearest port."

Perceval nodded. "But who wouldst tuck the tail between my legs as I turn and run?"

Brother Bob expected something along the lines of this retort. He sighed and looked up to the heavens. "When ye wert formed in thy mother's womb, didst she eat briars, thistles, and prickly pears in order to make thee so stubborn? Didst not sister Mary Angel tell thee of the King's rule?"

Percy nodded. "Aye, that she did. I be curious as to why thee never mentioned it afore now?"

The monk spit back his reply, "Afore now, I believed thou didst possess a modicum of intelligence! I never dreamed thou wouldst take leave of thy senses long enough to actually go through with this fool's errand. Thou didst have a bad run of luck. Truth be told, the worst. But put thy losses behind thee. If ye displease the King, he doth have the right to take thy head. Flee whilst it still be affixed to thy shoulders. There be no shame in saving thy own skin."

At this, all Perceval could do was shake his currently attached head. "And that, dear brother, art where we disagree. I believe the King be just, and I wilt stake my very life upon it. If there be no mercy in him, then my life be forfeit already, for I have served a King whom I do not know."

Perceval moved around to the back of the cart and surveyed the contents. "Whilst I thank thee for thy provisions, I shalt ask thee to hold on to them for, hopefully, one day more. With the exception of this." Spying a small, wrapped kerchief stuffed with bread, cheese, and fruit, the man reached in over the buckboard and claimed the sustenance as his.

At this point Brother Bob knew all his words of protest were moot, so he shook his reins, clicked his tongue, turned the cart around and slowly trotted off into the distance with nary a word or glance behind him.

When the monk was almost out of earshot, Perceval yelled at the top of his lungs, "I love thee as well, my good brother! Thank thee for thy many acts of consideration. I pray we shall see each other again."

After the monk's cold shoulders and his cart disappeared around a corner up ahead, Perceval the Altruistic walked over to Redeemer, slid one foot into the hanging stirrup, grabbed the saddle, and swung himself up onto his closest and most loyal companion. "Ye shall be in my service for just a bit longer. Soon, though it breaks my heart, I shall return thee to my servant, thy rightful owner."

He then bit down on a piece of the monk's hard cheese and lightly tapped his heels into the horse's sides, saying, "To the King's castle, my faithful friend."

✝✝✝

By the time Perceval arrived at the King's grey stone fortress, the wind had picked up considerably, and dark foreboding clouds began to effectively block out the sun.

Redeemer was visibly nervous. He shook his mane, snorted, and pawed at the ground. Percy patted the horse's neck and agreed with his assessment. "Methinks thou art right. A large storm be brewing. And the weather be a fright as well." A large raindrop on the man's nose punctuated his jest.

Swinging off of his horse, Perceval looked up at the blackening sky, grabbed the monk's small provision of food, and promptly gave Redeemer a mild swat on the rear. He had to shout to be heard over the encroaching storm. "To Brother Bob's!"

His ride needed no more convincing. The steed bolted off to find shelter.

Perceval turned to face his fate.

The King's castle was large, ominous, and in the darkening storm, quite intimidating. The immense wooden drawbridge was standing at attention, held in place by massively thick chains, protecting those inside from various nefarious intruders and whatever vile reptiles lived in the moat surrounding the castle.

No torches were lit, as only moments ago the morning sun shone, making it all the more difficult in the ensuing darkness to discern anything more than a huge block of stone sitting on top of a hill at the edge of the city.

Finding himself thoroughly drenched by the sudden downpour, Perceval trudged over to the front of the castle. He stopped at the edge of the moat, squarely situated at the point where the drawbridge would fall, if one were granted access to the King's home.

Squinting, Perceval was fairly sure he saw the bobbing head

of a guard or two, so he yelled to get their attention. The whipping wind of the squall was now so loud, even he couldn't hear what he was saying. He waved his arms above his head, but no one on the other side of the chasm paid him any mind.

Seeing no shelter of any kind, save one lone majestic tree, Perceval leaned into the battering wind and rain and struggled to retain his balance.

He was keenly aware he had now come full circle from where he was just one short year ago when he sat around a fire with his friends in between storms. At least when that deluge came, his barn provided some protection from the elements.

Today the only silver lining he saw was that he was reasonably healthy and blissfully alone. No townspeople would come out to harass him in this kind of tempest. For those small favors, he was grateful.

Percy tried crying out a few times more, but he knew his words were lost in the relentless, pounding cacophony. Every sane person far and wide was huddled up with their loved ones, inside, beside a warm fire.

It was at this moment that Perceval came to the stark realization that, in one way or another, all of his loved ones had been taken from him. This epiphany caused a surge of strength to well up within him.

Up to now, he had managed to keep a lid on his anger, biding his time. Some men, after they have been beaten down long enough, find all the fight has been drained from them. But in Perceval's case, he successfully nurtured and maintained his rage at a low boiling point, just waiting for the perfect opportunity to let it all spill out as he vented his spleen.

Perceval felt his time was close. The flood of painful memories stoked the flames of his ire. He saved his voice.

Sloshing through the mud over to the stately old tree standing guard by the path to the castle, Percy found some ineffective protection. He pressed his back up against the bark and used the large trunk as a shield from the pelting rain.

Percy slid down on his haunches and sat between two large, exposed roots. His bottom was immediately drenched, and the leaves above barely reduced nature's relentless shower. He wiped his face with his soggy sleeve and laughed. He felt as if the storm itself was trying to convince him of the foolish nature of his quest.

He yelled out, daring mother nature herself. "Do thy worst! For even ye shall not dampen my resolve."

Answering the man's hubris was a lightning bolt so close and powerful it shocked Perceval into silence. The accompanying explosion of thunder was so loud he instinctively covered his ears for their protection.

After his heart stopped pounding, the man peeked out at the black sky and meekly shouted, "Point taken!"

Waiting out the storm gave Perceval the opportunity to plot what he intended to say, should he survive the next lightning strike and be granted an audience with the King. He had gone over a few points in his mind while standing in the stocks for the last three weeks, but as he had finally reached the end of his journey, he was determined to make every moment count. Assuming he would be given any moments at all.

By mid-day the squall had lost a great deal of its strength, and Perceval felt if he were to try again, he could be heard over the remnants of the gale. He also found he was shivering and needed to get moving before he succumbed to the numbing effects of the thunderstorm.

Percy unwrapped the scarf from Brother Bob and salvaged what he could of the sodden bread, which came to about one meager bite. Fortunately, the cheese and fruit were not ruined, so he feasted on what he soberly realized could well be his last supper.

Satiated, the wet rat of a man stood and wove his way through the puddles to the castle entrance. He cleared his throat and yelled, "My name be Perceval the Altruistic, and I seek an audience with the King!"

When he received no response, he increased his volume and

191

tried again. "I say, my name be Perceval the Altruistic, and I seek an audience with the King!"

Again, getting nothing in return but silence, he tried a third time. "I humbly come naked before thee to ask my good and noble King why he doth treat me with such indifference. And also, to inform him of the cancer eating away at his kingdom."

The stonewall of abject apathy Perceval encountered only solidified his resolve. He raised the level of his voice. "I say, my name be Perceval. Ye doth know me! I be a good and loyal subject to my lord and master! I wish him no harm. I only ask for an audience to satisfy my own curiosity and to warn him of an encroaching plague that threatens all of his subjects."

Off in the distance, a bright light lit up the sky, and the accompanying crack of thunder slowly trailed off.

Perceval continued. "My King may ignore me. That be his right. But he doth need to hear what be happening under his very nose."

The sun came out just long enough for Perceval to see a number of heads hiding behind the protective stone on the castle wall. "I can see thee up there. One of you run to the King and tell our good and perfect master that his humble servant, Perceval the Altruistic, doth seek an audience."

The one-sided nature of this conversation was beginning to irritate the determined man. "An audience. That's where the King doth listen to what I have to say and then does whatever the King wants to do! I know not if my diatribe be worthy of a sentence of life or death, but I shall not leave until my litany of woes be heard. Although, for purposes of clarification, I believe a sentence of death would be a vast over reaction."

The only response was the soft pitter patter of a light rain falling into the moat.

Feeling his patience ebb, Perceval found himself sliding into sarcasm.

"Doth anyone on that side of the moat speak the King's

English? Or art I speaking to Martin the Mute, Dan the Deaf, or Sally the Slightly Dull? My name be Perceval the Altruistic, and I seek an audience with the King! The King who reportedly lives in yon castle! Unless I have the wrong address and he doth reside in another castle just across town. Doth I have the right place? Be this the home of the King? The one from whom all blessings flow? He wrote a book everyone uses as the basis for life? Ringeth any bells?"

And so it went until almost dusk. Perceval's voice was growing raspier by the minute. As a result, his rants became less and less demanding. By the end it took all he had just to squeak out his name.

Then, as if in answer to his silent prayer, just when darkness began to invade the land, the huge drawbridge suddenly started to clank as it was lowered.

Perceval was understandably excited. He believed that finally an answer to his petition was about to be heard. That briefest glimmer of hope lasted until he heard a group of women behind him.

Turning, he saw the sisters of mercy walking up the path, returning from their day's errand of compassion into the warm protection of the castle.

Knowing full well the welcoming was not meant for him, Percy acquiesced, moved away from the entrance, and stood off to the side with his head bowed.

Sister Mary Angel brought up the rear. When she saw Perceval, she was shocked. She blurted out, "Perceval? Thou art drenched! Didst ye take a swim in the moat?"

Percy nodded.

"Yea. I took a couple laps. 'Twas quite invigorating!"

Instinctively she moved towards her friend, but he held up his hand to stop her. "Nay, speak to me not. This be my fool's errand, not thine. Sully not thyself with my guilt by association."

Rebuffed, the sister reluctantly got back in line and followed her companions over the bridge and into the castle. She looked back at the soaked man standing in the castle's shadow, but he refused to acknowledge her.

Glancing up, Perceval caught the unmistakable glint of several lances held aloft by guards standing on either side of the castle entrance. If he held any thoughts of rushing across the drawbridge to gain entry, that formidable sight laid them to rest.

When all the sisters had passed, Perceval stepped back onto the path at the edge of the moat, croaking out the words, "My name be Perceval the Altruistic! I beg for an audience with my King."

The only answer to his heartfelt plea was the ten-foot door to the castle slamming shut and the cumbersome iron chains attached to the drawbridge slowly receding, subsequently raising his only possible path to the entrance back up and out of reach.

For Perceval, that was the final straw that broke his back. He no longer cared that he may well look and act as one who had taken leave of his senses. He had a point to make and he was determined to get it off his chest, audience or not.

This was the moment when Percy began his unbridled rant. He had managed to be reasonably polite up to this point, but that tactic was officially strangled and then kicked off to the side.

Of late a rather crude phrase had insinuated itself into the popular culture. The saying was, in fact, so base that polite people restrained themselves from saying it out loud in mixed company.

To protect sensitive, virgin ears, the populace collectively conspired to only use the first initial of each word.

The colloquialism was simply W-B-T-F. While a few precocious children appropriated the acronym in their ignorant attempts to appear more grown up, the adults in the area knew exactly what was meant by the popular slang.

Perceval bristled every time he heard it. But on this day, at this hour, in the twilight of his life, he seriously believed those four simple words perfectly expressed exactly what he felt at that very moment.

Staggering to keep his balance in the mud in front of the

King's castle, totally alone, wet, broke, bereft of strong voice, and inches from total exhaustion seemed to Perceval to be a classic WBTF moment, and it made him burst out with laughter.

Which caused him to shout, "If it doth please the King's court, may I humbly ask, what be thy f—?"

And then he stopped. He realized, regardless of how upset or self-righteous he felt, he could not blaspheme the King. There was also the not insignificant matter of keeping his head where it currently resided, so it was probably wise to refrain from needlessly upsetting the powers that be.

Perceval threw his head back and shouted to the skies. "I cry to thee, my life be relinquished! I have lost all hope and dreams save one. I pray for an answer and explanation for my plight. Nay, my series of plights, from my good and glorious King."

Though Perceval's throat was beginning to hurt, he coughed and continued, "Why dost thee hide behind these stone walls and thy Book of Acquired Wisdom? Art thou afraid to meet thy subjects face to face?

"Here be an idea: appoint some kind of representative. A figurehead, to be sure, but a faithful one who canst keep thy ideals alive and let thee know of the mood of thy subjects. For it be obvious to a blind man that thy statutes have fallen through the cracks, regardless of the tirelessly ineffective work of thy scribes."

Perceval found himself pacing back and forth at the edge of the moat. He began to pick up momentum. He was unsure how long his voice would hold out, but he wasn't about to coddle it long enough to find out.

"Art thee even there? Or doth the line to see thee be short because ye hast beheaded all who wert foolish enough to seek an audience?

"And be that even true? If thou doth desire thy subjects to love thee, art thou sure fear be the best tactic to inspire that love? Art I out of line? Undoubtedly! But doth I fear the consequences of my boldness? Nay, I say! Come what may, I say nay!

"Then there be the question of evil! If there be grievous wrongs committed in thy kingdom, why dost thou not stop them? For if thou doth have the power to stop said crimes, and ye doth not, art ye not guilty of committing such wrongs?

"Strike me down if I be wrong! But if the King dost not stop all that be evil, doth that not make the King complicit?

"May it never be! For I say the King be good! I stated as such in Pleasanton, and I state it here. It be no secret that I have pledged my life to thee. This doth not make me special for I know of many who have done the same. My only true desire wast to serve thee. Strike me down if I doth not speak the truth!

"Whilst I need not special accommodations for my loyalty, surely I be not out of bounds to expect the slightest acknowledgment that I doth even exist! But when my calamities didst occur, I heard from thee not. Not even a courier with the sentiment, 'it doth suck to be thee.'

"When all was lost, the first thing I sought be thy empathy. Be that wrong? Be that my weakness? Far be it for me to judge thee, so I stand here asking thee to explain thyself.

"I seek only thy direction. I be a man adrift in a sea of lost souls! I seek an answer. Any answer. If thou doth say all of it be of my own doing, I shall accept it. For I be too tired to debate.

"I know I live covered by the veil of self-deception. I told myself I only wanted to be happy, but perhaps thou doth know the true deceit of my heart; what I really wanted wast to have everything be easy and convenient."

This self-revelation stopped Perceval in his tracks. He looked up at the castle and yelled one last time. "Why be it so hard to find thee? Be that the test? To see if we still love thee even when thou art absent? Or art ye merely a hoax to keep the huddled masses in line?

"But assuming thou art real, and I hope with every fiber of my being that thou art, how canst ye expect anyone to love thee when ye doth freely give with one hand whilst stealing our joy with the other?"

Perceval had very little left to give. He stared up at the castle until his eyes grew bleary and then croaked out a final, "I only ask ye give me the simple courtesy of telling me—why?"

A few moments after his last unanswered pitiful query, the sun finally sank down behind the ramparts of the castle.

Thoroughly defeated and deflated, Perceval turned and walked back to the tree, muttering as he went, "Seriously, what be thy fornication?"

Chapter Twenty-Four
The King!

The second day went much like the first, with the possible exception that, instead of rain, on this fine day the heat was unbearable.

No one alive could remember a time when such extremes played out in the weather. At first the intense warmth of the sun was a welcome friend, quickly drying out both Perceval's clothes and the sea of mud surrounding the castle.

But a few hours into the morning it became clear the rising heat was intended to punish every living soul who was foolish enough to leave the shelter of their home.

The air was hot and sticky, and soon, so was Perceval. He began sweating profusely, causing his clothes to cling to him, all while he had the disquieting feeling of one who was slowly being baked.

At one point around noon, Perceval was so parched he was severely tempted to drink water from the moat, but as he drew closer to his hoped-for salvation, he saw a large pair of scaly eyes staring at him from just under the surface. Quickly retreating, Percy wisely decided it was better to live with extreme thirst than tempt possible death or amputation.

The unrelenting heat was the worst at the three o'clock hour. That's the time when Percy's lips were so dry and cracked, he gave up, limped over to the shade of the tree, and found himself wishing he was back in the torrential rainstorm from the day before.

At dusk Brother Bob brought the headstrong man both food and drink which were greedily consumed in a matter of moments. The monk felt it was not the time to ask Percy if he'd had enough, so he patted his wild-eyed, unkempt friend on the shoulder, let him know Redeemer was safe and sound in the monk's stable, turned, and made his way back home.

By sundown the heat was still stifling, and though exhausted, Perceval resisted the idea of giving up. He was like a child who, despite being overly tired, insisted they were wide awake.

That was when a severe depression set in that sapped what little strength Percy had left. He croaked out his pitiful pleas of desperation with little to no hope that any living soul could help him out of the abyss he seemed to have dug for himself.

After months of struggling against the relentless currents of depression, exhaustion, and oppression, Perceval the Altruistic had finally run aground. He was figuratively dashed against the rocks. He had nothing left to give.

Around midnight, despite his best intentions, the bone-weary man finally collapsed onto the hard, crusted ground and passed out in front of the entrance to the castle.

✝✝✝

On the third day, at dawn, something miraculous happened. An event Perceval almost missed due his dead-to-the-world deep slumber.

The golden silence of the morning was broken by the disquieting sound of the drawbridge being lowered and subsequently crashing onto the ground mere yards from where Perceval slept. Immediately after that, the immense castle doors creaked open on hinges that begged to be oiled.

Despite the disturbing volume of these activities, the spent man splayed out spread eagle on the ground apparently didn't hear a thing, as he moved nary a muscle.

It was the sunrise that woke him.

Asleep on the baked dirt with his head facing the castle, the morning sun that was blocked by the high stone walls broke through both the fog and the opening of the doors, blanketing

Perceval with blinding intensity. The man sluggishly squinted, doing his best to block out the light, but to no avail.

Something in the back of his mind began shouting, "Awake, ye fool, the castle doors be open!" That still, small voice, along with the light and commotion from the castle, slowly seeped into Perceval's brain.

Then, as if he had just received a bucket of freezing water to his face, the man bolted upright, sputtering.

Immediately he leapt to his feet and tried to stand, but his legs betrayed him. He staggered for a few steps and fell back down on his knees, which, he later came to realize, was where he belonged in the first place.

Looking up, Perceval saw the silhouettes of at least a dozen men walking out onto the drawbridge. Each of the tall, imposing figures carried a ten-foot-long lance.

Thinking the authorities had come to dispose of him, Perceval's blood surged through his veins. All thoughts of sleep vanished. He tried again to stand, struggled a few steps, and fell again, knees first, onto the rock-hard ground, just inches from the edge of the drawbridge. And there he stayed.

One man from the middle of the pack stepped forward and moved to the side of the drawbridge, shouting out with a loud, booming voice and punctuating the finish of each phrase by raising and then pounding the bottom of his lance against the reverberating wood on which he stood.

"Hear ye, hear ye, come one and all to bow down and worship the one who art worthy to be praised! The one from whom all blessings doth flow! The one whom doth embody grace and truth and love and charity! Come forth one and all, both great and small, and prepare to worship thy King!"

Signaling he had finished; the crier pounded his lance on the drawbridge twice and his backup corps of guards answered in kind.

Squinting, Perceval could make out some of the features of the King's backlit guard. Each man was stern of face and wore a military uniform unlike anything Percy had ever seen. They had ornately designed helmets, breastplates, and leggings of iron, with long swords hanging by each soldier's side. Painted in the middle of every suit of armor was a large red iron cross.

From the castle entrance and through a thick cloud of fog stepped a lone figure out into middle of their ranks. As he slowly came into focus, it was clear this man was dressed altogether differently and carried himself with a royal demeanor.

The stranger's robe and tunic were both pure white. Around his mid-section was a wide band of gold cloth. His boots came up to his knees and were made of burnished bronze. On his head was a golden crown laden with many jewels. His long hair and beard were pure white, matching his billowing outfit.

As an involuntary chill ran up his spine, Perceval knew in an instant he was now facing the King. He was torn between wanting to look up in order to take it all in and a sudden urge to fall on his face (and, as his children were wont to say, "sucketh dirt").

The sergeant at arms continued, "Hear ye, hear ye, come from far and wide, for thy King has arrived! Tell thy neighbors, friend and foe alike, that thy Lord and Master doth seek an audience with Perceval the Altruistic, for his petitions have been heard by thy great and powerful King!"

To Perceval, this time it seemed as if the pounding of the soldier's lance on the bridge wasn't nearly as loud as the thumping of his own heart. The soldier had announced his name! Instinctively he lowered his head until his forehead touched the ground.

His every desire was to look up and gawk, but he suspected he should not until he was given explicit permission to do so.

At the same time, Perceval recognized the fact that he was offering up his neck to be sliced in two. Surprisingly, some small part of him almost wished it would happen, just to be done with it all.

Percy noticed his entire body was trembling from a combination of fear, excitement, and exhaustion, but he was powerless to stop it.

Not even close to wrapping up his introduction, the soldier began another round. "Hear ye, hear ye, all from the town of Kingston and the surrounding kingdom of Goodania! Here stands thy goodly King and Master, the one whom ye all owe thy very lives! Come forth to pay homage! Come forth to worship! Come forth!"

The King smiled at the shouting soldier as a signal that he had reached the point of saturation with this particular pomp and circumstance.

That's when the trumpets sounded. Seven men stood in a row atop the castle wall and let loose with a blast so loud Perceval was sure those in the Outskirts could hear it. This was the official announcement that the King had arrived and everyone in the kingdom was now called to the castle.

After the head guard yet again pounded his lance into the bridge and was answered by his fellow guards, the King raised his hand and said, "By thy leave, good and faithful servant, I believe thy introduction be more than adequate. For unless I miss my guess, this man doth understand who I be."

In answer to his leader, the guard struck his lance down two more times and shouted, "So sayeth the King! Thy King has spoken!"

At that the King raised his hand up further in the air and was quite emphatic as he stated, "Oh, I do believe we may all live with a tad less pronouncements and pounding. I thank thee for thy enthusiastic service, but let us move on, shall we?"

When the soldier raised his lance yet again and began to shout, "So sayeth—" the King shook his head and cut him off. "Nay, my good man! Ye need not tell one and all I just spoke. If they have ears to hear, it shouldst be fairly obvious."

It took all the available restraint of the overly trained soldier to quiet himself and not pound down with his lance again. The man nodded and, though frustrated, did as he was told.

To lessen the blow, the King interjected, "Though I admire thy enthusiasm! Thy training has come through in flying colors.

Well done!" The soldier bit his lip, reverently lowered his head, and reluctantly took a step back in line.

Needing to clarify, the King continued, "However, if I do mention an edict or some such thing and the throngs doth get unruly, or someone rushes at me with a blade, then that wouldst be the perfect time to reinstate order and afterward, by all means, add thy punctuation to my pontification. Art we clear?" The guard raised his head a bit and nodded.

Satisfied that minor debacle had been smoothed over, the King turned to the scraggly man bowing before him, walked directly to the edge of the drawbridge and queried, "Now, who here be the one who speaks endless words without knowledge or counsel?"

Afraid to utter an answer, Perceval remained in his position of reverence, frozen in place, save one timid hand that ever-so-slowly raised up in the air.

To which the King said, "Good. Now sit thee up, gird thy loins like a man, and I shall ask thee some questions."

Those words sent a shiver through Perceval. He had gotten his wish. He finally had an audience with the King, and he was currently regretting the day he was ever born. He also regretted his idiotic idea of demanding anything from the picture of royalty currently condescending to stand before him.

Perceval wished he could get up and run away but was afraid his legs would betray him again. So he leaned back and braced himself for what he was sure was going to be, at the very least, a series of knock out blows to the chin or gut.

Instead, the King let out a loud sigh, allowed the silent tension to rest in the air, and then dove in.

"Good Perceval the Altruistic, wert ye there when I established my kingdom? Surely you understand all I did and how I didst do it. When I leveled the land and carved my castle out of the mountain, didst ye supervise and direct my creation? Speak up, for surely thou doth know!

"Was it ye who didst change the course of the river so that

it fed the trees and crops of my kingdom? Were ye there when I stretched out the measurements of the city? Surely thou dost have full knowledge of the particulars of my labors.

"And if it pleases thee, remind me, wert ye responsible for bringing in the first cows and horses and livestock so that all within my fair country might be fed and flourish? I recall thee not, but perhaps I art mistaken.

"Wert ye the one who didst create the monetary system? Or write out the rules of wisdom that be enclosed within my book? And doth ye protect the borders of my kingdom so that all art not overrun? Speak now, for surely thou art the one whom we should praise for all the goodness that we see both far and wide!"

Perceval quickly caught on to the sarcastic drift of the King's diatribe, and as he could not argue with the logic, found himself feeling smaller and more inconsequential with each and every rhetorical question.

The King was on a roll. His voice was strong and carried a great distance as he queried, "Advise me if ye know! When I built the roads and the sewers and stocked the lake and built the bridges, what part did ye play? Surely ye were instrumental in all that we see and hear and touch? Tell me if ye know!

"Perhaps ye invented the printing press, or the loom, or the thresher! Surely it was ye who trained the butcher, the baker, and the candlestick maker! Remind me of all that ye have done, for it seems to have slipped my mind."

As the King continued to reprimand Perceval, reaction to the trumpet announcement as well as word of the gates opening and of their lord and master's appearance spread like wildfire. People rushed out from the city in various stages of undress and unkempt hair in order to gather around the castle gate to see the show.

This kind of spectacle was a once-in-a-lifetime event and anyone who was able to walk, run, or crawl made their way up the hill.

The villagers were astonished and amazed at the dressing

down Perceval was receiving. A few gloated, but most were just happy they themselves were not under the judgmental glare of the King.

"I beg thee to correct me if I be wrong, but if I doth own the cattle on a hundred hills and I allow ye to earn thy living by selling and trading what be my property in the first place, what right have ye to complain when I take back or misplace what be rightfully mine? Speak now, for my curiosity be at a fevered pitch!"

That particular arrow of guilt sunk directly into Perceval's heart. Had he ever actually owned anything? For if everything did truly belong to the King, as he had known from the time he was a child, then, at best, Percy was merely managing it for the briefest of seasons.

And since whatever he lost or gained was merely on loan from his master, how could he have the gall to claim he lost anything at all?

Percy wanted to ask the King to stop for a moment in order to process all the thoughts and feelings currently rushing through his head and heart, but the lecture continued unabated.

In the midst of his reprimand, Perceval noticed a peculiar thing. While the King's words may have indeed sounded harsh, his tone was anything but. In fact, the feeling behind his soliloquy was unquestionably parental, almost soothing.

It was if the King was directing his lecture to Perceval, but the bulk of his advice had subtly shifted its intent toward the ever-increasing curious voyeurs in attendance.

It appeared as if the most important lesson to be gleaned that day was righting a lax impression of the one who truly be in power, to be sure, but at the same time, to let everyone know that behind the chastisement was a strong feeling of love.

The emotional underpinning for the man who had overstepped his bounds was inexplicable.

It was at that time that Perceval no longer feared for his life. He felt assured that regardless of the final outcome of this meeting, he would be leaving with his head intact.

He also came to the conclusion that, when confronted with real greatness, humility is incredibly easy to achieve. He felt small and stupid and wondered how he ever got it into his head that he had any rights at all.

He was ashamed he had behaved like a petulant child and swore, if he was ever allowed another chance, he would never make that mistake again.

Not long after those realizations, the King's comments came to a close. In the ensuing silence he looked down at Perceval.

Finally, the King asked, "What say ye, Perceval the Altruistic?"

Percy could only shake his head and mumble, "I beg my King's forgiveness."

The King let him know it was all right to continue. "For—?"

"For forgetting who thou art and who I be. For forgetting thy words of wisdom and believing I had any rights. For my hubris at demanding ye explain thyself when ye hast already told us all we need to know."

"Which be—?"

"Thou art our Lord and Master, and we art not. We serve and live and breathe at thy behest. To demand any answers or cry that we have been treated unfairly is to behave as a fool! I art the king of dunces, and I beg thy forgiveness."

Satisfied with Percy's answer, the King extended his hand with a warm, "Stand, my son."

Surprised, Perceval tried to rise up on his own but found he needed to grab the King's hand to steady his wobbly legs. As he did so, the King opened his arms and brought Perceval in for a hug.

Knowing how filthy he was, Percy tried to pull away saying, "Nay, for I doth stink!" But the King's strength overcame him and drew the man in.

The monarch held Perceval tightly for quite some time before he gently whispered into his ear, "I be so sorry for thy many losses. My heart didst break."

Hearing these kind words broke Percy. Lost in the comfort of his redeemer's arms, the hurting man broke down and cried. And then he sobbed. After carrying his pain for so long, he was finally free to release the loss of all that he held dear.

Watching the tender scene was cathartic for many of the villagers. Tears streamed down the faces of the majority of the King's subjects, and to a man, the lips of the stoic guards were seen quivering with emotion.

When all of Perceval's feelings were sufficiently cried out, the King released his subject. The man held his throat. The pain he felt only moments ago was gone. In fact, he felt renewed. Not understanding how any of this was possible Percy wiped his eyes and nose and face as best he could and then looked at the mess he had made upon the King's pure white robe and tunic.

Percy apologetically burst out with, "Oh, no! My Lord, I am so—"

The King stopped him with a wave of his hand, saying, "Pay it no mind." Then he simply brushed off his shoulder and all of the dirt and stains Perceval imprinted there seemed to disappear, leaving the Master's robe and tunic completely spotless.

Raising his eyebrows while wrinkling his nose, the King said, "But ye *art* the slightest bit ripe." He snapped his fingers, and within moments two well-dressed men emerged from the castle and rushed up to Perceval.

The King simply said, "Prepare this man for his reward." The underlings nodded and whisked away a clearly confused and unprepared Percy.

As he stumbled over his uncooperative feet to exit, Perceval exclaimed, "Reward? What reward? If it pleases the King, might I—?" And then he was out of earshot.

The moment Perceval was gone, the King turned his attention to the many people who had come out from the village.

His eyes crinkled, and his mouth smiled as he bowed his head.

In response, a few people near the front felt the urge to bow before their Lord and Master and subsequently did so.

When others saw the handful of kneeling faithful, they responded in kind. The overwhelming feeling of being in the presence of greatness as well as the need to give all due respect to their provider and protector spread out like a wave, and soon all the people of Kingston, small and great, rich and poor, fell to their knees in homage.

Seeing the populace bowing before the King in reverence, the head guard relaxed his aggressive stance. He nodded appreciatively and lowered his lance.

Chapter Twenty-Five
Judgment Day

Before the King said a word, he extended his arm out with his palm up. In response, a soldier from the middle of the line took a giant step forward and placed a scroll in the ruler's waiting hand.

The King unrolled the parchment, took his time perusing the contents, then rolled it back up.

Looking over the crowd, he spied the person he was looking for, turned to the lead soldier, and whispered the servant's name. Immediately the sergeant at arms shouted out, "Augustus the Giant! Come and kneel before thy King!"

From the middle of the gathering, as if he had springs in his legs, the sheriff's body popped up. Clearly flustered, the small man snaked his way through all the kneeling bodies while doing his best to straighten his collar, smooth out his tunic and hold on to a shred of his dignity as he approached the drawbridge.

The instruction to bow down was totally unnecessary. He immediately assumed the position, crossing his arms across his bent knee.

The King spoke in a voice loud enough for all to hear. "My dear Augustus, I have seen thy deeds. Thou art an honest and goodly sheriff. Where there be dissension, thou doest thy best to instill peace. Where there be chaos, thou dost use the power of thy office sparingly to instill order. In all things, first and foremost, ye seek not revenge or punishment, but my justice. This warms my heart. If ye continue in thy goodly ways, ye shall be a welcome addition to my kingdom. Well done, good and faithful servant."

When the King finished, Augustus didn't move. Understandably, as he was frozen in place, waiting for the other shoe to drop.

The guard let him know his time was up by slamming his staff onto the bridge and yelling, "So sayeth the King! The King has spoken!"

Relieved, the sheriff jumped up, whirled around, and practically ran back to his spot in the center of the crowd, causing a small titter of laughter from all in attendance.

Though the mood was now considerably lighter, when the King turned to the guard and whispered another name, a hush fell over the gathering.

The soldier yelled, "The King's scribes! Come and kneel before thy King!"

The town's religious leaders were currently huddled in a small circle at the far back of the crowd where they could properly observe and critique everyone deemed not worthy enough to be in their clique. They helped each other stand and sauntered up to the castle as if they had been invited to attend their own coronation, gently nudging, pushing, and subtly kicking aside all who were inconveniently in their way.

Assembling before the King, they gave a cursory nod of their heads, but none of them felt the need to kneel. The self-appointed leader of the brood cleared his throat and announced, "We lowly scribes art honored to stand before our revered Lord and Master. It hath been our distinct pleasure to serve thy—"

He was cut off before he could get out another word.

The sergeant at arms lunged towards the black-robed men with his spear at the ready. His tone left little wiggle room for the self-satisfied scribes. He spat out, "I said kneel before thy King!"

Following his lead, the soldiers at the back of the drawbridge all lowered their lances and assumed a battle stance.

Shocked, surprised, and not a little terrified, the scribes dropped to their knees. You could almost hear the entire town gulp in unison. The event in Kingston had just taken a turn. In an instant it had become what is known by parents and authorities the world over as a "teachable moment."

From that point on, not a single person had to be reminded of the proper stance when they were called before their Lord and Master.

The King nodded at his commander, and both he and his fellow soldiers slipped back into their at-ease formation.

Looking at his scribes, it was obvious the King was not pleased with the men before him. He shook his head as he said, "My poor, pitiful scribes. Thou art naught but a gaggle of noisy gongs. Ye have memorized every jot and tittle of my law, but somehow ye have lost its meaning. The trial of Perceval be just the most recent example. Were any of ye looking for justice that day or merely anxious to extract thy pound of flesh? It doth appear ye have lost thy first love. I shall give ye one more chance to find it. If ye do, ye may enter into my kingdom and reap all my rewards. But if ye continue on the path thou art currently on, I shall remove ye from thy positions and cast out one and all into the outer darkness. But to him who overcomes, they shall have a seat at the table of my banquet. Be I clear?"

The six chastised heads clustered nearest to the King vigorously bobbed up and down.

"Have thee any confusion as to what I demand of all of thee?"

As one, the scribes all shook their heads.

Satisfied, the King looked over at his commander, giving him the high sign. The man pounded his spear into the bridge and announced, "So sayeth the King! The King has spoken!"

Taking their cue, the humiliated scribes practically leapt up and did their best to disappear into the anxious audience, finally making their way back to relative safety at the rear of the pack.

Next up were the namers. After being called, the entire Naming Day committee made their way up to the drawbridge, their knees knocking the entire time.

When they had all assumed the subservient position, the

sergeant at arms called out another name. He cried, "The King doth call Beatrice the Belligerent!"

Off on the side a tiny irritating voice called back, "That's princess!"

Before the guards could rush the naysayer, the King looked over in the young girl's direction, smiled, and waved for her to come forward. The ignorant young thing practically skipped up to the front.

The King smiled as he said, "Thou wert out of earshot. Canst thou repeat what ye said?"

The girl flung her hair back over her shoulder and proudly declared, "That's *princess*. He called me Beatrice the Belligerent." The precocious pre-teen indicated the people bowing down on the ground behind her. "That's what they wanted to call me. That not be who I am. I be a princess!"

Understanding, the King nodded.

Several in the crowd as well as the King's own guard grimaced, waiting for the boom to be lowered.

The King baited his hook and asked the young girl, "Refresh my memory; be I your father?"

The girl looked at the King as if he were a complete imbecile. She scoffed and said, "Nay! My parents be over there!"

The King looked over at the girl's mortified parents and waved. The couple's eyes were as wide as saucers. Nervous sweat was visibly dripping down their faces. All the father could do was give an apologetic shrug.

Nodding again, the King turned to the girl and said, "Unless I be mistaken, only my daughters have the right to be called princesses. Now, if thou doth pledge thy loyalty to me, and live accordingly, one day thou shalt become a true princess. But until such a time, thy namesake shalt be as the naming committee rightly decreed: Beatrice the Belligerent."

Hearing the news, the young girl stomped her foot on the ground and began to give a repeat performance of the show she'd given just a few weeks earlier on Naming Day. She screamed, "Nay, I say! Forever and a day I shalt be known—"

As they had done with the scribes, the guards nipped that particular tantrum in the bud. In unison, all the soldiers assumed a battle stance, pointed their spears at the diminutive brat, and shouted, "Thou art Beatrice the Belligerent! Thus sayeth the King! The King has spoken!"

Shocked into submissive silence for the first time in her young life, the girl's eyes welled up with tears. She then nodded, stepped back, and wandered away, clumsily tripping over to her mortified parents.

The King looked down at the trembling group of women who formed the Naming Day Committee then softly declared, "My dear ladies, take heart! Thou art well suited for thy task and have carried out thy duties admirably for lo these many years. But of late I have noted a surprising lack of backbone. Let not the vitriolic self-absorbed opinions of children or their families sway thee from the wisdom of thy choices."

At which point the King looked over the crowd and made a pronouncement. "These selfless women doth constitute my Naming Day committee. Whatever names they choose for the fine underlings of Kingston shall be henceforth honored, for they speak on my behalf and with my authority."

Staring into the eyes of the women before him he added, "Though it would be good of thee to not take quite as much delight in the power ye hold over thy charges."

Nodding toward the soldiers, all of men rhythmically smacked their lances down on the surface of the bridge two times and called out, "So sayeth the King! The King has spoken!"

When the naming committee stood up, most had tears of happiness streaming down their cheeks. Their unbridled relief was evident. Without thinking, the shortest one ran forward to hug the King. Immediately two of her friends thrust out their arms, grabbing the impetuous woman, in order to hold her back.

One and all were shocked when the King opened his arms in response. The eyes of the naming committee grew wide. The two women holding onto their friend let go of her cloak, then watched the tiny brave woman run onto the drawbridge and into the King's arms.

When the King wrapped his arms around her, all the women from the naming committee rushed forward. The guards made no move to stop them. The King let out a hearty laugh and opened himself up to a group hug.

From the back, at the bottom of the hill, one of the jealous scribes smacked his compatriot and said, "Fool, why didn't we do that!"

After a few moments of comforting bliss, the women reluctantly released their collective grip and moved away, constantly bowing before their King as they backed up. When they stepped off the drawbridge, the entire committee turned on their heels and scampered off, giggling like schoolgirls.

From the run of highs and lows on display that day, the crowd was on pins and needles, having no idea what to expect next.

The King opened his scroll one last time, scanned the contents again, rolled it up, and handed it back to the head soldier. When he whispered the next name to his sergeant at arms, all could hear the labored sigh that accompanied it.

When the soldier cried out, "Priscilla the Obstinate, come bow before thy King," only confusion rippled through the crowd as no one seemed to be familiar with the name.

But a few moments later, when the leader of the terrible teens begrudgingly stood, a visceral rush of excitement could be felt. More than one who had been burned by the scullery maid were secretly hoping the time of her comeuppance had finally arrived.

They got their wish.

The reprehensible persuader slowly and defiantly made her way to the front. She stood before the King for the longest time, glaring at him.

Sensing the soldiers were about to demand she physically acquiesce before her ruler, the King looked at his guards and subtly shook his head.

When they obeyed and stood down, the town of Kingston was treated to a staring match. There was little doubt of the outcome, which made the open defiance of the young girl all the more astounding.

The teen's shoulders shifted as if she were thinking of making a run for it, but when the King raised his eyebrows, she had a change of heart.

The majesty's voice became very soft, barely raised above a whisper. He shook his head and said, "My dear, dear Priscilla. The hopes I had for thee. But ye rejected my path and instead insisted on closing off thy heart to my truth. Even now, ye refuse to release thy pride and acknowledge there be a better way."

Unable to escape and unwilling to bow, the girl's body started to shake.

Ever so slowly, the teen leaned forward the slightest bit. She then bent one knee, then another. When her torturous submissive fall to the ground was complete, she punctuated it with a loud, piercing scream of frustration.

She shouted, "I feel unsafe! Thou art emotionally raping me! I beg for an advocate! Who wilt help me stand against the cruel and malicious unfair judgment of the King?"

None stepped forward. Seeing she was alone, she screamed again, "Most vile cowards! I shall see thee burn with me!"

Making her final play, she shrieked, "The King be most unfair! I have suffered as a chambermaid, with naught but pain and humiliation cleaning the droppings of vile rich pampered people whom he didst bless over me! I cried out for any crumb of privilege but ye turned thy deaf ears to me! So I took it upon myself! I deserve all that I have! I have made my way in the world, no thanks to thee!"

With a wave of his hand, the King raised his voice to full volume, shouting out, "Enough!" And she was silent.

The Lord of the country of Goodania looked upon the angry child and said, "Priscilla the Obstinate, I see that ye have been rightly named, for I have seen thy deeds. I perceive there be no goodness in thee and that thy heart hast grown as black and cold as coal. As such, ye shall be cast into the outer darkness where there be great weeping and gnashing of teeth. In this way ye shall get thy most fervent wish: to be as far away from me as possible."

Hearing this, the chambermaid let out a loud and long, "Nay! I beg of thee! Have mercy upon me!"

The King was incredulous. "Mercy, you say? Wert ye merciful to the restaurant owners ye slandered, whose families lost their only livelihood? Wert ye merciful to Perceval, as ye stuffed rotting fruit into his mouth to the point of suffocation? When be the last time ye showed any mercy to anyone, be they man or beast?"

The girl's silence spoke volumes.

Having his answer, the King signaled his guards, and one man from either end broke ranks, strode to the girl, picked her up by her elbows, and escorted her off of the hill. Defiant to the end, she screamed out how callous and cruel the King was, until her protests diminished to little more than distant echoes bouncing off the hills.

When her unanswered accusations finally faded away, the King turned to his subjects and said, "Wilt all of Priscilla's friends please rise?"

Trembling, a handful of frightened teens stood to their feet. First up, ready to take his lumps, was Victor the Healer (whose real namesake was a sight better than the scullery maid's cruel nickname, the Homely).

To them, the King showed mercy. "As for ye, I offer forgiveness. Tear down the social boards scattered throughout the city. They have become a blight upon my land. Then seek out those whom ye have maligned and shunned and beg their forgiveness. Walk in my ways and it shall go well with you. But continue to walk in darkness and ye shall receive thy just reward."

The troubled teens quickly shouted back their wholehearted agreement and practically dove out of sight.

As the King wrapped up what became known as "Judgment Day," he turned to the crowd and said, "And everyone didst say of one accord..."

The entire assembly shouted back, "So sayeth the King! The King has spoken!"

In answer, the guards slammed down their spears onto the drawbridge two final times.

Chapter Twenty-Six
The Reward

After the conclusion of Judgment Day, when the King asked everyone to rise, the relief was palpable.

Being properly subservient is a good thing, but there's only so much obedient knees can take, be they old or young. Amid the cracking of joints, stretching of backs, and sighs of relief, Perceval returned.

The version who walked back onto the drawbridge was wholly unrecognizable to nearly everyone. He had been washed, buffed, and primped within an inch of his life. His hair was cut and styled, his beard trimmed, his clothes regal.

While he was clearly uncomfortable in his ornately tapestried long coat, puffy shirt, laced up boots, and tied scarf, to one and all the man looked better than he had in years.

When the King saw him, he urged him to come forward and stand by his side. Reluctantly, Perceval did so.

Turning to the people of the kingdom, the King made an announcement. "Hail, good people of Kingston, Perceval the Altruistic hath returned!"

A murmur of appreciation swept over the crowd. This did not appear to be the same man whom they had cast out. The gentleman standing before them looked nothing like the one who had been, right up until that very morning, standing upon the precipice of the shadow of death.

Uncomfortable being ogled, Percy tried to back away. The King put out an arm to stop his retreat and asked a very loaded question. "And what, pray tell, hast thou learned on thy long journey?"

Unsure how to even begin to answer, Perceval was uncharacteristically tongue tied. He hemmed and hawed for a bit, and apologetically came up empty.

Seeing his hesitation, the King reframed the question. "Surely through all of thy trials and tribulations, ye hast come away with some nugget of wisdom? Something from thy adventures that might, perhaps, help the good people of Kingston? Something ye hast noted my people seem to be, perhaps, lacking?"

Put on the spot, Perceval swallowed hard, mustered his courage, looked out at his former friends and neighbors, shrugged his shoulders and simply said, "I suppose, compassion and gratitude."

The King nodded and waved his hand, indicating Percy should elaborate.

The man who had come through his own crucible of fire took a moment to collect his thoughts, then dove in, although very softly. "It's what be needed when asked to love the King more than oneself. It's what be needed when considering thy neighbor's needs above thy own."

The King smiled at his subject and said, "Speak up, so even the scribes can hear ye."

Perceval over compensated, then found the right modulation. "I said! Compassion and gratitude! It's what be needed to appreciate the innumerable gifts ye hast given us. When both gratitude and compassion be the order of the day, society thrives. Without them, it cannot help but decay and die."

Smiling, the King remained silent. He merely indicated Perceval should continue.

And so Percy did.

"More? Then I suppose, perhaps this." Percy turned to the crowd and felt the old fire creep back into his bones, a fire he hadn't felt since he left the Outskirts. "What the King asks is for his people to love him and our neighbors more, or at least as much as, ourselves. To a man, every person here believes that command to be nigh impossible.

"It be impossible, for it goes against our instinct for self-pres-ervation. If that be so, then why this command? Doth the King not know our basic nature? He must not, for he asks for the impossible!

"May it never be! In his wisdom, he hast given us a directive which he doth know be difficult, if not impossible to attain without his help! Ah, could that be the method behind such apparently mad advice?"

Perceval glanced back at the King to make sure he should continue. His majesty's smile urged him to do so. Percy said, "Be it not obvious that our lord and master's ways be higher than ours? That he doth know something, nay, everything we do not?"

The King looked both bemused and intrigued. He gave a very large wave of his hand, in essence commanding his subject to elaborate.

Believing it could well be his last chance to truly lay out what he had concluded, Perceval continued unabated. "I believe with all my heart, mind, and soul that the King's command be not just wise, but the true secret to happiness!

"The King doth know this but be patient enough to let his entire kingdom fail time and time again as we stumble towards the light, in the hopes that a few of us might actually catch on."

Feeling he'd said his piece and had come close to wearing out his welcome, Perceval again tried to slink back into the shadows, but the King wasn't having it. He nodded to his guards.

Immediately Perceval felt the sharp tip of a spear poking into his back. He quickly adjusted his trajectory accordingly.

The King bellowed, "Pray, good Perceval, enlighten us."

Upon that pronouncement, the King moved back, forcing Perceval to take center stage. Knowing he had no choice but to obey, Percy stepped forward and unveiled his theory.

"The King has asked what I have learned over this past year. Beyond gratitude and compassion, three things have been impressed upon my head and heart!"

"First and foremost, and ye won't like this, but we have no

rights. Our very existence be naught but a gift of the King's good grace. Everything we have belongs to him. We art little more than caretakers of his vast fortune. The sooner we all learn and live by that simple rule, the better."

Perceval looked back at the King, begging with his eyes to be excused. Again, the ruler of all urged him to continue.

Percy reluctantly turned back to the assembly. "As ye all know, I have been rich, and I have been poor. Rich be far better. But it be also a trap. For my fortune became a distraction. It took my eyes off of what should have been my main focus. I see now I needed to be stripped down to nothing in order to become the man the King needed me to be."

A few heads in the crowd began to nod in agreement.

"As it says in The King's Book of Acquired Wisdom, the benefit of tragedy and loss is that they can soften us. It gives us an empathy towards others so stricken that we didn't have before. It saddens me to know that I was so deficient in empathy that drastic measures had to be taken. For others, pain and loss can harden one's heart. Methinks we all know those people. So, don't do that."

When the audience laughed, Perceval knew his story was landing. Emboldened, he moved on.

"Secondly, every man, woman, and child be seeking happiness. But it not be found in getting everything ye think ye want. That be the lie of places like Pleasanton.

"To clarify, I be all for the occasional pleasure. But what I be talking about is lasting happiness that cannot be purchased one mug at a time by over-imbibing in Brother Bob's fine casks of ale!"

The people hooted and hollered, and Brother Bob called out to defend his order. "Though fine casks of ale they be!"

Perceval looked over at his friend and bowed in his direction. "We art in total agreement. But I believe happiness and contentment be found in pouring yerself out for someone or something else. That be the secret! That be how we're made. Our instinct be selfishness. Our first word be 'Mine!' But when we rise above our base nature toward altruism art when we be on the right and true path.

"I thank the naming committee for naming me as such. I be hereby ashamed it took my entire life to understand that my name actually be a map, a destination toward true fulfillment. That I be so dim, that such a fact eluded me, I can only beg all of thee for thy forgiveness.

"Third, and this be my final point, of late, we all seem to be divided. Can none of us agree on anything?"

To lighten the mood, Brother Bob called out again, "Only, perhaps, on the high quality of thy local monk's fine ale and furniture!"

Perceval laughed along with the town. "Rightly stated, good sir. Please understand, I do believe our differences art what make us great. How boring life wouldst be if we all looked at it from the same viewpoint or agreed on every jot and tittle.

"But so many of our disagreements be nothing more than petty distractions. We need to set aside our minor differences, and agree to disagree, in order to accomplish our main task. Namely, to go out and help those who need it; be they the poor, the hurting, or the hungry.

"After that, feel free at any time to go back to thy irritating hobby of pitching a bitching.

"To love one another, serve one another, to grieve or laugh with one another, surprisingly, that be when the afterglow of satisfaction be most pure.

"Sadly, over this past year I have wasted a great deal of time crying over my rights. What happened to me was unfair, to be sure, but returning to my disappointments day in and day out only succeeded in diminishing my joy. I wasted a year rehearsing the hurt in my heart. I shall not go down that path again.

"In truth, I wish a dark and terrible storm might come into all of thy lives so that ye may all emerge out the other side as happy and joyful as I art! Or, better said, as happy and joyful as I plan to be, once I finally get over my own fine self."

When the crowd laughed and he felt the King's hand on his shoulder, Perceval knew he was done.

To the assembled crowd, the King said, "Well said, good Perceval!"

In response, the people gave Percy a hearty round of applause.

He let loose with a mighty exhale, smiled and happily transferred the center stage back to the King.

That's when another thought jumped in his head. He tentatively stepped forward, tapped the King on his shoulder and said, "If I may?"

Amused, the King nodded and backed away in order to give the center of attention back to Perceval.

With boldness, Percy called out a challenge to the entire kingdom. "So sorry, just one last thought! Good people of Kingston, I believe it be not just about serving others, for that be our second command. First and foremost, it be about worshiping the King. It be not about obeying the rules, it be about worshiping the King. It be not about work, or love, or play. It be about remembering who gave us the ability to work and love and play! I say this not because he was gracious enough to spare my head but because I am grateful for all that he has given me. Above all else I say, worship the King! There. I be done."

The head guard beside Perceval shouted out, "Hear, hear!" All the guards pounded their lances down two times, and as one, all the people said, "As it has been said!"

For good or ill, Perceval had finally unburdened himself. For the first time in over a year he felt lighter. He no longer carried the weight of his trials. That alone was a true blessing.

All he wanted to do now was to be allowed to leave in peace and find some faraway place where he could live out his days with his memories and wait for his broken heart to heal.

The King, however, had different plans.

His majesty turned to the head guard and nodded. The soldier stepped forward and yelled out, "The King doth call forward Brother Bob, Stephen the Sarcastic, and Richard the Conveniently Brave!"

Surprised, the three men made their way through the crowd and assembled in front of the drawbridge.

Unsure of the protocol, Richard went down on one knee. The King shook his head. "Nay, good Richard. Methinks we have all had our fill of bowing and scraping."

As he stood, the conveniently brave one leaned over to Stephen and said, "He called me *good*."

To which his sarcastic friend quietly muttered, "Which only doth prove he knows thee not."

The King raised his voice and spoke to his subjects. "It has come to my attention that the governance of my kingdom perhaps doth leave something to be desired. The people need a strong and available hand to guide and persuade and be a judge in my stead. As such, I am appointing one who shall be governor over all the land. He shall be my voice, and ye shall obey him as ye would me."

For a split-second fear ran through Richard's veins. He turned and pointed a finger at his friend, then Brother Bob, and mouthed, "Me? You? Him?" To which Stephen vigorously shook his head.

Smiling, the King turned to Percy. "I give ye Goodania's new ruling judge and governor, Perceval the Altruistic!"

To say Percy was shocked by the announcement would be a vast understatement. As the majority of those in attendance broke out into applause, the wide-eyed man coughed in surprise and shook his head. "Ah, thank ye, my lord, but I desire this not. Not at all!"

The King replied, "Which doth make ye the perfect candidate."

Percy continued his attempt to weasel out of the assignment. "Truth be told, I was half expecting to be executed today. I would far prefer that over this."

In response, the King laughed.

Perceval tried again. "I know I have no rights, so I canst argue with thee not, but I beg of thee, please reconsider. This not be a reward. This be punishment!"

To which the King nodded, "I wholeheartedly agree. Which is why I art assigning yon three trusted friends as thy assistants. Tried and true dependable deputies to which ye can delegate thy duties."

Perceval looked at his beaming friends, then back at the guards and remembered the gentle poke of one of their spears in his back. Turning to the King, all he could say was, "Please. I be not the man ye need."

The King shook his head. "Nay, thou art. Ye have been applying for this position for the past year. Do to Kingston and the rest of the country what ye did in the Outskirts. Bring my people back to their first love. Steer them back onto the path from which they have strayed."

Slowly resigning himself to his fate, Percy asked, "Have I any choice in the matter?"

The King shrugged. "If ye refuse, I foresee the entire country shall be ransacked by a series of plagues and pirates that wilt make your woes seem pale by comparison."

Percy grabbed for his last straw. "Which should lead them all to happiness!"

At that the King let out a belly laugh and brought Perceval in for a bear hug. "My boy, thou art only proving I hast made the right choice."

Close to the King, Perceval whispered his true reticence. "My Lord, ye cannot know, but there be too much pain for me here. Every day be a reminder of what I can never have. I beg of thee for my release, for all I want to do is leave."

When the King let him go, he stepped back, waved toward the castle and said, "Then perhaps ye need one more helper."

From the open door walked a grouping of young women whom Percy recognized as the sisters of mercy. Each was dressed in a stunning gown of red silk, and each cradled a bouquet of white flowers in her arms. The soldiers parted ways to allow the enclave to pass.

Seeing the women, Stephen elbowed Richard.

"Percy gets a harem? I call first dibs on the rejects!"

The women proceeded in two parallel lines on either side of the drawbridge. When they came to a stop, as one they turned and looked back at the castle entrance.

From the open doorway emerged a solitary female dressed in the most elegant white ceremonial gown. Like the King, her waist was wrapped with a wide band of golden cloth, accentuating her womanly figure. In her arms, she carried a lovely bouquet of white flowers. Her face was covered by a sheer veil, held in place by a small crown of many jewels.

The woman stepped up to the King and bowed before him. The ruler of the kingdom took a moment to admire the vision of beauty, lifted the veil off of her face, gently pushed her long blonde hair aside, and leaned in to place a gentle kiss her upon her cheek.

When he stepped back so that all could see the stunning figure, Perceval was shocked to realize the woman dressed as a bride was none other than the love of his life!

He couldn't help himself. He shouted out, "Sister Mary Angel Face! Thou art out of uniform. And ye have hair."

Sister Mary shook her head and laughed. She looked at the King and said, "What did I tell thee?"

The King nodded and said, "He be everything ye described and more."

Turning to Perceval, the King asked a very straightforward question, "Dost thou love my daughter?"

Later his friends teased him mercilessly about his delayed reaction. At that point, one could have easily knocked over Perceval with a feather. As if the day had not already held enough shocks and surprises, this one beat them all.

Perceval sputtered and stuttered, "Your—your—daughter?! Sister Mary?"

The King nodded. "That she be. Dost thou love her?"

Percy practically shouted, "Love her? I adore her with every fiber of my being! She be the reason I need to leave."

When the King looked quizzically at Percy, the man exclaimed, "She be one of thy sisters of mercy. She hast taken a vow of celibacy. She be—dressed as a bride."

Hearing this, Sister Mary laughed again. Perceval still hadn't entirely caught on as to what was happening, but it did his heart good to see the young woman express such unbridled joy.

The King patiently explained, "My daughter has spent a lifetime looking for someone worthy enough to take her hand, and according to her, she hast finally found such a man. Doth thee agree?"

At that declaration, there was not a sound in the entire kingdom. Sister Mary's face flushed as she shyly looked down at the ground. One and all, great and small, looked over at Perceval, waiting for his response.

After a tortured silence, Percy spit out, "Oh. Ye mean me! Oh. And I be dressed as groom! Not as a governor! That be a relief. I thought I'd have to wear this to work every day."

Not even hearing the laughter from the crowd, Percy began to shake with the realization, "I get to marry her? Art thou kidding? I am to be Mr. Sister Mary Angel Face?!"

When his awareness finally came lunging and tripping out of the dark and into the vague light of understanding, the entire town erupted in shouts of excitement and applause.

Unable to hold himself back, Perceval ran over to Mary, swept her up into his arms, and gave her a such a kiss that now, years later, it is still talked about as the standard by which all other kisses are measured.

To this day, throughout the land of Goodania, it can oft be heard said, "By all accounts, ye be a fine and most respectable suitor, but thy kiss doth not equal the passion of Perceval and Sister Mary."

After the kiss to end all kisses, Percy twirled the laughing woman around in the air a time or two before he remembered where he was and let her feet touch the ground.

Staring deep into her eyes, he earnestly asked, "Thou doth

love me? Ye would take me?" All Mary Angel could do was beam and nod.

When she did, Perceval went in for another kiss to evidently seal the deal.

When he came up for air, the King asked the new governor, "Art this plan acceptable to thee?"

Squeezing his bride-to-be's hand while loudly sighing, Perceval said, "Acceptable? Yea! As long as you allow her to renounce her vows, as I would hope the whole celibacy thing be a non-negotiable."

Smiling from ear to ear, the King nodded, swiftly turned to the town and proclaimed, "Then let the festivities begin! Everything be prepared for the wedding feast. The banquet be ready. Come one and all and attend the wedding of my daughter, Sister Mary Angel Face, and thy new governor, Perceval the Altruistic!"

Upon the King's grand announcement, the entire village roared their approval, then rushed into the castle for the surprise wedding of the decade, if not the century.

The last ones who made it across the drawbridge were Percy and his bride. He kissed her again and again until he was told he needed to come inside to make it official.

Later Perceval said he was kissing his new fiancée like there was no tomorrow because, up until that very morning, he wasn't sure he was ever going to see another one.

Every time that part of the story was retold, the King couldn't help but smile.

Chapter Twenty-Seven
Thy Conclusion

For all intents and purposes, thus ends the long and sordid and hopefully uplifting tale of Perceval the Altruistic.

As many of ye have surmised by now, I be none other than everyone's favorite monk, Brother Bob. While I have spent the last decade working by his side as one of Percy's deputy governors, I truly believe I have been able to adequately glean the gist of the tale's various ups and downs and whys and wherefores (though, admittedly, I wert not privy to all the comings and goings of our protagonist's arduous journey).

In case ye were wondering, despite his original reluctance at taking the job, Perceval became a fine governor and judge of Goodania. Which only goes to show, once again, that the King doth know what he be doing.

At the same time, it should be noted that in no way was the governing easy. The turnaround was not an overnight affair. Kingston, especially, was mired in self-satisfied complacency that took quite some time to shake off.

Even today, the old entitlement rears its ugly head now and again. But Perceval is nothing if not patient, and with the sage advice of his wife and three deputies (all guided, of course, by the King's wisdom), he has managed to herd the city of temperamental cats toward a brighter day.

Concerning Percy's marriage to sister Mary Angel Face, only superlatives may be used. Their love blossomed and grew by leaps and bounds to the point of nausea for many a bystander.

She stayed with the sisters of mercy in a part-time consulting position, and Perceval came to see his first impression was dead wrong as all of her sisters truly did love her, despite how unbelievably gorgeous she was.

Fortunately, fertility was not an issue for the married couple, and over the years the pair has added four bouncing baby citizens to the kingdom, with another on the way.

Nothing makes Percy happier than spending time with his many children. He taught them all to read using his prized King's Sacred Book of Acquired Wisdom, and each child signed their name at the end of their favorite chapter, alongside their long-lost half-brothers and sisters.

It should come as no surprise that when the King offered to restore all of Perceval's past fortunes, the man turned him down. First and foremost, he had his hands full ruling the entire country. But perhaps more importantly, his greatest desire was to spend every free second doting on his wonderful wife, his ever-growing family, and serving his neighbors, whatever their needs might be.

The governor built his manse on several acres of land directly between Kingston and the New Outskirts. It was a much smaller home than he had before, but he told Mary Angel that he actually wanted his family to practically live on top of one another.

Rather than desiring privacy, the man explained to every visitor that he had lived too long in pampered silence and had come to love the perpetual chaos of his brood. Perhaps it was because of his great losses, but he honestly relished every scream, cry, burp, and fart that his children manufactured.

Percy loved to wrestle with his offspring, and more often than not, serious state business was conducted with one or more child climbing over the governor or slaying dragons at his feet.

As for me, I built a small abode on Perceval's property. It was cozy and close to the action. Because there happened to be the occasional late night when the governor and his trusted advisors had yet to reach a consensus, I built a fire pit between the two houses. There we chewed the fat, talked over the issues, and were all grateful for our delivery from the (thankfully short lived) angry, boil-ridden Perceval of the past.

Concerning the long-lost secret to happiness, well, that be the rub. Over the years Perceval thought long and hard about what constituted this nebulous, but much sought after prized possession.

In order to adequately summarize our leader's many thoughts and ponderous pronouncements, I decided the best course of action was to add my own inklings and record them all in a book. Yea, another book. It be a companion piece, if you will, to the one thou art currently perusing.

While my humble efforts pale in comparison to the King's Sacred tome, I be the teensiest bit proud that my collection of wit and wisdom has become the second most popular book in the new Kingston library.

Worry thee not, I shall not test thy patience any further with a reading herein of my offerings, but if ye desire a deeper dive into all that doth bounce between my ears, please pick up a copy of my labor of love, The Book of Bob.

Please forgive me for inserting myself into Perceval's story, but other than making ale and the occasional rocking chair, prattling on with endless advice be my favorite way of shining a light in these dark times.

I also get two farthings for every copy I sell!

As for Perceval, what he learned could fill ten other books and then some! But I believe his greatest lessons be quite straightforward and somewhat less verbose than my endless pontificating.

Firstly, have compassion.

Secondly, be grateful.

Also, understand that all wealth be an illusion. Thou art really little more than a steward of thy maker's resources, and for only a short time at that.

Lastly, do thy level best to out serve and out love all those ye hold dear.

That be about it. While the advice listed above be deceptively simple, it also be undeniably hard. But as Perceval would say, it be the hard what makes it good.

If ye want easy, throw in thy lot with Todd the Odd or Priscilla the Obstinate. But if ye want thy best life, and true, lasting happiness, ye could do worse than to follow the path of my friend, Perceval the Altruistic.

Acknowledgements

Every script goes through a long series of tweaks, shifts and revisions as the author fails forward on the arduous journey toward their discovery of what the story is meant to be.

This tale was helped immeasurably by my wonderful editor, Rita Warren, and my faithful friends June Colson, Cory Edwards, CJ Foss, John Isaacs, Bill Parrott, Jennifer Schuchmann, Daren Streblow, Michele VanDusen, and Beth Wetherill.

Each one of them contributed a little more light onto the path I was attempting to blaze. I thank you all from the bottom of my heart.

I would be remiss if I didn't mention my amazing wife, Anne Lee, who patiently listened to, read, and encouraged every thought, notion and half-baked idea along the way.

And to you, dear reader, I hope this story brought you half as much joy as entering Perceval's world has brought to me.

After you finish the last page, if you could find it in your heart to leave a semi-glowing review on a dozen or so social media platforms and then buy a copy or two for absolutely every single person you know, you would have my eternal gratitude.

About the Author

Robert G. Lee's inventive, clean humor has been on display for over three decades.

Well known in the entertainment industry as Hollywood's top warm-up comic, Robert's a veteran of over 1,500 episodes of such shows as The New Adventures of Old Christine, Just Shoot Me, Becker and the reboot of One Day at a Time.

In addition, Robert has written several episodes of the popular Veggie Tales video series as well as ten of his own full-length comedy projects.

Robert's stand up can be heard nationwide thousands of times a month on SIRIUS radio's Pure Comedy channel and he recently recorded his second comedy special for DryBar.

Robert also wrote and directed a faith-based screwball comedy feature called, Can I Get a Witness Protection?

His first book, What's The Big Idea? A Comedian Explains God, the Universe and Other Minor Stuff, looks at the intersection between faith and science.

To follow Robert, visit his website:

www.RobertGLee.com

which holds all the heretofore hidden keys to his booking information and social media.

Also Available From
Wordcrafts Press

Gretchen and the Bear
Carrie Anne Noble

Demimonde
James E. Cressler

Tears of Min Brock
J.E. Lowder

A Pale Horse
Michelle A. Sullilvan

Beauty Unveiled
Paula K. Parker

www.wordcrafts.net

www.ingramcontent.com/pod-product-compliance
Lightning Source LLC
Chambersburg PA
CBHW061125310726
48974CB00002B/688